MW00476763

SANTORI REBORN

THE SANTORI TRILOGY BOOK 2

MARIS BLACK

SANTORI REBORN
Copyright © 2018 Maris Black
All rights reserved.

No part of this publication may be reproduced, distributed, or transmitted, in any form or by any means, without prior permission. For information regarding subsidiary rights, please contact the author: maris@marisblack.com

Cover design by Maris Black

Model: Mike Chabot

Photographer: Alfred Liebl

This book is a work of fiction. Names, characters, places, and incidents are the product of the author's imagination or are used fictitiously. Any resemblance to actual events, locales, or persons, living or dead, is coincidental.

For my Beast.

PART I

CHAPTER ONE

JAMIE

MY ALARM WAS an unwelcome intrusion on a fitful night's sleep. I swatted frantically at my phone, somehow managing to get the snoozed activated before the alarm woke Kage. He was finally sleeping peacefully, and I wanted him to stay that way.

After I'd left him the night before, I had done some research online about treating his bruises. Then I drove to Walmart and loaded up on bags of frozen peas and rolls of compression dressing. We should have started treating the injuries the night before when they were fresh, but I figured it was better late than never.

When I returned, much to his dismay, I covered him with the bags as he lay in bed, treating the front of his body first and then the back for twenty minutes each. Then I wrapped the worst spots in the compression bandages. By the time I was finished, I'm pretty sure he'd wanted to kill me, but he kept his mouth shut and let me nurse him.

After that he had tossed and turned all night, moaning so often and so heartbreakingly I had begun to suspect he was having another dream about the death of his brother. Several times I'd had to pull my hand back from shaking him awake.

Maybe it was the drugs that had him unable to quiet his mind. Maybe it was the mugging, which I suspected wasn't a mugging at all. Kage had secrets, of that I was certain, but the true nature of those secrets was still a mystery to me.

I rolled out of bed, careful not to disturb Kage, and crept across the room to the picture window that framed the city beyond. The balcony called to me, and I answered, stepping out onto the clear surface and feeling the familiar twinge of fear. Of suspicion that it might give way at any second and send me careening to my death.

Cool morning air chilled my skin, and I grabbed onto the edge of the balcony and watched as dawn's light slid over the city, washing out the deep blacks of night. If only that light could somehow get inside me and illuminate the worry-shadowed corners of my soul. I felt so lost. So out of my depth as I white-knuckled the balcony rail and pondered the confusing mess my life had suddenly become.

The note I'd found shoved into Kage's desk drawer had been nothing more than a hint, a tiny clue with no context. *Watch yourself.* To me, those words could only mean one of two things; Kage was being harassed, or he was being warned. Either way, someone was not happy with him.

Could the note really have to do with Kage coming out as gay? Though the timing of its arrival had coincided perfectly with the now-infamous Grace Howard interview, I had a feeling the two were unrelated and that the note was meant to communicate something much more sinister than homophobia. And what about the so-called mugging, during which nothing was stolen and all of the injuries seemed to be strategically placed to be hidden by Kage's clothing? I was leaning toward the theory that both the beating and the note were warnings, and they had absolutely nothing to do with sexual orientation.

But Kage seemed reluctant—no, unwilling—to share any details with me. As if he thought we could coexist in the same living space while leading separate lives based on two opposing realities. Did he really think he could get away with keeping me in the dark? And why would he want to? If I had something scary going on in my life, I would definitely want him to know about it.

Unless...

Oh, my God. Could that be it?

I covered my mouth with my hand as my brain seized on another idea—one that made me panic, my breaths quickening. What if this was all my fault? What if Kage was being threatened because someone knew I had killed Santori? What if this was something like blackmail? An *I Know What You Did Last Summer* intimidation plot? All because of me.

My stomach tightened as my mind filtered facts through a different-shaped sieve. I'd been keenly aware of Kage's growing agitation over the past weeks. He was absent more and more often, and even when we were together, he would get a faraway look in his eyes. As if his body was right in front of me, but his mind was somewhere else entirely.

I had thought seeing a therapist would fix the problem. Kage had been at least partially dependent on therapy since he was a young boy, and now that poor Dr. Tanner was missing and presumed dead, Kage's mental health had been left unattended like an innocent little latch-key kid. Who knew what trouble he might get into while he was left to fend for himself? What emotional aberrations might manifest, especially in the wake of Santori's death?

Murder, my mind corrected, as it always did. It couldn't let me forget. I kept telling myself it had been self-defense. That Santori had been an awful man, and I had really performed a public service by taking him out.

Of course I had, because the alternative was unthinkable. And yet it was always there, lurking on the periphery of my thoughts. Leering at me. Taunting me. And if I ever looked directly at it, or listened to the insidious little voice that whispered—

Shut up, shut up, shut up. I buried my fingers in my hair and pulled hard enough to bring tears to my eyes. My head was still vaguely sore from the last time I'd done this, and the familiar ache comforted me in a strange and unexpected way. I clamped my teeth tightly together, and there was an ache there, too, from long nights of clenching in my sleep.

I had tried to stay upbeat and keep a smile on my face while I watched Kage drift away, trying to pretend it was just a temporary bump in the road caused by stress. I had encouraged him to seek therapy under the guise of concern, but the truth was, deep down, I was resentful. Tired of playing second fiddle to his demons. I needed him more than ever, and he had left me flapping in the wind like so much forgotten laundry.

But now I had to entertain the possibility that the resurfacing of his demons and the very real threat of physical danger were all *my* fault, because I had committed murder and then made myself a permanent fixture of his life. Was I a liability? A tool to be used to punish or manipulate him? If that was the case, then maybe I deserved to be hung out to dry.

Whatever the case, this was my life now. I needed to man up and take control of it. If I was a liability, there was nothing to be done about it now except to move forward and try to fix it. Kage was strong, and I was coming to believe that I was strong.

Wow. When had that happened?

I got dressed for *work*. It still felt funny calling it that, even though I was getting more confident and productive every day. Running an MMA blog wasn't as easy as it had seemed when it was an abstract idea, but I was actually loving every minute of it. Kage may have funded it and gotten the ball rolling, but the blog was mine. I'd even called it *Jamie's Corner*.

It was the first thing that had made me feel like a man instead of a fumbling college student, and I had begun to think of it almost like my child. An adorable little bundle of potential for me to nurture and love and help grow into something more. It depended on me, and I wasn't about to let it down.

After I was dressed in a white button-down and slacks, I pasted my unruly curls into some semblance of order and walked through a light spray of Creed cologne, which I could admit I was addicted to. Then I left Kage a note, along with my cell phone, his pain pills, and a bottle of water.

I bent to kiss him on the forehead, but I swerved away at the last second for fear of waking him and brushed my lips lightly against his hair. Then I grabbed my laptop and headed off to the office.

God, I loved the sound of that. I was officially adulting, and despite the rest of the bullshit, it felt amazing. I was beginning to think maybe I could do this real life thing after all.

STEVE WAS in my office before I'd even gotten my laptop fired up, looking vibrant in a peach shirt, skinny khakis, and a tie striped with shades of raspberry. His blond hair had new highlights and a streak of lime green that swooped elegantly across one eye.

"Channeling your inner rainbow sherbet today?"

He smiled, unperturbed. "Are you saying I look good enough to eat?"

I rolled my eyes and hit the power button on my laptop. "If that's what you want to tell yourself, I'm cool with it."

"Hmmm..." Steve said. "That's pretty close to an admission. I'll take it." He sat down in the chair facing my desk and sighed. "I'm bored."

"Your shift just started. How have you had time to get bored?"

I logged in and scrolled through my email inbox, which was getting really busy since I'd started the blog. Fan mail, requests for coverage of certain fighters, offers for interviews. There were even people asking about advertising on my site, and I had enlisted a developer to create an ad system for me.

It was shocking how quickly things were moving. I was actually already receiving ad revenue—okay, I had sold two ads so far. It was only a drop in the bucket compared to the amount of money Kage had invested and was still investing to make me a success. But still...

I was nervous about my next step, which was posting regularly on my YouTube channel. Fortunately I already had a great camera, which Kage had bought me in the early days of our professional relationship. I had fashioned a little makeshift studio, with my camera mounted and ready to go on the edge of my desk, a ridiculously expensive microphone, and a backdrop with different scenes I could pull down behind me. I mean, I had a green screen, for Christ's sake. *A green screen.*

Steve leaned forward and rested his elbows on my desk, refusing to be ignored. "After last night, anything would be boring. I had a date with an investment banker."

Oh, yeah, right. We were talking.

"An investment banker?" I asked, not looking up from my

laptop. "That's different. I'd figure a suit who handles money for a living would be a little sedate for you. The firefighter, the DJ, the rock climber... Those seemed more your type."

I refrained from mentioning the MMA fighter, because though Jason and Steve had hooked up once, it had not ended well. Steve was my new bestie, and Jason was the closest thing Kage had to a friend, so we all avoided that touchy subject like the plague.

"Hey, alphas come in all shapes and sizes," Steve said. "As long as they're not afraid to explore their kinkier side in the bedroom, they're my type."

I didn't even want to know what Steve got up to in the bedroom. He made it difficult not to try to imagine, though, because he loved to throw out suggestive comments. He never got graphic, but I often found myself picturing him—against my will, of course—playing the submissive bottom for some big, rough dude. And wearing lingerie, of course. The way he dressed during the day pretty much guaranteed he'd like to dress up in pretty things for his partners.

I thought maybe it was a good time to ask.

"Do you...ummm...dress up for sex like you do for work?" That wasn't exactly how I'd meant to word the question, but I was suddenly shy.

Steve grinned knowingly. "I don't wear khakis and button-ups to bed if that's what you mean."

"Nooo..." I felt a blush coming on. "I mean colorful things. Fancy things." Why was this damn question so hard to get out?

"Colorful or fancy? You mean like clown suits or tuxedos?"

"Stop fucking with me, Steve. You know what I'm talking about. I mean do you wear..." I fluttered my hand awkwardly. "Pretty undergarments?"

That made him laugh. "Why yes, grandma. I do wear pretty undergarments. Last night I was rocking a pair of black silk panties with black stockings and a lacy garter belt. Wanna see the pictures?" He pulled his phone out of his pocket.

"Do *not* show me that." I held my hands up in front of my face, warding him off.

He put the phone away with a shrug. "Fine, but the investment banker sure seemed to like it."

"I'm sure you were very lovely," I said. "But please don't make me look at panty pics. I have a hard enough time ignoring your sex life as it is with you telling me about it all the time."

"Hey, I have to hear about you and Kage all the time, too."

I gaped at him. "Because you *ask*, asshole."

Steve regarded me for a moment, the smile finally falling from his face. I had a moment of regret, thinking maybe I had gone too far and hurt his feelings. But nope, he was only gearing up to hurt mine.

He looked at me with pity in his eyes. "Oh, my poor boy. You and Kage are having trouble in bed, aren't you?"

"What? God, no." His comment made me feel uncomfortable, probably because it was so close to the truth.

Steve sat back in his chair, putting more distance between us, and held up a hand to mute my protests. "Don't lie to me, Jamie. I've noticed you've been getting awfully snippy and closed down about sex lately. It's like you've been possessed by the spirit of some sexually frustrated spinster. Before long you'll be knitting cat sweaters and wearing sensible shoes, and I am not going to stand by and watch that happen. I had thought maybe it was the blog. That you were trying to be all *mature* or something, but I just realized it's not that at all. You're just hard up."

"I am not hard up," I huffed. "Besides, everything isn't about sex, Steve. Some of us have priorities and stuff. Goals and shit."

Steve got up out of his seat and rounded my desk. I braced for him to slap me for being a colossal dick. Instead, he threw his arms around me and squeezed.

"I'm sorry, Jamie. Is there anything I can do? Would you like me to speak to Kage?"

Oh, God, this was worse than a slap. His pity and lovey-dovey bullshit made my skin crawl. I wasn't weak. I wasn't some emotional charity case. Kage loved me, and I loved him, and I didn't need Steve feeling sorry for me.

"Hell, no, I don't need you to talk to my boyfriend." I extracted myself gently from his hug and nudged him away. "I'm fine. I told you Kage has been stressed out for a while, and things have been strained. It's nothing a little therapy can't fix."

Steve nodded. "Well, that Dr. Key is certainly cute."

"Cute?" I gave Steve my most genuine what-the-fuck look. I was about to launch into an inquiry on why he thought Dr. Key's looks had anything to do with his ability to counsel Kage into a better frame of mind, but then I realized it wouldn't do any good. Steve had a very unique way of thinking, and a bit of logic wasn't going to change him.

Besides, I kind of liked him just the way he was. Confusing, annoying, snarky, and sweet.

I groaned and gave in like I always did. "Okay, we're having a little trouble, but it's not so much sexual as communication-related. Kage and I have never been the most efficient communicators, and lately it's even worse. I've already told you he seems distant, and I don't know how to draw him back in. That's pretty much the gist of it."

Confiding in someone who could only know a small part of what was going on was sort of pointless. I knew that, but the alternative was shutting Steve out.

I'd had something of a breakthrough that morning as I stood in our bedroom contemplating everything. After all of the fear and freaking out, a sense of peace and of certainty had settled over me. Kage and I were meant to be together, I was absolutely sure of it. And we were strong, both separately and as a couple. It might take a while to get everything sorted out, and things might get worse before they got better, but I was in it for the long haul.

If things had to get bloody and messy, then so be it. Kage was my man, and I wasn't giving him up without a fight.

"You know I'm here if you need me, right?" Steve said. "I may not be able to do much, but you can at least count on me to listen and to watch movies with you."

"And to pop into my office fifty times a day to gossip."

"Don't even try to pretend you don't like it. You'd be lost without me."

"If by lost you mean oblivious to the color of Catwoman Cathy's new glasses or the fact that Alicia's new boyfriend has a receding hairline, then yes. I'd be completely lost. Thank you."

"You're welcome," Steve said with an endearing grin.

"Now get your lacy bloomers out of here. I've got actual work to do."

CHAPTER TWO

KAGE

I WOKE to a throbbing in my head and an aching body. Rolling over was a chore, and my muscles groaned in protest as I maneuvered myself into a sitting position on the side of the bed. For a disoriented second, I wondered if I'd been hit by a train, and then I remembered. Four trains had hit me, and they'd been wearing steel-toed boots and carrying guns.

I shuddered, remembering how calmly Theodore Brown had smiled as he'd told me goodbye, all the while knowing what I was walking into. Knowing that he had ordered an ambush on me, and that the only mercy I'd be shown was getting to live afterward.

Fucking bastard.

I spotted the bottle of hydrocodone on the bedside table where

Jamie had left it for me, along with a bottle of water, a note, and his cell phone. Even when we weren't particularly getting along, he was thoughtful.

I went for the pills first, shaking two into my hand and then adding a third before gulping them down with water. I needed to be careful. This kind of pain was the stuff overdoses were made of.

Jamie's note was short and to the point: *I'm downstairs working if you need me. Ice yourself when you get up.* He'd drawn a cute little heart and kissy lips under the words, and that made me smile.

Yeah, he still loved me.

I shuffled to the bathroom to take a much-needed piss, removed the uncomfortable compression bandages, and made a detour on the way back to bed to grab the dreaded frozen peas from the freezer. Without Jamie's help, icing my back wasn't easy, but I managed. I read a little more in Santori's journals while I was immobilized. I had a burning need to discover everything I could about his life, and hopefully more about my own. It was tough knowing that a huge chunk of my life was just random snippets and fuzzy images, as if I'd barely existed before puberty. I was going to have to learn about myself through someone else's eyes. That is if my family or I was even mentioned at all.

Just before time to remove the frozen peas, a text message notification sounded. It was a reminder for a doctor's appointment I hadn't made, with a doctor I'd never heard of. The message said they were expecting me there in two hours.

For a split second, I was upset. I'd told Jamie no doctors, but apparently he had taken it upon himself to make an appointment for me anyway. I knew he was worried about me, but it was ultimately my decision whether or not to see a doctor. Not his. He had no idea what was at stake here.

I had enough of a conscience to admit it was partly my fault for not being honest with him about the attack, but goddammit why couldn't he just listen to me? I wasn't angry. Just disappointed.

After returning the bags of peas to the freezer, I called the front desk and had them transfer me to Jamie's office. He picked up on the third ring.

"Jamie Atwood." His voice was all business-like, and I took a second to be impressed.

"It's me," I said. "What are you doing?"

"Just working. Going through these millions of emails and wishing I had an assistant." He paused, then started backtracking. "Not that I'm asking you to hire me an assistant or anything. I don't really need one. It was a joke, because emails are just annoying."

"Jamie, I know you're not hitting me up for an assistant. But if you ever really did need one, I hope you would feel comfortable asking me. I told you I would get you whatever you need for your business, and I meant it."

He let out an audible breath. "I know. Forget it. I'm just being an idiot. How are you feeling?"

"Shitty," I admitted. "But I'll be leaving for the doctor's office in about an hour and a half."

I waited, letting my words sink in. It didn't feel right just launching into a tirade, because I knew he was only looking out for me. He didn't deserve my anger, but we did need to talk about it.

"Are you okay?" The naked alarm in his voice was a surprise. "Something bad happened, didn't it? Are you coughing up blood or something? Just sit tight, and I'll be there in just a minute to help you to the Rover. Wait, I should probably pull it around to the front door. No, I'll get Steve to pull it around while I come up and get you. Or maybe we should just call 911 and let them take you to the emergency room."

"Slow down, Jamie. I'm fine. But—" Confusion set in. There was no way he would be that shocked if he had made the appointment.

"Don't lie to me," Jamie said, his voice wavering. "If there's nothing to worry about, why did you change your mind about going to the doctor? Please don't shut me out, Kage. Not when it has to do with your health. I'm scared."

Fuck. If Jamie hadn't made the appointment, then who the hell had? I needed to figure that out, but first I had to calm him down. I felt guilty for having scared him, and even more for having doubted him.

"Hey," I said firmly, raising my voice to cut through his heavy breathing. God, it sounded like he was going to hyperventilate. "I'm fine, baby. When I woke up this morning all stiff and uncomfortable, I just decided it wasn't such a bad idea to go and have someone take a look. Maybe they can suggest something to help me recover faster."

It was a lie, but it was for a good cause. Just until I could figure this shit out. Eventually I was going to have to come clean to Jamie, but for now...

His breathing slowed and quieted. "You promise you're okay?"

"I promise I'm not any worse off than I was yesterday. Quit worrying and get back to your emails. I'll stop by your office in a bit, but right now I need to get dressed."

Jamie reluctantly got off the phone, and I clicked on the mysterious text message again. If Jamie didn't make the appointment, and I didn't make the appointment, then who did? It was too big much of a coincidence to be a mistake. So the logical question was, who all knew I was hurt?

Theo knew, of course. And his goons. But it didn't make sense that any of them would make a doctor's appointment for me. Were they planning to finish me off in a public place? Have a doctor administer a fatal dose of something during my examination? It was just totally implausible.

But who else knew? I hadn't spoken to Dr. Key since the attack. Had Jamie told Steve? Maybe, but it was highly unlikely that Steve would have made an appointment for me, and certainly not without at least consulting Jamie first.

No one else knew. Except... Oh, God.

Aaron knew.

My heart jumped into my throat. When we'd talked on the phone, he said he would be seeing me soon, but he'd been mysterious about the details. He was always mysterious about everything.

Aaron. That had to be it. This whole thing smacked of his down-low espionage shit. Then again, maybe I was just tripping. I *had* been eating hydrocodone like candy. Hell, there was even a slim chance I'd been so altered by the drugs that I'd made the appointment myself. It was the most unlikely of all the scenarios I could come up with, but I had to admit it wasn't outside the realm of possibility.

No, it almost had to be Aaron. And if there was any chance it was him, I had to go. He had answers I needed, and after the vanishing act he'd pulled after my uncle's death, I was pretty sure he wasn't just going to waltz right in through the front door of the Alcazar.

With a deep sigh, I pulled on a loose pair of gray sweats, a dark blue t-shirt, and sneakers. Too late, I noticed the pile of compression dressings I had forgotten to put on. They were uncomfortable anyway, so I said fuck it and left them off.

I brushed my teeth, ran a hand through my hair, and headed downstairs with Jamie's cell phone. I limped into the elevator and pressed the button for the lobby, trying in vain to pretend my tenderized flesh wasn't about to fall off the bone.

Damn, I hurt all over. Thank goodness the meds were starting to kick in hard, the familiar tingle beneath my skin promising relief.

When I stepped off the elevator, I made my way through the lobby as quickly as I could, keeping my head down. I didn't want to talk to anyone. I wasn't in any mood to play boss man today. Thank God Steve was away from the desk. If he saw me, I'd be stuck in an endless conversation.

I got through the lobby without incident and headed down the small hallway that led to Jamie's office. I pushed his door open and stepped gingerly inside, sucking in a sharp breath when I caught sight of him sitting behind his desk.

His beauty caught me off guard, as if it had been months instead of hours since I'd last seen him. He was fresh-faced beneath the boyish waves of his dark hair, and he was wearing those damned sexy glasses. My own personal Clark Kent, and only I knew how freaky he could get when the glasses came off.

His warm brown eyes stretched wide when he saw me, and he smiled, melting me with that unmistakable air of innocence he always carried. It was just like the first time we met, when I'd felt the undeniable pull of something rare and precious. I needed his innocence. Needed to own it, eradicate it, and preserve it all at the same time. I didn't understand my own conflicting feelings, but it was a conundrum that I'd happily spend the rest of my life trying to work out.

All thoughts of my mysterious doctor's appointment evaporated. Right now all I could think was that Jamie looked like he needed a good fucking—to be bent over that desk with his dress shirt and perfectly-fitted slacks torn off and lying in a heap on the floor. I wanted him naked and begging for my cock. Unfortunately, with my injuries, I was pretty useless at the moment.

Maybe tomorrow...

Jamie removed his glasses and set them on the desk, but his bright smile morphed into a smirk as he noticed I was hobbling around the desk to get to him. "Great. I'm dating an old man."

I used every ounce of willpower I had to straighten my gait and pretend I wasn't about to fall down. "Trust me, babe. I may walk like an old man, but I fuck like a cheetah."

Jamie laughed. "A cheetah? That is the most disturbing analogy I've ever heard. What does that even mean?"

"You know... old men are slow, cheetahs are fast." My face colored. "Fuck, I don't know. I'm thinking with the wrong head right now. Just go with it."

I bent down over him with some effort, my face coming to hover just above his as he gazed up at me. So much better than the last couple of days when we'd been arguing. He graced me with another of his innocent smiles—something I hadn't seen enough of lately.

It made me fucking hard.

I covered his mouth with mine and forced his soft lips apart with my tongue, invading him and taking every bit of pleasure I could. He opened wide for me, making slutty little moans with every pass of our greedy tongues, getting off on me as much as I was on him.

I knew this feeling. It was *us*, and I hadn't felt *us* in a while.

His fingers wound tightly in my hair and pulled, grinding my mouth down hard on his as if he thought I might try to escape. I groaned long and low and redoubled my efforts to ravish his face off.

"I want you so bad," he panted between kisses. "Feel how hard I am." He pulled my hand down beneath the desk and pressed my palm to his crotch, grinding against me like the little slut he was.

The hardness I found between his legs was too much to resist, and with no care for appropriate workplace behavior, I wrapped my fingers around his cock as best I could through the fabric of his pants and started to stroke. He shuddered against my lips and giggled.

So fucking adorable.

"You weren't expecting this, were you?" I asked playfully.

"Not even close. Did you just stop by to mouth-rape me in my office?"

"Hell, no. If I'd had any idea this was going happen, I would have worn underwear."

He got that little mischievous glint in his eyes I knew all too well. I had about half a second to realize this was about to get serious before he drew his head back and eyed my dick, which was currently snaking its way down the left leg of my sweats.

"Is all of that for me?" he asked, licking his lips.

"Mmm hmmm. Every inch of it."

He tore into my pants like he was unwrapping a gift and freed my cock, drawing it up and out and straight into his mouth.

"Jesus, Jamie," I cried out, as much from shock as desire. "You don't mess around, do you?"

He was hungry for it, pulling off of me and murmuring, "Not today," before gobbling it down again.

Watching him lose control that way was a total high, affecting me even more than the painkillers that were slowly spreading through my system. My instinct was to close my eyes and lose myself to the sensations—the wet warmth of his mouth around me, the slick glide of his tongue along the underside of my shaft, the drag of his soft lips against my aching flesh.

But as soon as my eyes fluttered shut, they flew back open again. I wanted to watch. There was nothing I'd rather see than my sweet Jamie swallowing my cock.

As usual, he made it very clear with every movement and every sound that he wanted me to use him—to rough him up and make him take more than he thought he could. So I obliged, shoving my entire length down his throat and making him choke on it.

"That's it, baby. Take that dick." I grabbed him by the back of his head and locked him in place while I gave a few rapid-fire pumps into the back of his throat. "You love it when I use you like that, don't you?"

When he gagged hard, I pulled out, watching as a thin string of saliva stretched from his mouth to the head of my cock before breaking and disappearing. I wound my fingers into the fine hair just above the nape of his neck and pulled. Jamie yelped in surprise, but then his lashed lowered, and his eyes went unfocused as he responded to the pain.

"You know I love it," he said in a low, lust-slurred voice. "Don't stop." He darted his tongue out and dragged it slowly over the head of my dick, pausing to kiss the slit and lick into it. He was shameless. Wild-eyed. Completely undone with need.

"Take your dick out," I told him. "Get it out now. I want to see it."

He scrambled to unfasten his slacks and pull out his flushed and straining cock. Not waiting for any command or suggestion from me, he started stroking. Hard and fast like he was trying to beat me to the finish line. And I'll be damned if his mouth didn't open right back up in a blatant invitation for me to fuck it.

I did, pushing in without preamble and picking up right where I left off—buried deep in the back of his throat. He sputtered and moaned, yanking mercilessly on his own dick.

I watched him work himself, turned on by his own rough treatment of his equipment. I'd never seen him so desperate to get off. The level of his need was staggering, and my own body responded to it with a feral hunger of its own. The sensation grew inside me until I thought I would explode from the sheer magnitude of it... and still, it wasn't enough.

Words spilled out of me. "Yeah, jerk it, baby. That's it. So fucking hot. I'm gonna tear that tight little ass up tonight. You won't be able to walk straight for a week."

He moaned in response, unable to speak with his mouth stuffed full of me, but I could see how frantic my words had made him. His hand blurred over his cock, moving so fast in his desperation to get off that I thought he might hurt himself.

The sight of it sent waves of impending orgasm rippling through my belly and my balls, and I wanted to scream, *No! Not now. Not when he's so fucking beautiful.*

But then he groaned around my cock, eyes rolling back in his head in blissed-out surrender, and came all over my sweats.

God, it was sexy and messy and so damn filthy. There was no way I could see a thing like that and not spontaneously unload in his sweet mouth. I filled it up with spurt after spurt of hot come, my orgasm so forceful it felt like it was being ripped out of me.

Jamie was so dazed and lethargic from his own orgasm that he couldn't possibly swallow it all down. I watched from beneath leaden eyelids as a thick stream of semen spilled out of his mouth and dribbled onto his slacks.

Jesus...

I pulled out of him slowly and reluctantly, my knees wobbly and my breath coming in harsh gasps.

"Uhhh..." Jamie groaned before slumping back in his chair, so boneless I thought he might slide onto the floor. "Wow. That was —" His head lolled toward the door as though he might pass out from satisfaction, but then he flew up from his seat and started frantically stuffing his dick back into his pants.

What the hell?

Dimly, through my post-orgasmic hydrocodone haze, I

heard a yelp and turned to see Steve standing in the open doorway. The shock on his face told me all I needed to know, and I flipped my damp sweats back up over my still-stiff cock.

I think I was too medicated to be startled. But I *was* pissed off. Jamie rested his forehead on his desk and groaned, draping his arms over his head in utter embarrassment.

"What the fuck, Steve?" I demanded, hearing the sluggishness in my own voice.

His kohl-lined eyes nearly bugged out of his head as he stared, opening and closing his mouth in an unsuccessful attempt to form words.

I glared at him. "Have you ever heard of knocking? Jesus Christ."

"I was trying to be quiet," he wailed.

"You were sneaking up on us?" I was getting more furious by the second, and his explanation wasn't helping.

"No, no," Steve said, looking like he was about to piss his khakis. "I just—I heard voices through the door. I thought Jamie was in one of his video chats, so I tried not to make any noise. Oh, shit. I'm so sorry."

"Video chats?" I looked over at Jamie, who was still face-planted on the surface of the desk. "What kind of video chats?"

I knew I sounded jealous and paranoid, but when I heard *video chat*, all I could think about were the ones Jamie and I had shared during our time apart. If I found out he was having video chats like *those* with anyone else, things were about to get really uncomfortable.

"I do interviews," Jamie said. "Watch live streams, sit in on conference calls. Business stuff."

His voice was flat. Traumatized. He was clearly still reeling from being walked in on in such a compromising position.

"Oh, yeah. You mentioned something about live streams before."

I felt like an idiot for even allowing such a crazy thought to enter my mind, but I was a relieved idiot nonetheless. When I turned my attention back to Steve, he was still shell-shocked in the doorway.

I glared at him. "Why do I get the feeling you're not getting much work done since Jamie's been spending time down here?"

Steve's eyes got even wider, and he put a hand to his chest. "Kage, you know me. I'm great at my job, and good luck finding anyone as dedicated as I am. Do you know how many shifts I have to pick up when other people call out? I practically live here."

I ran a hand through my hair, suddenly feeling like I needed to sit down. The meds were kicking in pretty hard. The edges of my vision had gone a little fuzzy, and there was Steve in the center, looking like a pastel martyr all shocked and hurt. And I'd just practically accused Jamie of webcam cheating.

"I guess I could have locked the door," I admitted begrudgingly. "But you don't need to be spending all of your time in here, either. Save the socializing for after work hours, okay?"

Steve nodded and walked stiffly away, leaving the scent of God knows how many beauty products in the room with us.

"Well, that was embarrassing," Jamie said after he'd gone. "How much do you think he saw?"

I laughed as the absurdity of it all finally caught up with me. "Well, I'm pretty sure he saw you drooling my jizz all over your pants. Oh, and my dick. He probably got a good enough look at it to identify it in a police lineup."

Jamie smirked. "Well, let's hope you your dick doesn't ever have any reason to be in a police lineup."

"I don't know..." I leaned down and kissed his lips until he moaned against me and relaxed. "It gets pretty crazy when you're around. No telling what illegal things it might end up doing."

Jamie laughed quietly. "Now I'm just intrigued."

"We'll explore those possibilities later." I stood and stretched a little, the pain having dulled to a persistent ache. "But right now I have to leave. Somebody got my pants all messy, and now I have to go change."

Jamie furrowed his brow and looked down at his own pants. "I have to do the same, but I'll let you go first. If we go up together, you might never make it to that appointment at all."

"Good idea. I knew that college degree would come in handy."

I kissed him again and left him with a big grin on his face that matched the one on mine. All things considered, this day hadn't started out too badly.

That is until I stepped into the elevator and received a text from Steve. I clicked on it without thinking, and a selfie popped up. Steve in black lingerie. The caption read, *Payback for what I just had to witness, you perv. I'm seriously traumatized.*

After the urge to bleach my eyeballs subsided, I replied. *This is Kage. Why are you sending my boyfriend sexy pics?*

To which he responded, *OMG. Forgot you had Jamie's phone. I am so embarrassed right now. But you really think it's sexy?*

I shook my head and laughed against my will. *Fucking Steve.*

CHAPTER THREE

KAGE

SOMEWHERE BETWEEN LEAVING Jamie's office and flopping into the backseat of the Uber, my apprehension had returned. I was under no illusion that the doctor fairy had felt sorry for my busted up body and dropped a magical appointment into my lap, so that only left my theory that this was some sort of cloak-and-dagger meeting.

I offered up a silent prayer to please let it be Aaron and not another ambush, because I had no doubt that another meeting with Theodore Brown's Matrix crew would mean certain death.

I looked out the window of the Uber car and noticed a man standing across the street. There was nothing particularly remarkable about a guy in a baggy hoodie and jeans, but my gaze had snagged on him before I realized I was staring.

Something about him... The posture. The stillness. The way he seemed to be staring right back at me, even though his face was almost completely hidden within the shadows of the too-large hood.

My car pulled away before I could study him too closely, but as I turned to look through the back glass, I was disturbed to find that his head had turned to follow the car.

Fuck. A chill went through me.

I tried to forget about the strange man, but even Cliff-the-Uber-Driver's babbling couldn't wipe the unease from my mind. I thought about him all the way to the doctor's office.

I did manage to pick up snippets of Cliff's one-sided conversation. He talked about Las Vegas traffic, his girlfriend's unwillingness to commit to marriage, and his brother-in-law's drug addiction among other things. It made me think of bartenders and hairdressers, who were known to be sort of lay-therapists to their customers, and I had to wonder why it always seemed like the roles were reversed with Uber drivers. Maybe it was just my luck to get the mouthy ones.

By the time we reached the doctor's office, I was so stressed out from worrying about Cliff's issues on top of my own, I was out of the car before it even came to a stop.

Fuck you, Cliff," I thought. *You think you've got problems? Try walking in my shoes for a day. You'd be in rehab right alongside your brother-in-law.*

As the car pulled away, I stumbled into the sparsely populated waiting room and gave it a quick scan. There was a lady with a walker, a man in a Braves cap, a bald man reading Cosmo, a businessman tapping on his cell phone, a woman with a sleeping baby, and a man in a leg brace.

No men in trench coats, thank God.

With no other obvious options, I approached the receptionist's desk. She was on the phone, so I stood on unsteady legs and waited. When I heard her say goodbye to the person on the other end of the line, I took a step forward, and that's when I felt the hand on my shoulder.

Aaron's voice.

"Follow me out the back door," a familiar voice said close to my ear.

Aaron's voice.

He stepped in front of me, wearing an Atlanta Braves baseball cap, jeans, and a pink Polo. He'd dropped about thirty pounds, and his dark brown hair, which I'd only ever seen buzzed, had grown long enough to reach the collar of his shirt. It was full and lustrous, and he was sporting a neat jaw full of stubble that could almost be classified as a beard.

"I didn't even recognize you," I called after him, trying to keep up as he practically sprinted down the hallway. My words came out thick and slow, like the last bit of syrup from a bottle, and I found myself wishing I wasn't so dulled from the pain pills.

Once we were through the door, Aaron got into the backseat of a waiting black sedan, and I followed him inside. The driver wasted no time getting us out of the parking lot.

"You look so different," I said, gaping at him. "I figured you were the one who sent me the text, but I looked straight at you in that waiting room and didn't recognize you."

Aaron smiled. Not a full-on smile, but at least the hint of one. "I'm dressing a little differently these days."

"Yeah, in someone else's body. Jesus, man. I mean, I still know your face when I look closely, and your voice is the same, but—" Words finally failed me, and I just threw up my hands and laughed.

"You look a little different, too," he said, his dark brown eyes flicking down and back up as he gave me a quick once-over.

I shrugged, feeling a little judged. "I'm carrying about twenty extra pounds these days. Nothing a little cleanse won't fix."

"You got any fights coming up?"

I heard echoes of Marco's bitching and looked out the window. "Yeah, in a couple of months."

He whistled. "And you went and got yourself all jacked up by Theo's boys."

I nodded. "It'll be fine. I'm Michael Kage."

"Well, Michael Kage, you're making some pretty stupid decisions these days. You know that, right?"

"How do you figure?" I was being purposely obtuse as I mentally waded through my ever-deepening pile of colossal mistakes.

His laugh was a low rumble in his throat. "Well, let's count them off. One, you pissed Theo off. Two, you're not training like you were. And three, what in God's name were you thinking getting fucked up before coming here today? I could have been anyone."

I met his gaze and raised my t-shirt, revealing the nasty bruises all along my side. "Does this answer your question?"

He nodded slowly. "Yeah, okay. I guess you get a pass. But you need to be more careful, Kage. If they come after you again, that first beating will seem like fun times."

I dropped my shirt and stared out the window again, noticing we were pulling into a parking garage. "I know I'm fucking up, Aaron. But I'm confused. I don't know what to do to fix things, and every move I make seems to be the wrong one."

"For starters, you can tell me everything that you said to Theo Brown. And everything he said to you."

I struggled to remember and to articulate. "Basically, he just told me he'd known my brother and me when we were kids. And my dad. We had a drink, and I asked him a few questions about my family. Then I told him I was thinking about shutting down the art gallery, the horse stables, and his hotel. I told him he could come work at the Alcazar as the casino manager because I was thinking about firing the current one."

"So you were going to strip him of his current position in the company and obliterate his income. Sounds reasonable. I can't imagine he didn't go for it."

My face colored. "Well, I did tell him he'd still make the same salary he's making now as a hotel manager."

Aaron laughed, but it was a harsh and humorless sound. "You thought he was just a hotel manager? How could you have been living with your uncle all these years and still be so clueless? It's a wonder you made it this far without stepping off in it."

"Nobody ever told me anything," I said defensively. "You think Santori ever gave me the time of day? The only time he had anything to do with me was when he wanted to bitch or threaten me. You of all people should know that."

"I did know you were oblivious. I just never could understand it. You were aware that your uncle was involved in illegal activities, and you knew he wasn't a good guy. The two of you rarely got along, he had you watched like a hawk, and he controlled every move you made. Yet you just—" He shook his head. "I don't know."

My eyes watered, but I willed the tears away. "I ignored it all because it was easier that way. Fighting was my way of coping. I could pour every bit of my focus into that one thing, and everything else didn't seem so bad."

"Fighting wasn't your only outlet," Aaron said, eyebrow raised.

I glared at him. "Now you want to talk about my sex life?"

"No." He had the decency to look chagrined. "I'm sorry. I

shouldn't have said that. You were a good kid in a bad situation, and you did what you had to do to get through it. Believe me, I get it."

I slammed my fist down on the armrest of the car door and growled. "I thought when he died, it would all be over. I thought Jamie and I could get married and run the Alcazar together. I could fight in the UFC for a while and maybe get that fucking belt my uncle was gagging for. But now it seems like things are worse than they were before."

"That's because they are," Aaron said. "Much worse."

I laughed. "Don't try to sugar coat it or anything."

"I'm not here to sugar coat anything, Kage. I'm here to pull your head out of your ass and tell you exactly what's going on."

"And what exactly *is* going on?" I was pleading now, because this bullshit had gone on long enough. I needed help, and it seemed like Aaron was the only one in any position to give me that help.

Aaron turned his entire body to face me, hitching a knee up onto the seat. The driver had pulled into a parking space deep in the garage, and we were just sitting there in the semi-dark with the car running.

I turned to face Aaron, mimicking his pose and wincing when I twisted a little too far for comfort. "So are you gonna tease me or tell me?"

"What do you think of the journals?" he asked.

"I read some of the first one. It jumps around a lot, and it seems like an emo teenager wrote it, but it's very enlightening. I got to the part where Peter moved in with Gio Rivera, and... well, I had to read all about him losing his virginity, because he spared no details in describing that." I shook my head and chuckled at the memory of his words. "Are we even sure my uncle wrote that stuff? He drew hearts, Aaron. Cheesy little

31

hearts with arrows through them. And *Peter Loves Gio 4-Ever* in bubble letters."

Aaron smiled. "I thought it was kind of sweet. In the beginning, anyway. Enjoy the hearts. They'll be gone soon enough."

I swallowed hard, dreading what was to come when the hearts were gone. I may have been flippant when speaking to Aaron about the journals, but deep down I was rooting for eighteen-year-old Peter Santori. The guy whose father had abused him all his life deserved some happiness, and it seemed like Gio truly cared about him. At least from Peter's point of view. When I compared the young man in the journal to the man who had raised me, I knew the rest of the journals couldn't be all hearts and bubble letters and declarations of love. Mainly because I'd never heard of Gio Rivera, the man whose hotel I now owned.

What had happened to him? Had my uncle bought him out? *Forced* him out? It was a question I wasn't sure I wanted answered, because the Peter Santori I knew didn't seem to have much of a conscience to speak of.

As for the rest of the crew mentioned in the journals, none of their names rang a bell. Except for Theo, of course. He was still hanging around like the after-effect of a bad meal.

"So what's Theo's deal?" I asked. "How do I get rid of him?"

Aaron laughed. "Get rid of him? My poor, deluded boy. You can't fire the boss."

"Boss?" My head was suddenly spinning worse than before. "What are you saying?"

Aaron shifted a little in his seat and looked me in the eyes with an expression so serious it scared me. "Theo has always been the one running things, Kage. Your uncle was nothing but the money man. Peter Santori never wanted to get his hands dirty, but Theo...

Let's just say he doesn't have a problem with it. He was Gio Rivera's right-hand-man."

"But I thought he was just some kid. Peter's best friend."

Aaron shrugged. "Apparently, he was a fast learner. He started out as Peter's best friend, but after Peter got him hired on with Gio, things changed."

"And what happened to Gio? Why haven't I ever heard of him? I didn't even know my uncle was gay or had ever had a lover. And now I find out I have his hotel."

"You'll have to read all of that for yourself in the journals."

I groaned. "Aaron, stop being mysterious."

"I'm not trying to be mysterious," he said. "It's not my story to tell. I think you will understand it all better coming directly from your uncle, however *emo* his delivery may be. Besides, you may discover some things I failed to notice. I was reading with a detached professional eye. You actually have some emotional investment in the story."

"Fine. But that can't be all you're going to tell me."

"It's not," he said. "The most important stuff has to do with what you're going to do for me. And for yourself."

I swallowed. "And what would that be?"

"Are you sober enough to retain information, or do we need to reconvene at a future date?"

"I can't wait for a future date. Things are getting real for me now if you hadn't noticed."

His gaze flicked down to my rib cage, where the damage was lurking beneath my shirt. "Yes, they are. More real than you know." He took a deep breath and stared out through the window at the darkened parking garage. "What I'm about to tell you cannot leave this car. Do you understand me?"

I nodded, knowing that I was making a pact of secrecy that

was going to be hard not to break. "I promise. It doesn't leave this car."

"The entire time I was working for your uncle, I was actually undercover with a certain government agency I'm not at liberty to name. Your uncle was laundering money for some big-time players in the crime world. Drug dealers, gun runners, and just all-around bad guys. We'd been looking at him for a while, and when he put out feelers for someone with surveillance experience, I happened to fit the bill. It was a perfect setup. I could get in close to him, monitor things, and keep my eyes open. The goal was to find out who his clients were, bust them, and get out. Peter Santori was supposed to be the gateway to a wealth of information about who we needed to be targeting, only he proved to be a dead-end."

"A dead-end?"

"Yes. He was a slick bastard, your uncle. Believe it or not, the Alcazar is a legitimate business. There is absolutely no illegal activity tied to it. Theo is the one running the show, and somehow Peter always kept his nose clean. But getting in close to Theo Brown is next to impossible. If there's one thing I learned in the last few years, it's that he trusts no one."

"Great," I breathed, feeling the clock of my own mortality ticking. "If he doesn't trust anyone, what am I supposed to do?"

"Well, I may have misspoken when I said *no one*. He did trust your uncle. And that's why you're our only hope if we want to salvage this operation."

My mouth dropped open, and I stared at him. "Why me? I'm not my uncle. Far from it, in fact."

"True," he said. "But you are the official owner of everything Theo holds dear, and you are his last connection to his best friend, Peter Santori. *And...*" Aaron scrubbed his fingers through his baby beard. "You look an awful lot like Peter."

"Well, there was definitely a family resemblance, but I'm hardly his doppelganger."

Aaron chuckled. "Have you never seen any old pictures of your uncle?"

"He didn't exactly keep framed photos of himself on the fireplace mantel."

"No, but there are some tucked away in the folder flaps at the backs of those journals." He cocked his head at me. "You're really not very observant, are you?"

That pissed me off.

"I'm extremely observant. Just not where my uncle is concerned. I spent too many years wishing he'd disappear."

"And you finally got your wish. Unfortunately, as it turns out, your uncle was the only thing keeping you safe. He kept you sheltered from the harsh realities of his business, presumably until the time was right to initiate you properly. He just died before that could happen. The man was clearly deluded about his own mortality."

"But in the end, he was going to kill me," I said.

Aaron shook his head. "It was all a ruse. I happen to have the inside track on that situation, remember? That man never intended to kill you, Kage. You were his heir, and he took that very seriously. I doubt he gave you the entire contents of that syringe."

"But I think I remember seeing him empty it into me."

Aaron raised a brow. "You don't think he could have squirted some of it out before he gave you the shot?"

"Oh. That never occurred to me. I guess he could have."

"I'm sure he wouldn't have risked killing you. I know for a fact he was only stalling until he could get you under control. Things just got out of hand."

"But... Jamie." My mind was frantically trying to hang onto the crumbs of truth he was feeding me.

"Oh, he fully intended to hurt Jamie if it came to that. He was certainly no humanitarian. But the original plan was for us to talk Jamie into leaving. The drugs were just to scare you. If you hadn't come barging into his apartment that day, things would likely have played out very differently."

"But why did he have such a vendetta against Jamie?"

Aaron shook his head. "Love was never supposed to be in the cards for you, Kage. At least not like that. Santori was convinced that your proclivities toward men were going to be your downfall, and then when you actually developed feelings for one of them... Well, he couldn't abide that. Not when your affection for Jamie had you rebelling in earnest. For the first time, your uncle felt like his control on you was slipping. He needed to rein you back in."

"So he never even planned to kill me?"

Aaron scoffed. "Not even a little bit. He just wanted to scare you. To scare you both. He had Aldo and me keeping tabs on the two of you all the time, looking for anything to drive a wedge between you. When that didn't work, he resorted to hardcore scare tactics. In the end, it was just too much for him, losing control that way. He flipped out, and I had to step in. Especially when Aldo started waving that gun around. He would have put bullets in us all if he'd thought it was what Santori wanted."

"And you saved us."

Aaron chuckled humorlessly. "Make no mistake, kid. I like you and Jamie, but I would never have compromised my mission or my safety to save you. This thing is bigger than us. Bigger than me. So I had to make a judgment call: back up a dead-end lead by helping to murder an innocent young man, or salvage what I had left."

"And that was?" I thought I knew the answer, and it made me sick to my stomach.

"You," he said simply.

And then all of it made sense. My part in this twisted drama.

My destiny. The truth sank deep into my guts like a rusty hook, and I wanted to jump out of the car and run until I couldn't run anymore—until my insides burned and my muscles gave out. But I couldn't, because I didn't want a fucking bullet in my back. I was caught, and all I could do was allow Aaron to reel me in by that rusty hook.

I took a deep breath, suddenly much closer to sober than I had been moments before. "What do I have to do?"

Aaron told the driver to head back to the doctor's office, then leaned casually against the car door. "It's pretty simple, really. Make friends with Theo and get me a list of everyone he's working with."

"Ummm... make friends with the man who trusts no one? How the fuck am I supposed to do that?"

Aaron shrugged. "I'm sure you'll figure out a way."

"And if I refuse?"

"I'm sure you can imagine. This is an important operation, Kage. We have the opportunity to take down some really big drug and arms dealers. After all of the time and money we've invested, we can't afford to fail."

I didn't have anything to say after that. My words dried up, and I was left with nothing but images of what might happen if I didn't go along with Aaron's plan.

As I climbed silently out of the car at the back of the doctor's office, Aaron leaned across the seat and called after me.

"Remember, Kage. No one can know about this. Not even Jamie. I'd hate for anything to happen to him because you can't keep your mouth shut."

I swallowed hard. "Are you threatening him?"

Aaron's gaze didn't waver when he said, "I hope I don't have to. He's a sweet kid."

CHAPTER FOUR

KAGE

WHEN I STEPPED into the Scepter Hotel on the following morning, you could have knocked Theodore Brown over with a feather. His brown eyes widened, and he excused himself from talking to the girl behind the check-in desk.

"Little Santori." Theo's voice was purposely casual, but the fine edge of wariness was unmistakable. "I didn't expect to see you here today."

Somehow I managed a smile. "I would have come sooner, but I was a little under the weather." I touched a hand discreetly to my rib cage, my smile never faltering. "Can we talk, or did you have other plans?"

"No, it's fine." He gestured for me to follow him to his office, and we had to sidestep a ladder and paint supplies in the hallway. "You'll have to excuse our progress. We're doing a little touching up. You know how old buildings are."

"As a matter of fact, I do. Since I've taken over the Alcazar, I've made some improvements myself. Our spa is nearly finished."

"Spa?" he asked with a laugh. "Sounds like you're getting fancy over there."

"We are. As I explained before, I plan on making the Alcazar a destination rather than a place to sleep off a Vegas drunk."

As we entered Theo's office, he offered me the same chair I'd sat in during our previous meeting. I lowered myself into the cushioned seat with a shudder. This felt too much like déjà vu, and I wasn't itching to have a replay of what happened last time. I did glance at the liquor cabinet, though, because that part of the memory wasn't too damn bad.

"You're thinking about that forty-year-old Macallen we shared last time, aren't you?" Theo asked with a tentative smile.

I nodded. "Yeah. Might take the edge off of these bruises your goons kicked into me."

Theo paused as he reached for the bottle and shot me an astonished look over his shoulder.

I shrugged. "The elephant's in the room whether we like it or not. No sense trying to tiptoe around it."

After a tense few seconds, the astonishment cleared from Theo's features, and he smiled. He took his time pouring up a couple of glasses of Macallen on the rocks, handed one over to me, and took his seat behind the desk.

"You surprise me, Michael. I had no idea you would be so straightforward. Most men who had received a beating like that would have stayed far away."

"I'm not most men. I make a hell of a punching bag, and I learn from my mistakes. I also know how to admit when I've been beaten."

His eyes glittered. "So I've beaten you then? Is that what you're saying?"

"You won this round," I admitted, nearly choking on the words. "But if you ever get the urge to hurt me again, I do hope you'll do it yourself. Getting a smackdown from your hired men is so impersonal. I'd much rather go hand-to-hand with you."

Theo laughed and took a swallow of his drink. "You kill me, Little Santori. So damn ballsy. I like that."

I downed my drink and shifted forward to set the glass on the desk, wincing slightly at the sting in my ribs. Damn my body for betraying me. I had hoped I could keep the pain hidden.

Theo noticed and leaned forward reflexively, his shrewd gaze scanning my body and lingering on my side where the pain was the worst.

"May I—" He cleared his throat and took another swallow of whiskey. "May I see?"

I couldn't check myself before my mouth fell open, revealing my shock. "You want to see the damage your goons did to me? How they wrecked my body with their boots?"

The way his eyes lit up at my description was downright disturbing. "Yes. I would very much like to see it. If you don't mind showing me, that is."

So he got a kick out of seeing his handiwork. I could work with that. I was always looking for any chink in my adversary's armor, anything that would indicate a weakness I could exploit. After I found that chink, I was damn good at using it to bait them in.

Real life wasn't so different from being in the cage, I supposed. Weakness was weakness. I wasn't sure how I could use this particular bit of knowledge to get the upper hand with Theo, but I needed to latch onto anything I could.

As much as I hated it, I was now the government's pawn, and my one mission was to gain Theo's trust and get him to reveal his secrets. It sounded like a fool's errand to me, but Aaron hadn't given me any other choice. He'd thrown me into the lion's den, and now I had to figure out how to survive.

Following my instincts, I looked Theo in the eyes... and pushed.

"Come over here and get a close-up, Mr. Brown. It's pretty gruesome. I don't think you can get the full picture from all the way over there."

He chuckled. Hesitated. Then he was on his feet and moving around the desk, looming over me with his superior height.

"Get on your knees," I said. I was being cocky, but I couldn't help it. I had him now. The knowledge echoed through my entire body like the resounding click of a deadbolt sliding into place, and I succumbed to the urge to keep the upper hand if only just a little bit. It was in my nature. And besides, if I seemed too much of a pushover, Theo would never buy my performance.

The incredulity in his eyes when he met mine was priceless, but I could see in the twitch of his long fingers and the slight sway of his body that he wanted to do it.

"Are you planning to club me over the head when I get down there?" he asked, dissembling with humor in a weak effort to camouflage the magnitude of his need.

"Only one way to find out," I said. "But I'm not showing you unless you get on your knees. You made this mess, and I had to lie there and take it. If you really want to see, I figure it's a fair trade. Your dignity for mine."

Theo nodded. "Alright, Michael. My dignity for yours. And then we're even."

I repressed the urge to shudder as I lifted the front of my T-shirt and tucked the tail into the neck like a teenage girl's improvised halter top, channeling a young Britney Spears. Not my best look, but I wasn't trying to win any fashion awards. I was trying to bait Theo Brown, and at the moment, his bloodlust was all I had to work with.

He pushed his lion's mane of hair back from one shoulder and dropped to his knees, settling back onto his calves as if he planned to stay a while. The pose was incongruous with his regal demeanor. He was a prideful man, and his willingness to debase himself for such a cheap thrill was as exhilarating as it was unsettling.

You have him on his knees, my own pride whispered. Adrenaline surged through my veins at the thought, and it occurred to me to wonder who the real animal was here—him or me.

My torso was on display now, the purpled flesh mottled with patches of sickly yellow and a deceptively pretty shade of pink. Theo's eyes grew wider, his pupils expanding to take in the sight, and his lips stretched into a languorous grin. He didn't even try to hide his reaction from me.

When his eyes raked over my exposed skin with a savage hunger, my sense of self-preservation tried to kick in. Power was a pendulum between us, swinging first one way and then the other. When he'd hit his knees, the pendulum had swung my way, but now I found myself wanting to cower from the gaze that was stripping me down to nothing. I wondered if he felt it, too.

I let the animal have his fill of looking. Then, when looking was no longer enough for him, he reached out and gently clasped both of my flanks. There was a sting of nerves where his fingers grazed the surface of my skin, and I gritted my teeth.

This is easy, I told myself. *And it will all be over soon.*

But then he pressed in with his thumbs just enough to make me suck in a breath.

"Still tender," he said, not bothering to feign concern. "They really worked you over, didn't they?"

"I thought that was the point."

"Of course. What good is a message you don't understand?" He studied my face closely for a moment, biting his bottom lip before he continued. "You *did* understand it, yeah? My message was clear?"

He pressed his thumbs into me again for emphasis, a big cat toying with his prey. This time it didn't catch me off guard, and I was able to mask my reaction. So he tightened his grip on me until I squirmed and let out an involuntary whimper.

Then he let go, satisfied.

"Are you finished playing yet?" I asked, irritable and a little breathless. "We have things to discuss."

He ignored my comment and looked up at me with softening eyes. There was wonder in his expression, and something akin to affection if I was reading him right.

"So much like your uncle," he mused. "I'd noticed the resemblance before, but only from afar or in pictures. Now that I have you so close, it's almost as if a ghost from the past sitting in my office. I can't get over it."

First Aaron and now Theo. Did I *really* look that much like Santori? In my drugged-out stupor, I'd forgotten to look at the photos Aaron had mentioned the day before.

"Of course he was never as fit as you are," Theo went on. "We were skateboarders—you know, back when it was a social statement—so he was always athletic. But he was never muscled up like *this*." His eyes ate up my biceps, following every curve. "The hair is the same, though. And the eyes. Even your face is remarkably like his."

Before I could think of a response, he stood up and returned to

43

his seat with a dismissive shrug, as if the moment had passed. His expression went blank, and he was all business again.

"So what was it you wanted to discuss with me?" he asked.

I shook my head, struggling to change gears as quickly as he had, and covered myself with my now-wrinkled shirt. "Isn't it obvious from the fact that I'm sitting here in front of you after you set your goons on me? I'm not backing down, Theo. I want in."

One corner of his mouth came up as he tried to feign ignorance. "I'm confused. What is it that you want into?"

"My own business," I said. "Quite frankly, I was pissed that you and some of the others seemed intent on keeping me out of the loop. I figured the best way to control something I couldn't understand was to shut it down."

"And now?" Theo steepled his fingers beneath his chin.

"And now I want in. I want to be a part of it. I don't like being shut out. My uncle kept me that way for my entire life, and I'm sick to death of it."

I hoped I sounded a little bit like a petulant teenager, because that's exactly how I wanted Theo to see me. As someone he could control. If he perceived me as a threat to his position as king of our dirty empire, he might try to push me out again. Or worse.

"I'm afraid you don't know what you're asking, Michael. Do you even have any idea what we do here?"

The question caught me off guard. How could I tell him I knew about the business without saying too much? I certainly couldn't let on that I'd spoken to Aaron, or I'd be leaving this office in a body bag.

I took a deep breath and decided to tell him about the journals.

"I know a little," I said. "I've been reading my uncle's journals, and he describes some of what he was into. I haven't gotten through them all, but I've read enough to know it's not entirely legal, and I'm fine with that. You and my uncle have been running this business for years, and neither one of you ended up in prison. That's all I was concerned about, and now—" I bit my lip and met his inscrutable gaze, playing to his ego. "I don't want to be on your bad side, Theo. I want to learn. I want to be your protégé."

He laughed. "My protégé? I don't have protégés."

"Well," I said in my sincerest voice. "Don't you think it's time you did? I'm a fast learner. And I'm strong." I flexed my bicep and laughed almost shyly, realizing too late I was fucking *flirting*.

When Theo's eyes nearly bugged out of his head, I realized I needed to dial it back a bit. I was desperate to gain his trust, but I had to be careful what signals I was throwing.

But he was considering it. I could practically see the gears turning, and my heart skipped a beat when I thought I saw something change. The skepticism seemed to drain from his expression, replaced by genuine interest. I couldn't push too hard, though. This had to be his decision, and he had to feel secure in it. In me. It was my only hope of slipping past the near-impenetrable security system that had become a part of who he was.

Aaron had warned me that Theo didn't trust easily, if at all. There was still a chance—would always be a chance—that he'd have me maimed or killed when I walked out the door. His complacency meant nothing and his smile even less.

But I had no choice but to try. I was now the backup quarterback for some mysterious government agency, and this was my Hail Mary pass. If I came up even a little bit short, or if Aaron and his men dropped the ball, I knew it would probably be lights out for me.

Theo leaned forward, and I thought he would give me an answer about working together. Instead, he asked, "Did your uncle mention me in his journals?" The expectant, almost hopeful look in his eyes helped to guide my answer.

"Of course he did. That's how I knew you two were so close. You were his ride-or-die."

He smiled. "Ride-or-die. I like that."

I relaxed in my seat, confident that I'd said the right thing to put Theo at ease. "That's the impression he gave in his writing. I've learned a lot about him in those pages. Things I never dreamed of. I had no idea he could be so sensitive and caring, but I guess maybe that's because he raised me. I suppose I always had a chip on my shoulder toward him, and now that he's gone, I feel... regret. Does that make sense?"

"More than you know," he said, his eyes fogging with emotion. "I just wish I knew why—"

I had a bad feeling he was about to bring up Santori's alleged suicide, and that was one thing I did not want to talk about. I hoped maybe if I kept my mouth shut and didn't prompt him to continue, he'd just leave his thought unspoken. But I didn't have very good luck where Theo Brown was concerned, so of course, he went there.

"I just wish I knew why he killed himself. We had made it through rougher times than that. Hell, he didn't even seem that sad before he died."

Hearing the word *sad* used in a sentence to describe my uncle was strange. Sadness didn't seem like something he would ever have felt, much less shown. But I thought back to the boy in the journals, and I had to acknowledge that he'd once had emotions. Theo Brown had known him then and had witnessed him actually feeling something other than the disdain he'd worn like a second skin.

I wanted to pick Theo's brain. He was closer to my uncle than any other person in the world, and he would know things about the man that no one else could tell me. But I couldn't risk the tentative connection we were forging. Maybe in time I would be able to get some answers from him, but today was definitely not the day.

"Alright," Theo said, jogging me out of my thoughts. "I'll take you on and teach you the ropes, but only because Peter would have wanted it. However disappointed he was in the choices you made, you were his heir. He knew he was putting the two of us in this position when he chose to end his life, but he did it anyway. He must have had faith that we could work through this without him, and so that's what we should do. But if we do this, you will defer to me in all things whether you agree with me or not. I won't be as lenient with you as Peter was. You fuck up, you pay. Got it?"

"Got it," I said, swallowing around a lump. Because, oh god, what was I getting myself into?

"Be back here tomorrow morning at nine." Theo pulled a stack of papers from the side of his desk and started reading through them as if I wasn't even in the room.

Apparently, I had been dismissed.

I got up from my seat, considered trying to tidy up my glass, then decided that hanging around might anger him. He hadn't texted anyone this time, so that was a good sign. I needed to make my escape while I could and come back the next morning with a fresh outlook. I pulled open the door and started out, but Theo wasn't quite finished with me yet.

"Get rid of the boyfriend," he said. "There's no room for him in our arrangement."

I spun around, mouth agape and my heart pounding like a million war drums. My brain scrambled in search of something—anything—to say to make him change his mind.

Several desperate pleas rose to my lips: *I can't do it, Theo. Please don't ask that of me. He won't get in the way, I swear it.* And finally, *He's my ride-or-die, like Santori was yours.* I was seriously considering going off script and risking everything, because Jesus Christ, *not this*. Anything but this.

In the end, I settled on the lamest thing I could have said. "Is that really necessary?"

"It's non-negotiable," Theo said without even looking up from his papers. His tone was flat, as if he didn't give a good goddamn whether or not he was crushing my fucking soul.

Then again, what had I expected? To pluck the heartstrings of a man whose heart was long dead?

He would be utterly delighted to know he was causing me pain, because as we'd established at the beginning of our meeting, the sick bastard got off on it. Next time I saw him, he'd probably ask if he could crack open my chest and have a look at my broken heart. Then he'd dig a finger into it and watch me squirm.

The torture was coming whether I liked it or not. I'd signed a devil's pact with Theo Brown, and there was nothing left to do but shut up and walk out of the room. The click of the door closing behind me was loud, like the sound of a hammer striking the final nail into my coffin, but this was only the beginning, and I knew it.

I wanted desperately to fight for Jamie. How in the hell would I get through this without him?

But Aaron had already threatened Jamie's safety if I told him I was working with the government. Now Theo was telling me I had to cut him loose. Months before, my uncle had literally died trying to get rid of him.

What was it about that clueless little Georgia boy that inspired such strong feelings in people and made them want him out of the picture so badly?

I didn't have to think long to come up with the answer, as Vanessa's words from the UFC party we'd attended a lifetime ago came back to me. She'd told me that Jamie was my kryptonite. A weakness. Now it was finally clear what that really meant, even if Vanessa hadn't fully grasped the weight of her statement.

Jamie was definitely a weakness, but not to me. He was my strength. In reality, the only threat he posed was to those who would seek to control me, because he was the only thing that could truly inspire me to buck the powers that be and fight for my autonomy.

In being who he was—a simple young man with realistic hopes and dreams—he was tempting me to stray from what others would have me be: a loveless monster who would do their bidding without a second thought.

Even the shit we had already been through—the stuff with Santori, the fears that Jamie was now a murderer—hadn't brought the reality of the situation quite home to me. Now that I finally saw it in high definition, all the sex and love and blind denial in the world couldn't make it go away.

Jamie Atwood, whose only crime was being loved by me, was a huge threat to some very powerful and ruthless men. He had the potential to fuck up their plans in a big way, and if I didn't do what they said and remove him from my life, he was going to end up dead.

Not just being harassed. Not just rotting in a prison cell somewhere. But fucking *dead*.

The walk to the parking lot felt more like my final walk to the electric chair as I tried to work out a plan to try to save the only man I'd ever loved. I couldn't tell him the truth about who I was really working for because Aaron had made it very clear he wouldn't tolerate his mission being compromised, and without that tidbit of information, my working with Theo made no sense. Even if I was able to make him understand that it had to appear we were broken up, we couldn't risk meeting in secret. There was far too much at stake.

No, I had to make him want to leave, and to do that I was going to have to make him hate me. God help me, I didn't want to break that sweet boy's heart, but what other choice did I have?

I bent over next to my car in the parking garage and puked what little was in my stomach onto the pavement. Then I drove around town and did everything I could think of doing that didn't include going home.

CHAPTER FIVE

KAGE

WHEN I FINALLY COULDN'T DEAL WITH my own morbid thoughts rattling around in my head anymore, I found myself back at the Alcazar, stumbling around like a crazy person. It was after seven, so I knew Jamie would be upstairs. I took the elevator to Dr. Key's floor and banged on his door.

He answered a moment later in nothing but a pair of plaid pajama pants and fuzzy purple slippers, running a hand through his crazy brown hair. He squinted at me, his eyes bleary as if he'd just been sleeping.

"Kage. I was beginning to wonder if you were ever going to come see me."

"Is this a bad time?" I asked. "I can come back some other time if it is. I just—"

"Not at all. You're paying me to be at your beck and call, remember? I've been feeling a little guilty taking your money for nothing." He cocked his head at me and took in my state. "Besides, you look like you need to talk to someone. Please come in and make yourself at home."

The place looked like it could use a visit from housekeeping, with food cartons and papers scattered everywhere, but I didn't care. It was better than being cooped up and claustrophobic in my Corvette with no one to talk to but myself.

Dr. Key went to the kitchenette without a word and came back with two bottles of Japanese beer. He popped the top on one and handed it to me, then opened his own and sat down on the sofa, tossing the cap into the cluttered mess on the coffee table.

"It's great to see you again," he said, patting the seat next to him in invitation. "What have you been up to?"

"Nothing." I sat down beside him and took a swallow of beer, hating the taste. I almost gagged, then took another swallow. It wasn't the most distasteful thing I'd experienced that day. If I could let Theo Brown feel up my bruises, I could stomach a little nasty beer.

"Nothing?" Dr. Key repeated skeptically. "Well, I've been trying to get some work done, but I'll admit it's difficult with the temptations of Vegas beckoning me night and day. I went out to have a drink last night and woke up this morning on the floor just inside the door of my suite with only one shoe on. Not my proudest moment."

I tried to chuckle, but it was so weak it sounded more like a raspy breath. "Did you ever find your shoe?"

"No, that's the crazy thing. I have no idea where it could be. I even checked with lost and found here in the hotel, and they said they hadn't seen it."

"Maybe you shouldn't drink." I knew it came out sounding rude, but I was beyond censoring myself. My mind was still flying a mile a minute trying to figure my own shit out.

Dr. Key held up his beer and looked pointedly at it, laughing. "That was my first thought, but as you can see, I didn't even last twelve hours. To be honest, I rarely get drunk, but I've been holed up in here for a while working. It's made me a little stir crazy, especially since I haven't heard from you. It's a good thing you didn't need me last night. No telling what kind of advice I might have given."

I thought about telling him that I *had* needed him last night. That I needed him at my side twenty-four-seven these days and was just too proud to ask for help. I settled for a partial truth. "A lot of shit has been going on lately, Dr. Key. I feel like I'm drowning sometimes, you know? My life is... Well, it's spinning out of control. I don't expect you to be able to help me, but I had to talk to someone because I can't go home. At least not yet."

"Why can't you go home?"

I sighed. "Because Jamie's there, and I have to tell him something." I spun my beer bottle in my hand and tried to read Japanese. "I need to break up with him."

Dr. Key's eyes widened. "What on earth for? You two seem so good together. Of course, that's just an outsider observation. I don't know everything that goes on between you."

"I love him," I said. "More than anything in the world."

Dr. Key waited a moment, and when I didn't continue, he prompted me for more. "But..."

"But it's complicated." I paused and bit my lip. "How much can I tell you about my life, Dr. Key? We haven't signed any papers or anything, and I'm worried. I don't lead what you'd call a normal life. There are things about me that would probably make your hair stand on end. Things that could compromise me in a *legal* way."

"I'll sign whatever you want me to sign, Kage. I'm not here to report you to the authorities or sell your secrets to the press. You're paying me a lot of money to be your confidante, and I take that very seriously. Short of murdering kids or planning to shoot up a McDonald's, there is nothing you can tell me that will shock me or make me go running to the police or the media. So I'm telling you now if you *are* killing kids or planning a mass murder spree, you'd better keep that to yourself. Otherwise, we're good."

I turned this information over in my mind. "What if I was a drug dealer?"

Dr. Key shrugged. "No problem."

"What if I was laundering money for the mob or planning to rob the vault at the MGM?"

He shrugged again.

"What if I was an assassin?"

There was a barely noticeable twitch at the corner of one eye. "Is this your way of telling me you're here to kill me?"

"No!" I said, shocked that he'd even gone there.

"That's good to know," he breathed. "Are you killing innocent people?"

I took a swallow of beer and grimaced at the taste. "I didn't say I was killing *anyone*. I'm just throwing hypothetical shit out there. But no. As a hypothetical assassin, I am not killing any hypothetical innocent people."

It occurred to me that I had indeed killed an innocent child, but I had been an innocent child myself at the time, and I wasn't planning on sharing that information with Dr. Key anyway. I had more pressing matters to deal with. Things that hadn't happened eighteen years before. This shit was happening right fucking now, and I needed some advice on how to deal with it.

"Well, those are my hard limits," Dr. Key said. "No killing innocent people, and no killing me. Feel free to throw anything else on the table, and we'll sort through it together."

I thought for a minute, hesitant to move forward, but I needed to trust someone. Living with all of this shit in my head was going to drive me fucking insane. But when Dr. Key only sat quietly waiting for me to continue, putting no pressure on me and showing no signs of being overly enthusiastic to get me to confess my secrets, I gave in to the need to unburden myself.

"Okay," I said finally. "My uncle left me a lot more than a hotel when he died. Apparently, he was involved in a lot of shady business, and now by default, so am I. The thing is, I don't want to have anything to do with it. I'm an MMA fighter. I just want to do my own thing and enjoy the money I inherited, but there are people who don't want to let me do that. I'm sort of stuck dealing with these guys who are way more powerful than I am, and they don't want Jamie involved. Hell, I don't want Jamie involved in anything that's going to put him in danger, and we're talking a lot of danger. Not just from the police, but maybe... mortal danger. I'd love to get him out of harm's way, work my way out of the mess I'm in, and then live happily ever after with him. I just don't know how to do that. I hope to have everything straightened out within months, or maybe a year at the most, I don't know. But what if he doesn't want me back when it's all over? I'm so confused right now. Part of me wants to make him hate me so that he'll disappear off their radars completely, but the larger part of me wants to figure out how to keep him close."

Dr. Key didn't say anything immediately. He seemed to be trying to make sense of everything I'd just told him. His forehead wrinkled, and he got a faraway look in his eyes. Finally, he spoke.

"Could you explain the situation to him? Maybe the two of you could pretend to separate with the promise that you'll be together when it's all over. He could live somewhere else for the time being, and you could possibly even see each other on the sly."

"But what do I tell him?"

"What you just told me." He bit his lip, considering his next words. "Is there something about the situation you can't tell him?"

"Yes. There is a sensitive bit of information that I'm not allowed to tell him." That same bit of information I wasn't allowed to tell anyone, even Dr. Key. That I was an unofficial spy for the good old US of A.

"Well, I say leave that part out and explain it to Jamie just like you explained it to me. It seems pretty simple. If he loves you and values his freedom and his safety, he'll understand and back off. Is there a reason you don't want to do that?"

"Hell, yeah," I said, grabbing my beer off the coffee table and taking an angry swig. "I don't want any of this to be happening. I don't want to risk him thinking badly of me for joining forces with some really bad people. He'll try to talk me out of it. He'll think I'm bad, too, for even considering it. I don't know how to make him understand *why* I'm doing it without telling him about the other thing. The thing I'm not allowed to tell him. I have to make it seem like I'm cool with everything."

Dr. Key settled back against the sofa cushions, took a deep breath, and got lost in thought again. I closed my eyes and felt myself swaying on the seat.

"You can't *secretly* tell him the other thing?" Dr. Key finally asked. "Maybe no one would have to know."

I was already shaking my head before he'd finished the thought. "Absolutely not. It would put him in too much danger and potentially compromise my chance to get out of this mess. These people... They have eyes and ears everywhere. Trust me, I know this from experience. If I told Jamie, there would be a very good chance they'd find out about it, and that's something they're not going to put up with. Quite frankly, I don't blame them. If Jamie slipped up and inadvertently put them in jeopardy—" A fine tremor of fear shot through my body. "Let's just say that a lot is riding on no one finding out this secret."

"At the risk of prying, I need to ask you one question because something isn't adding up for me. I understand that someone has a secret that you can't share, but the fact that you seem reluctant to tell him you're going along against your will makes me think—" His eyebrows came together in confusion. "Are you dealing with two people, or maybe two groups of people? It seems like you need to pretend to go along with one while keeping a secret for the other. Am I reading that right?"

I nodded. "Yes. And Jamie can't know about either of those things. Knowing one gives away the other. And like I said... Eyes and ears everywhere. Probably on both sides. The only reason I feel halfway comfortable talking to you about this right now is I just got a new cell phone, and I'm not in my apartment or my office where there might be bugs or something. This is some pretty serious shit, Dr. Key."

He ran his index finger back and forth along his bottom lip. "Without specific details to go on, it's hard for me to form an opinion. But from everything you've said and the fact that you seem scared shitless, it seems to me you have two options. You can do like you said and make Jamie hate you, thus ensuring that he'd willingly remove himself from the situation and out of danger. End of story. Or you can explain that you love him very much but there's something you need to do that necessitates a temporary split. I know you're afraid he won't understand your motives, but I think the second option is your only bet if you want a future with him. In that scenario, you're risking him thinking badly of you, but in the first, you're guaranteeing it."

I leaned forward on the sofa, elbows propped on my knees, and buried my face in my hands. Dr. Key was right. Hearing it spelled out so succinctly from a third party who had no skin in the game had really cleared things up for me. The situation was still fifty kinds of fucked up, but at least it made more sense now.

I stood up, resolute for the moment. "Thank you for your advice. It's really helped me see things more clearly. You've really earned your money as well as my gratitude tonight."

He smiled. "No problem, Kage. That's what I'm here for. I hope you'll continue to confide in me. I have a feeling things are going to get tougher in the days to come, and I'd like to help you work through them. I wish you and Jamie only the best."

I nodded and headed for the door, but something occurred to me as I pulled it open. I looked back over my shoulder. "You know, I really like you, Dr. Key, and I've chosen to trust you with some very sensitive information. But I need you to understand one thing. If you even *think* about fucking me over, be prepared for some dire consequences. I may be desperate and confused right now, but I'm nobody's bitch. If you become a threat to me, I will have no problem making you pay. Are we clear?"

Dr. Key swallowed hard enough that I heard it from the door. "Crystal."

I left, pulling the door closed behind me, and headed up to my apartment. I was a little shocked at myself after delivering that threat to Dr. Key. I'd heard shades of my uncle in the cold, unwavering delivery. And of Theo Brown. The worst thing was, I'd meant it with every cell in my body. I had to protect myself, and that wasn't going to happen if I let people think they could walk all over me. I was a badass motherfucker, and it was time I started acting that way.

When the elevator stopped on my silent floor, I stepped off with newfound resolution. I was about to break up with my boyfriend, but it was for his own good. If he couldn't wait for me, then so be it. At least he would be safe, and that's all that really mattered.

I slid my key card through the door and stepped inside. There was no movement in the apartment, and the lights were off, but a cartoon flickered on low volume on the TV. I shook my head. Jamie and his fucking cartoons. I hated that it was so adorable.

As I got closer and prepared to turn the TV off, I stopped in my tracks when I got a good look at the sofa. Jamie was lying there asleep in the semi-dark, face unlined and innocent, long limbs slack. He was completely naked, wearing nothing except for the choker I'd given him. I was seized by a feeling of love so powerful it ached in my chest, followed by a crushing sense of grief at what I knew I had to do.

He was mine, goddammit. He belonged to me, and now I was just going to send him away? I wanted to gouge my fucking eyes out when I thought of the way I had been acting lately. I'd been preoccupied and distant. How many days had I squandered when I should have been proving my love for him? How many nights that I could have worshiped his body? I couldn't go back and change any of it, and for that, I would be eternally sorry.

I spotted his cell phone on the end table and took a moment to transfer Aaron's number to my new phone and send him a quick text that said, *Kage's new number*. I sent one to Jamie that said, *I love you forever*, then I placed my phone beside his.

With that out of the way, I sat down on the edge of the sofa next to Jamie and watched the gentle rise and fall of his chest as he breathed in sleep. That he could find peace when it so thoroughly eluded me was comforting. I had not destroyed him yet. I admired him so much. How could he remain innocent and vulnerable and *good* in a world that was so full of evil? I'd never had the luxury of being good.

Perched precariously on a sliver of sofa, I watched him for a long time, until the aching in my chest became too much and I was suddenly overcome with the need to have him open his expressive brown eyes and discover me there. I needed him to *see* me and to look at me like I was something other than damaged goods.

I reached out a tentative finger and touched the Claddagh at his throat, then dropped lower to trace a circle around one of his pale nipples. He stirred a little, pulling his knee up to bump against my ass, but it wasn't enough. I needed him awake. I trailed my finger down the line of his sternum, tickling all the way down to dip into his belly button before following his tantalizing happy. I stopped at the base of his dick, which at the moment lay sleeping on in its bed of dark hair just waiting for my touch.

The fact that Jamie was stark naked was proof that he'd been thinking of me. He had positioned himself here on the sofa like an offering, hoping I'd take him when I came home. Desire flared up in me at the thought. He was mine, and I was going to have him.

I dropped to my knees on the rug beside him and leaned over, lapping ever so gently over the flesh of his soft cock. At first, it remained oblivious to my ministrations, but after a minute it began to firm up, filling out slowly from the purely physical sensations. He stirred again and let out a soft moan—a promise that he would soon be awake. I pressed my tongue to the underside of his balls and dragged up over them, loving the feel of the crinkles and ridges, as I licked my way stealthily back up. He tasted so good. So clean.

He mumbled something in his sleep and turned a fraction toward me, still oblivious but beginning to respond more lucidly. I paused, not wanting to wake him until I'd made him hard. I wanted him to wake up wanting me.

When I couldn't wait any longer, I opened my mouth and took the entirety of his barely aroused dick all the way into my warm, wet mouth and began to suck gently. That was when he started to show the first significant stirrings of arousal. His erection grew fast inside my mouth, and the harder it got, the more I sucked, until I had to reposition myself to move my mouth up and down his solid length.

At some point, dazed as I was with lust, I realized that Jamie's fingers had wound into my hair, and he was actively thrusting. His hips pistoned up and down, dragging his cock over my tongue in smooth, long strokes punctuated by ragged breaths.

He let out a throaty moan that vibrated through me like an electric current. "Kage," he gasped. "I was waiting for you."

"I know, baby," I said, pulling off of him with a reluctant slurp. "You were laid out for me like a virgin on the altar."

He chuckled quietly and ran his fingers through my hair. "I'm hardly a virgin."

When I smiled up at him, I felt the sadness in my own expression. "You are to me. Every time." I wrapped my fist around his cock and stroked, slowly and firmly, determined to drag a response out of him.

He didn't disappoint, pushing up into my grip and shuddering. "Guess I need to work on my naughtiness factor."

"Wouldn't matter," I said. "You'll always be my sweet college boy, and I'll always be the monster who can't wait to get inside of you. To stretch you and wreck you. To turn you out until you can't see anything but me. I'm selfish that way."

To illustrate my point, I sucked him into my mouth again and worked my tongue and throat over him until he was panting out my name. He bent his knees and dug his heels into the sofa, legs trembling as he battered the back of my throat with his dick, seeking more contact, more friction, more sensation. Like me, he seemed to need something he couldn't quite reach.

"You're going to make me come like this," he cried. "I don't want to come like this."

"You should be so lucky," I said in a hoarse whisper. Then I squeezed the base of his cock hard and sucked him, using everything I had at my disposal—tongue, lips, throat—for maximum sensory overload. The trembling in his legs increased until they were wavering uncontrollably, and then I stopped. I let his dick slip from my mouth while keeping firm pressure on the base of his dick and looked up at him. "By the time I'm finished with you tonight, you'll wish I'd let you come the easy way. I plan on using you until you're begging for mercy."

When his legs stilled to an intermittent twitch, I released his dick. He went limp, his bent knees falling to either side of him, and he stared up at me with glazed, dark eyes.

He shuddered visibly. "Is that a promise or a threat?"

"Depends on how you feel when I'm done. As hard as I am, and as many things as I want to do to you, I'm betting on threat."

He caught his plump bottom lip between his teeth and held my gaze as he reached down between his splayed thighs and stroked his dick lightly and deliberately. "Sounds good to me."

He was so dewy-eyed. So precious. So fucking irresistible to the animal inside me. Would he have been so quick to invite my attention if he'd known what was in store for him? There was a terrible desperation building inside me, driving me to own him before I pushed him away. I had no intention of letting this man go until I'd branded him irrevocably, body and soul.

CHAPTER SIX

JAMIE

THE LOOK in Kage's eyes was fierce as he gazed down at me, and it turned me on like nothing else. I hadn't seen him so passionate in a long time, if ever, and for Kage, passion usually took the form of extreme aggression. The rougher he got with me, the more cherished I felt. Making him lose control of his dark side was my aphrodisiac, just like defiling me was his.

I loved his sweet side, too. The rare glimpses of vulnerability were special in a way that was hard to describe. It was like stumbling upon a long lost pharaoh's tomb and getting the first peek at the treasures hidden within, knowing all the while you're doomed for having been the one to break the seal.

All of his personalities were gold to me, especially the one that was running the show tonight.

He reached down and took my hand, pulling me up to a standing position. We were so close I could feel the heat coming off of him, and his presence was so strong I suddenly had trouble making eye contact. When I looked down, overwhelmed, he widened his stance and bent his knees, ducking his head down and capturing my lips in a kiss. His lips tasted like beer, which surprised me because he didn't ever go out drinking without me. I had to wonder just what he'd been doing all day, because he certainly hadn't been at work or at home.

"Have you been drinking?" I asked, pulling as far away from his mouth as he would allow. I tried not to sound accusing or suspicious.

"A little," he said before wrapping a hand around the back of my neck and crushing our lips together. He was ferocious. Single-minded. But he did pull back for a couple of seconds to say, "I had one beer with Dr. Key."

All I could think was, thank goodness he'd finally started utilizing Dr. Key's services. He needed to talk to someone, and that someone obviously wasn't me. Maybe we'd be okay after all. I sighed and leaned into his kiss, sucking on his tongue with renewed abandon.

Before long, he broke the kiss, leaving me breathless and lost in a cloud of rapture. I made a little surprised sound at the sudden absence of his mouth on mine, but he grabbed my hand and pulled me toward the bedroom.

He'd said he was going to make me beg for mercy, and I couldn't wait. I was down for any pleasure or pain he wanted to bestow on me. I'd missed this Kage so damn much.

He pushed me roughly onto our bed and clicked the bedside lamp on. Then he rummaged in the drawer and round the lube, tossing it onto the bed beside me. I watched him as he moved. My gorgeous fighter. My sexy hotel owner. His dark hair was slightly wild, as if he'd been running his fingers through it or riding with the top down. The look in his eyes added to the wildness, his lust-dilated pupils making the green of his eyes appear darker, the irises reduced to a thin band of color at the edge. I thought of a cat, which was so fitting at this moment. Kage was on the prowl, stalking me down in the low light of our bedroom.

The night sky glowed with the reflection of city lights through our window, and shadows danced on the walls as Kage started to remove his clothing. First the sneakers and socks, then the sweatpants he'd taken to wearing since the mugging. His thighs were thick and powerful, his calves a perfect swell of muscle, and the hair on his legs was all male and enticing to me in a way I had never thought possible before I met him. The bruises marred the perfection of his skin, but my eyes had feasted enough on this man that I knew him by heart. When he pulled his shirt over his head, the bruising was a little harder to ignore. Shades of yellow, purple, and fuchsia...The colors mixed and swirled over his naturally tanned skin like a sick watercolor painting.

"Are you sure you're good to—"

Kage narrowed his eyes at me in a way that made me shut my mouth. The look said he wasn't playing, that he could take the pain, and that he wasn't going to put up with any pity or worry from me. He was such a sexy beast, strong and fearless in a way I'd never be.

When he was completely naked and looking down at me, all gorgeous and damaged, I shivered with anticipation. For a moment, he just stared at me where I lay back sideways on the bed, propped up on my elbows.

When he spoke, his voice was rough. "Lie down," he commanded, brooking no argument.

I settled flat on my back and waited.

"Spread your legs," he said. "I want to see what's mine."

I drew my legs up onto the bed and flattened the soles of my feet on the mattress, positioning as far apart as I could so that I was completely bared.

"Not good enough," he said. "Pull your knees up to your chest and show me my hole, Jamie."

His hole. God, that sounded hot.

I pulled my knees up and banded an arm around them to keep them secure. The air was cool on my hole as I opened myself to his gaze. I chanced a peek around my legs, and Kage just stood there looking, as if he'd never seen anything quite so fascinating. It was almost embarrassing being that objectified.

He flipped the cap on the lube, turned it upside-down, and began to drizzle it straight onto my ass. I sucked in a breath as my muscles spasmed from the cold shock. He didn't stop, and he didn't apologize. Didn't even flinch until my hole was obscenely coated with lube. I could feel it pooling beneath my ass on the covers.

"God, you're making a mess," I whispered, my voice sounding strange and out of place with Kage so quiet and intent on his goal.

"I'm only getting started," he said. "Tonight we're not worried about the mess. Or noise. Or what's right or wrong."

What's right or wrong? A chill moved up my spine.

"Reach down and finger yourself," Kage said. "It's good and wet now. Slide one finger in, slowly. Let me see you."

Keeping my knees tight against my body with my the left arm, I wrapped the right around my ass and found my hole with my index finger. Jesus, there was a lot of lube down there. I was covered in it. When I slipped the tip of my finger inside, it was almost like moving through warm butter—hardly any resistance at all, and only a slight little burn to let me know I'd breached myself. "Fuck, that's wet," I said.

"Push it in," Kage growled. "All the way in."

I pushed in and moaned as my finger slid home.

"Now fuck yourself with it," Kage continued, his voice low and husky. "Give me a show, baby. I need to watch you get yourself ready for me."

I did as he asked, screwing my eyes shut and moving my finger slowly in and out, going all the way in each time. As turned on as I already was, my desire increased exponentially, and I imagined replacing my finger with Kage's big cock. I was glad he was letting me get myself ready, though. It had been a while, and I knew there would be a tremendous stretch when he finally entered me.

"Two fingers now," he groaned, and the sound of his voice made me pause and open my eyes. He was stroking himself while he watched, his touch gentle and unhurried. He was obviously pacing himself for the long night he had promised.

I added the second finger, feeling the burn a little more this time. "God, that feels good," I said. "Can't wait to have you inside me."

"You want me to stretch that hole?" he asked, his movements over his dick increasing in speed just for a few seconds before slowing back down.

"Yes," I whispered.

"You love it when I wreck that thing, don't you?"

His words caused my ass to clench around my two fingers as I fucked myself. "I can't get enough of it," I admitted.

My fingers made a squelching sound, and Kage hummed his approval. "Yeah, that's right. Get it all nice and messy for me. Three fingers now."

I contorted my hand into the odd position required and worked the third finger in alongside the other two. It was a tight fit, stretching and burning me deliciously.

Kage stroked himself harder. "Keep going. Don't slow down. Fuck yourself good, Jamie. I love watching you."

I plunged my fingers in and out of myself, ramping up the speed until it almost felt like I *was* being fucked. "God, Kage. That feels so good. I'm so ready for you."

"You're not ready yet," he said. "I want to see that thing stretched out, baby. I want you gaping for me. I'm getting so fucking turned on watching you."

I whimpered and slammed my fingers into myself harder, needing so badly to please him. I wanted him rock hard and aching to get inside me.

"Now four," he said.

I swallowed. Bit my lip. Pressed that fourth finger in and was rewarded with a low, tortured moan from Kage that echoed my own as I stretched myself to the point of pain. I tried to imagine what he was seeing. The scandalous sight of me practically fisting myself was obviously turning him on like crazy. He had a dazed look on his face as he took in every move I made. The lube was consistently making those obscene squelching sounds now. It was dirty as hell, and it made my insides quake.

"Love that sound," Kage said. "God, you're so dirty, Jamie. My dirty little slut. You'll do anything for me, won't you? Anything at all."

"Yes," I panted. "Anything, Kage. I love you so much." My voice was thick with the strain of trying to take my fingers. Kage's cock was huge, but there was something about shoving four fingers inside me that felt deceptively big. Maybe it was just the sheer nastiness of it that made it seem like more. Or maybe it was the angle or the shape. Whatever the reason, I was laboring on them, breathing hard like I'd just jogged the Vegas Strip.

"Okay, baby," Kage said, dropping his hand from his cock and taking a deep, shuddering breath. "That's enough. Pull them out and let's see how stretched you are."

I removed my fingers from my ass with a wet slide, and Kage grinned wickedly.

"How do I look?" I asked, feeling a little shy.

"You look like you're ready to get fucked. Pull those ass cheeks apart for me. Stretch yourself."

I gripped my cheeks, digging my fingers into the mounds of flesh hard enough to bruise. It was difficult to hang on with all of the lube smeared everywhere. The fingers of one hand were especially slippery, but I managed to get myself splayed out for his viewing pleasure. He showed his appreciation with a smile and a satisfied nod.

"You are so sexy, Jamie. Do you realize that? I couldn't imagine a better partner. Not in my wildest dreams, baby. Every inch of you was made just for me."

I blushed at his confession. It was a little odd for him to be professing his undying love while staring at my stretched ass, but this was Kage. He had needs that transcended the norm, and I had no doubt that my willingness to do whatever he asked of me made him love me just that much more. I was the yin to his yang, and he wasn't the only one catching feels at how well we fit together.

With me in this position, there was room for Kage to get onto the bed on his knees. He climbed up and rubbed the tip of his cock against my stretched hole, only tentatively at first, but it was enough to set my bared nerve endings alight. He teased me with it, slicking the tip against my sensitive flesh, pressing just a bit until I was dying for him to push his way inside and take me already.

While I writhed on the bed, driven by impatience to get thoroughly fucked, he just looked down at me like I'd hung the moon. Like I was his most precious possession. I wished he could look at me that way twenty-four-seven. It made me feel so powerful that I could command the affection of Michael Kage Santori. Me, of all people. How had that happened? I didn't deserve it, and yet he bestowed it freely upon me.

"Pinch your nipples," he said. "I want to do it, but I'm about to be really busy down here." To illustrate, he tapped the head of his dick against my waiting hole.

"Yes, sir, Mr. Santori." I latched onto my nipples with lube-slicked fingers and pinched gently, groaning at the sensation. "Jesus, why does that feel better when I'm doing it for you than when I'm alone?"

"Because you live to bring me pleasure, just like I do for you." He teased the head of his dick against my hole, and I pinched my nipples harder. "Of course I do a hell of a lot more taking than giving, but that's all part of it, isn't it?"

I nodded, feeling breathless. How could he look into my soul like that and understand what it was he did for me? That his taking brought me infinitely more pleasure than if he had been the most stereotypically thoughtful lover in the world. For me, his demands were gifts. That dynamic was one of the reasons we worked so well together.

"What do you think about when you jerk off, Jamie? Do you ever think of me?"

"All the time," I said, reaching out for him as he remained stubbornly out of my grasp.

"And what do you think about?"

"On my knees," I croaked, my mouth parched from all of the heavy breathing. "I'm on my knees for you or bent over while you pound me from behind. You're in charge. We do it a lot of different ways, but I'm always just taking whatever you want to give me."

"That's what I dream of, too." He pushed his dick hard against my hole, stretching me but not going in. "You're so damn good at taking it, baby. So perfect."

A little squeak escaped me, and a lump formed in my throat. When he called me perfect, it affected me profoundly because his praise was everything. It touched a place deep inside that no one else had ever been able to reach.

"Are you ready for me?" he asked, still teasing my hole.

I nodded frantically. "So ready." I pinched my nipples hard and wiggled my ass for him, trying to tempt him in, needing him so much.

The look in his eyes changed from turned on to ravenous at the sight of me wiggling, like a pit bull catching sight of its prey. He bared his teeth and latched onto my hips with biting fingers. Then he finally, *finally* pushed his thick cock inside me.

After the waiting and the teasing, the sensation of him entering me was overwhelming, and we both groaned out our pleasure simultaneously. "Fuck yes," Kage said. "That's what I need right there."

I was already so physically primed, my muscles responded violently to his every move as he pushed in and out of me. He watched our joining with every ounce of attention he had, leaning back occasionally to get a better angle. Then he brought his gaze up to mine and smiled.

"Feels good, huh?" I asked.

"So good."

"So *fucking* good," I whispered. I lifted my hips up and down, working them in tandem with his thrusts to create an added layer of mind-blowing friction.

He nodded his approval and bit his lip. "Mmm hmmm... That's it. I've been too preoccupied. Too worried to fuck. Forgot how amazing it feels to be buried inside of you."

"Just don't wait too long again," I pleaded. "I don't think I can take it."

Something crossed his face. A flicker of doubt or... something. I couldn't read it, especially with him working my ass with that talented dick. He was mastering me, owning me, and I couldn't think. Only feel.

His thrusts grew gradually faster until he was pounding me with the same kind of ferocity usually reserved for post-fight sex, when he had so much aggression and testosterone spilling out of him that the only place it could go was into me. I was moaning like a wild animal by then, not caring how damn slutty I sounded. Shame went out the window, because he was doing me so goddamn *right*.

A lot of time passed without my noticing as we got completely lost in the sex. I suddenly noticed that Kage had scooted me all the way across the bed with the power of his thrusts. He grunted each time he bottomed out in me, and my answering squeaks and cries were proof of how much he was wrecking my ass. He was fully on the bed now, hunkered down low over me to gain more traction for the thorough pounding he was unleashing on me. He looked like wicked, possessed thing with the bruises and the brutality of his expression. My own beautiful angel of pain come to torture me to the pinnacle of ecstasy. I'd never seen anything so sexy, so wildly gorgeous, and so out of control as Kage was in that moment. It was as if he needed to force every ounce of pent-up anger and yearning into me.

I was willing to take it for him. No, more than willing. Long ago I had figured out that Kage needed me to be a vessel for his demons. This is what I'd signed on for. It was what I wanted more than anything.

"Scream for me, baby," Kage said, as if I wasn't already loud and wanton enough. "I want them to hear you on the next floor. I want everyone to know what I'm doing to you. That I'm destroying that ass with my cock, and you can't get enough of it."

I let myself go even more, heightening the pleasure for both of us with my wracked gasps and incoherent pleas. I was speaking in tongues. When there were actual words, they were filthy and needy, jumbled up and disconnected, but the message was clear to anyone who might have heard. He was giving me everything, and I was begging for more.

I reached down to encircle my cock with my fist. I was leaking precum like a faucet, and I used it to get myself good and slick. I was so hard I knew I was going to blow at any second. A few strokes is all it would take, and then I'd be shooting off all over myself. I wanted that release. Needed it like I needed air.

When Kage noticed what I was doing, he stopped fucking me and pulled completely out, squeezing the base of his cock.

"Get your hand off your dick, Jamie. Didn't I tell you I wasn't going to let you finish until you were begging for it?"

I didn't move my hands, but I stilled my movements. "I *was* begging for it, Kage. I *am*. God, I'm so close I don't think I can take any more." My voice was pitiful, but I didn't care. The need to get off trumped everything. I was almost ready to go against Kage and stroke myself to climax while he watched, consequences be damned. My dick was throbbing in my hand, and the muscles in my ass quivered.

"I'm not ready," he said. "I plan on making this a night neither one of us will ever forget. When I said I wanted you unable to walk tomorrow, I wasn't kidding."

Reluctantly, I took my hand off of my dick. I had calmed down a little. His speech had given me time to get my second wind, which was probably his intention all along. He was hard, but he was using his iron will to last as long as he could. Dammit, if he could do it, so could I. I wanted what he'd promised. What he'd threatened. To have a hard time walking when this was all over. I wanted to feel the memory of him inside me for the entire day. I wanted to be so sore it would be almost like he was still there.

I took a deep breath and smiled up at him. Then I bent my knees as high up as they would go, nearly touching my shoulders as I offered myself up to him. "You're the boss, Mr. Santori. Do your worst."

"You're damn right I'm the boss," he growled, pushing into me again hard and fast. "Here, suck on these," he said, leaning over me and pushing two of his thick fingers into my mouth. "Let me feel that talented tongue. Pretend you're sucking my cock. I love watching you suck me."

I started working his fingers with my tongue, making dirty slurping sounds around them. I'd never imagined I could get off on sucking someone's fingers, but I was really getting into it. The illusion that I was blowing him and getting fucked by him at the same time felt surprisingly real, and that was such a turn-on. The way he was looking at me so raptly, his eyes dark and slightly hooded, made it infinitely more arousing.

His thrusts down below slowed as he watched. If it was a show he wanted, I'd give him a show. I brought my hand up to his and gripped it, pulling his fingers in and out of my mouth as I sucked. I kept eye contact with him the whole time, communicating with my eyes that I was loving what he was making me do. I ate his fingers like they were my last meal on death row, making the little noises he liked so much. I worked his fingers so thoroughly and made such a performance of it, I was pretty sure he could feel it in his dick. I could certainly feel it in mine.

Eventually, he pulled his fingers out of my mouth and grabbed onto my shoulders, leaning heavily on me and pushing my body down into the bed. I bucked and fought against him because it's just what felt right in the moment. He wrestled me down harder and leaned into me with every thrust, sending a jolt up my body every time he slammed into me.

That's when I noticed how hot it was in the room. Sweat

began dripping from Kage's hair onto my face, droplets plunking randomly onto my forehead and my cheeks. With him holding me like he was, I couldn't wipe it away, and I couldn't get away from it. I'd seen a YouTube show about water torture once. They said you could mentally break a person by dripping water onto their face at random intervals so that they never knew when it was coming. I thought of that now. This was torture for sure, but it was the sweetest kind of torture, knowing that I was suffering for Kage's pleasure. It only heightened my arousal and made me gasp out and clench hard around his cock every time a drop of sweat hit my face. A few times, droplets landed on my lips or near my mouth, and I darted my tongue out to swipe them away.

We had been going for a long time. Kage's stamina was ridiculous. I had no idea how he had lasted so long with such relentless friction on his dick. Determination to ruin me was the only thing I could come up with.

He pressed his torso against the front of my calves with most of his weight, and somehow I had the presence of mind to think of his comfort when my legs were bent and aching, stuck in the position they'd been in for so long.

"You're going to...hurt yourself," I managed to breathe out with my rib cage painfully constricted by his weight.

"All I feel is you," he said. "Nothing else."

He leaned up, though, taking his weight off of me, and I gasped in a breath. He continued to plow me just as hard as he'd been doing while holding me down, and within seconds I was hanging off the bed from the waist up, in danger of ending up on the floor.

"Kage," I gasped, reaching up for him and trying to find purchase on his broad, sweat-slicked shoulders.

He pulled out of me and hauled me back onto the bed like I weighed nothing. "Here. Get up on your knees."

I unfolded my painfully stiff joints and got into a kneeling position. When we were face to face, he smashed his mouth into mine, and we were kissing again. At this point, we were panting beasts, living only to devour each other in whatever way we could. I'd never been so mindless, and I'd never seen him so starving for me.

When our lips were thoroughly bruised and our lungs deprived of oxygen, he broke the kiss and pushed me against the headboard. Hard. My face glanced off the wood, sending a sharp pain through my cheekbone. He didn't apologize, but he turned my head and pressed an achingly sweet kiss to the spot. Then he forced me against the headboard again, a little more carefully this time, and slid his cock into me without warning.

"You'd better hang on," he growled against my ear. "This is going to be a bumpy ride."

I curled my fingers tightly around the top of the headboard and braced myself for the onslaught. Kage did not disappoint. I had to tighten every muscle I had to keep my entire body from slamming into the headboard.

"Fuck me, Kage," I gasped over my shoulder. "Give me everything you've got. I know you need this, and I want it. I don't care if I never get to come." Being close to him in this way and feeling the connection so strongly was overwhelming. I was probably delirious, but it felt like he and I had a secret, and this— the way were in bed together—was it. It defied logic and labels. I transcended mere sex. It was the unbreakable bond that kept us tethered to each other.

"You won't have to wait long now," Kage said as he plunged into me so fast and hard it made my head swim. I was dizzy from the pleasure, and from the pain. And from the blood that had been taken out of circulation in my brain and rerouted into my dick.

"Are you close?" I asked, know that he was.

"God, yes," he said, his movements getting frantic and jerky. "So fucking close. You need to grab your dick, Jamie, because I'm about to unload in you. Jesus, my balls are so damn tight. And my dick... Feels like I'm gonna shoot fire."

Spurred on by his words, I fisted my cock and started jacking furiously. My dick was hot and aching and more primed to blow than I'd ever been in my entire life. It was excruciating being this backed up and this turned on.

"You ready, baby?" he panted against my ear.

"Yeah. God, yeah. I've never been so ready." Before the words had completely cleared my lips, I was painting the headboard with spurt after glorious spurt of hot cum. Every time Kage plowed into me, more shot out. By the time I felt the pulsations of his dick in my ass and the forceful jets of his warm seed filling me, I was wrung out and dry, leaning over slightly and panting as I rode out the high.

Kage pushed in one final time and crushed me against the headboard with his exhausted body.

"I love you, baby," he said, his breath a warm breeze against my sweaty cheek. "Love you so fucking much."

He sounded so sad it melted me. Why did he sound sad? "I love you, too."

"I know you do. Listen, I—" He sighed. "I have something to tell you."

My heart seized, and suddenly it was really freaking hard to breathe. My mind swirled with unformed thoughts and unfocused fears about what he was going to say. From the tone of his voice and the fact that he was bringing it up on the tail end of hot sex when he should have been passing out, I had a feeling I wasn't going to like it.

CHAPTER SEVEN

JAMIE

"WHAT IS IT?" I asked, looking over my shoulder but not quite able to meet his eyes. I was nervous.

Way to go, Kage. Scare me half to death one time.

But I should have been scared. Scared and worried and distracted with the possibility of life as we knew it coming to an end. The look on his face told me all of that. I just didn't know why yet.

"Let's get some clothes on," he said. "I can't have a serious talk with my dick hanging out."

I let out a nervous chuckle. "Fair enough."

We got dressed in silence—he in the sweatpants he'd discarded on the floor, and I in a pair of dark blue basketball shorts. I settled into my spot on the bed, my back against the headboard I'd just been hanging onto for dear life, and Kage stretched out in the sticky puddle of lube that had soaked the covers.

Served him right.

"Do you know how adorable you look?" he asked, reaching over and running a hand over my abs, his fingers trailing into the low-hanging band of my baggy shorts. "If I could possibly get it up right now, I'd be attacking you."

I gave him a withering glare that was only half playful. "Stop trying to change the subject."

He took a deep breath as if steeling himself. "Well, you know how I said I got mugged?"

"I knew it," I said, knowing the triumphant gleam in my eyes was probably blinding.

"Well, it wasn't a mugging, but I think maybe you know that already."

"I had my suspicions," I admitted. "But there wasn't much I could do when you refused to be honest with me."

"I know, and I'm sorry for that. It's just that there are things going on that are so mind-boggling I didn't know how to explain it to you. Not to mention there's an element of danger involved. For you."

"Me?" I squeaked, not so much shocked as dismayed. "It's the Santori stuff, isn't it? Someone found out about my part in it, and they're blackmailing you."

He wrinkled his brow in confusion. "How on earth did you come up with that?"

"Well, the note you found. The fact that you're on edge all the time. And the way you've been treating me like I'm some heavy burden you've got to lug around."

"No." He ran a hand through his hair, looking guilty as hell. "Baby, I didn't mean to treat you that way. I'm really sorry. It's just

—I'm going to have to start from the beginning, so bear with me, okay? I need you to understand."

"The stage is all yours." I held out a hand, my body buzzing with agitation. This conversation was bringing up all the feeling from the past weeks. Of being left in the dark, of being ignored.

He took another deep breath and leaned against the headboard. "When I took over the hotel, I started to get really worried. We both knew my uncle was a shady bastard, but knowing it and being a part of it are two very different things. So I set out to discover exactly what it was that I was a part of now. I got paranoid. If my business wasn't on the up-and-up, then I was the one whose neck was on the line. I started thinking, what if something happens and I end up in prison? And what if I get into some legal trouble and someone finds out about—" He stopped talking and put a finger to his lips. Then he leaned into me and whispered, "You're never to speak of that thing again. Not even here in our apartment. Do you understand?"

I nodded, suddenly assaulted by palpable memories of the spying we'd been subjected to by Santori. Was that a danger again? And if Santori was dead, who was left to spy on us?

"Anyway," Kage continued. "I started asking around, and I discovered that there were other people involved in my uncle's business. They treated me like an outsider when I confronted them. One of them, Theo Brown, was my uncle's best friend. He runs the Scepter Hotel here in Vegas, which I own. I also own an art gallery and horse stables."

Already, I was getting confused by the new details, but I nodded for him to continue.

"I paid Theo a visit and told him I was going to shut everything down and just focus on the Alcazar. Since he was such a close friend of Santori's and had been with him from the beginning, I offered to give him a job here making the same salary."

"Seems fair."

"Does it?" Kage asked bitterly. "Because that offer is what earned me these bruises."

I gasped. "Really? Why? If you were going to keep paying him the same thing—"

"He doesn't just run a hotel, Jamie. He does a hell of a lot more than that."

"Ohhh..." My eyes went wide as realization set in.

"Yeah," Kage said in that same bitter tone. "So here's the deal. You know I can't sell anything for two years from the date of the inheritance, so I'm stuck with this situation. Theo is apparently part of my inheritance."

"But what are you going to do? You can't sell him after two years."

"No, but I can sell the business *to* him. In the meantime, I need to get a handle on what's going on so that I don't make another mistake and get myself fucked up even worse." He paused, presumably to let everything sink in. It didn't work. I was still just as confused as I'd ever been, but at least he was sharing with me.

"So you're going to..."

He studied the ceiling for a moment, as if either there was something really interesting up there or there was something he didn't want to tell me. Finally, he said, "I'm going to work with Theo."

"What?" I demanded. "Kage, that doesn't even make any sense."

"It does. I can't have him wondering what I'm doing and if I'm going to compromise his livelihood, Jamie. He and I need to be on the same page while we have to work together."

I shook my head. "But isn't this just guaranteeing what you

were originally afraid of happening? Now you'll not only own the company, but you'll be involved in illegal activities. If you got caught, you wouldn't even be able to claim ignorance."

"Jamie..." He was getting irritated now, but by God so was I.

"No, Kage. I can't even wrap my head around the stupidity of what you're saying." I scanned his face for something and found only stubbornness. He had made up his mind about this, and there was going to be no changing it. "Fine. If you're hell-bent on doing this, I need to be kept in the loop, too. We *all* need to be on the same page. Just promise me you'll be done with it as soon as the two years is up, and that you won't do anything you can't take back."

"Jamie—"

"Stop saying my fucking name. I'm not a child. We are a couple, and we're living together, and I need to feel like I have some say in this. It's my life, too."

"Well, that's the other thing," he said sheepishly.

My stomach dropped. "Don't say what I think you're going to say. Don't you say it, Kage. Don't you fucking say it."

"I need to keep you safe," he whispered, staring at that damn ceiling again. "This is not a good place for you right now. If I fuck up, it could be you with bruises all over your body. Or worse. Please, Jamie. Listen to me. Theo doesn't want you in the picture. He doesn't trust you."

"Well, I don't give a good goddamn if he trusts me or not. What, you're just going to let him dictate who you can have a relationship with now? Jesus, you fought Santori all the way, and now all of a sudden you're going to let this guy you barely know control you? I don't even know what to say. It's ridiculous."

I got up and started pacing the room, so close to exploding with rage it was ridiculous. I'd never felt quite so out of control.

"It's not that simple," he said, finally looking at me for a change. "I don't know what to do, okay? He wants you out of the picture. He said it's not negotiable."

"And you're just gonna lie down and take it. Why don't you tell him it *is* negotiable? That I'm your man, and I'm staying. Why won't you fight for me?" My voice trembled. "What do you expect me to do now? Go crawling back to Georgia? *Hey, Mom and Dad. I need to move back in because Kage dumped me. Why? I don't know. Something about turning to a life of crime.* I mean what the fuck?"

"You're getting too wound up," Kage said. "You need to calm down and listen to reason."

I shook my head. "You're unbelievable. Reason? You think this is reason?"

"It's as close to reason as I can get at the moment."

"Well, that's not good enough." I approached the side of the bed where he still sat, unmoving. Tears sprang to my eyes, and I wiped angrily at them. "Do you love me, Kage? Or was that all just bullshit to keep me in line?"

"Of course I love you." His eyes were beseeching. "I love you more than anything in this world, and I don't want you to go."

"Then I'm staying." I crossed my arms over my chest and planted my feet, daring him to make me move.

"You can't," he said simply.

"Then there's more to the story you're not telling me. That stuff you told me about Theo is flimsy as hell. It doesn't make any sense. And why do you keep acting like someone may be spying on us, yet you keep talking about it."

He picked nervously at the covers. "I'm not saying anything to you that Theo isn't aware of. He knows very well that I didn't want to get involved in the more shadowy areas of the business, but he also knows that I want peace between us. I tried to change things, he had me beaten up, and then I went to him and asked him to be my mentor. I can't be left out of my own business, Jamie, but I also can't put you in harm's way. Theo and I need to work together, and he says he won't do it unless you go. End of story."

"I can't believe you would let him do this to you. To us. I thought you were stronger than that, but I guess I was wrong."

I paced back over to the door, and I heard Kage getting off the bed. He came up close to me, his face inches from mine, and leaned in close. He whispered in my ear, presumably to avoid being heard by anyone who might be listening. "It's only temporary, Jamie. This is something I have to do. Believe me, if there was another way—"

"Get off me," I yelled, grabbing onto his broad shoulders and shoving him back as hard as I could. Every word and every sorry excuse out of his mouth pissed me off more than the last. "You know what's really bad? You came in here tonight and had sex with me knowing you were going to blow me off afterward. That was fucking low."

He physically winced away from my words, and I was glad. I had never wanted to hurt him before, but he was definitely hurt by my last comment. It was apparent in the subtle quiver of his lips and the way he suddenly looked defeated. It almost made me feel sorry for him, but not quite. I was hurting, too. So damn much. I wanted to fight to stay with him, but he seemed determined to get rid of me. Did he really plan on it being a temporary split, or was this all a complicated ruse to dump me without a fight? My head was spinning, and I couldn't trust a word he said.

Neither of us spoke for a long time. We simply stood there and avoided looking anywhere but at each other. Was there anything left to say? After all of the words we'd hurled at each other, we were no closer to a solution. Well, no solution that satisfied me, anyway.

"We'll talk about this when I get back from New York," I said when I couldn't take the awkwardness anymore.

"New York?"

"Yes, New York. I told you last week I'm going to the UFC fight. I need to get more experience at live events. Get out there and talk to people, take photos, do interviews. Blogs don't write themselves, you know."

"Sorry, I forgot about that. When do you leave?"

"Tomorrow afternoon. But don't worry, I'll make myself scarce in the morning until it's time to go. And I won't be back until Sunday afternoon. Do you mind if I sleep in here with you tonight?"

"Of course not." He moved toward me, and I got the feeling he was going to put his arms around me, but he stopped short when I took a step back. His shoulders sagged even lower. "Well, I'm tired. I'm gonna do my thing in the bathroom before I hit the sack."

"Fine. I'll go after you."

When we finally got settled into bed and the lights were out, the discomfort was so thick I was tempted to call Steve and see if I could stay at his place. It was a miracle I ever fell asleep. When my alarm went off and I dragged myself out of bed to pack for my trip, I decided I was more exhausted than when I'd gone to bed.

CHAPTER EIGHT

KAGE

TRUE TO HIS WORD, Jamie made himself scarce the next morning. He was gone when I got up. I thought about stopping by his office on my way out to meet Theo, but I changed my mind at the last second. His feelings were still raw, and he had said we would talk when he got back. Maybe in the meantime I could talk Theo into easing up. His insistence that I cut Jamie loose made no sense anyway. I figured he was just carrying out my uncle's wishes, which I was sure he had made known to everyone in his inner circle.

Theo was in his office when I arrived at the Scepter. He welcomed me in from behind his monstrosity of a desk, and I took my customary seat across from him. There was no Macallan this time—just an icy chill emanating from the man I now called mentor.

Well, I called him that to his face. In my mind, he was the bastard I was going to take down.

"So what's on the agenda for today?" I finally asked. I didn't want to push too hard or come off as too eager. If I had my way, Theo would spontaneously blurt out all of the secrets Aaron coveted, and I would be out of here. But that was far more than wishful thinking; it was high fantasy. Things like that didn't happen in the real world.

In reality, Theo would keep his secrets hidden, and I would work to discover them for years. Jamie would move on and marry Cameron or someone else more deserving of him than me, and I would die alone like my uncle had. The other likely scenario was that I would get a bullet in my back while I was rifling through Theo's drawers in search of some phantom list of clients that would have set me free.

"I'll just be giving you a tour of the hotel today," Theo said. "You *are* interested in seeing your own properties, right?"

What I wanted to say was, *No, I don't give a damn about my properties. Just tell me who you're doing business with.* Instead, I said, "Of course. I can't wait to see it."

So Theo gave me a mind-numbing tour of the Scepter, which was much less impressive than the Alcazar. It was in disrepair, with the entire top floor being completely closed off for renovations. Theo didn't show me that floor, and he didn't take me to the floor marked B for basement on the elevator keypad. That was fine by me. The dark basement of an old hotel was the last place I wanted to be alone with Theo Brown.

He explained that they didn't do nearly the business the Alcazar did. They housed the odd straggler who stumbled upon the place by mistake while looking for somewhere to stay that wasn't right in the middle of the fray. "Most people think we'll be cheaper here, but we don't want to encourage the budget crowd."

His comment sounded blatantly elitist, but I could read the subtext: *We're not really a hotel. We're a front for darker business.* I was fine with that. I just wanted his client list.

He finished showing me around and informed me that he had a meeting to get to. I took that to mean he was done with me for the day, but I needed more than a tour of the supply closet and an introduction to the bored desk clerk.

"Would you mind if I tagged along to your meeting?" I smiled, hoping he wouldn't sense the eagerness that was making me want to crawl out of my skin. "I don't have anything better to do today."

He regarded me with narrowed eyes. "I don't think we're there yet. I believe in baby steps."

Baby steps. Great.

"Besides," he continued. "I'm sure I'm keeping you from all of the fancy things you're doing at the Alcazar. Didn't you have a spa to finish or something?"

"I've got a great staff over there. They've really taken the ball and run with it. I hardly do anything besides check in with them every now and then."

"Oh, yes. I forgot you're just a beginner at all of this. I should warn you that letting your employees run the show is not a good thing and that you need to keep a close eye on every facet of your business, but you'll learn that for yourself soon enough. If you're letting someone else handle the decisions on this project, you're going to spend at least twice as much. People aren't nearly as conscientious about spending when it isn't coming out of their own pockets."

"I've been very hands-on with it up until now. It's in the final stages, so I'm not too worried. It's just a waiting game now."

"How are your injuries?" he asked.

Oh, God. I was not about to let him get another look at my body. I could still feel his hands on me as if I'd been molested. I suppose in some weird pain-fetish way, I had been.

"They're healing really fast, and I woke up with much less pain today than yesterday."

Theo nodded but said nothing. I supposed he was disappointed that I wasn't writhing in pain.

The truth was, I was still sore as hell, and the crazy sex with Jamie the night before hadn't helped. But I wasn't feeling quite as stiff, and that was a big plus. Hobbling around like an old man had been the worst. Hopefully, I would be fully recovered by the time I had to fight Anthony Rodriguez, who was a talented enough fighter to make me nervous. Not on a good day, though. If I were in the kind of shape I'd been a year before, I would have wiped the Octagon with him like I'd done everyone else, but I'd been shirking my training, and the weight cut already had me sweating bullets. I didn't need to be injured on top of it.

Theo nodded and tapped his index finger deliberately on the desk. My eye was drawn to it, and I marveled not for the first time at how shiny his nails were, and I wondered if they had polished as well as buffed. He was obviously a vain man, with that perfectly waving mane of lion hair, immaculate suit, and a thick gold watch glittering at his wrist. My uncle had been very much the same, though without the flowing blond hair.

Suddenly I realized Theo's finger was still tapping, and that it was a signal for me to stop wasting his precious time. Probably Morse code for *Get the hell out of my office.* Boy, when this man was done with you, he was done. No more chit-chat and no friendly smiles. Not that he was much of a smiler anyway.

I stood up and stretched, playing it off like it was my idea to leave. "You know, you're probably right about the spa. I really should get back and see what they're doing over there. I'm letting one of my employees handle the decorating, and he's pretty flamboyant. If I'm not paying attention, he'll probably have glitter paint on the walls."

My attempt to lighten the mood fell flat. Either Theo didn't appreciate humor, or I just wasn't funny. Probably a little of both.

"So when can we do this again? I'm fascinated."

Theo leaned back in his chair and steepled his long fingers in front of his chest. "I think a little get-to-know-you time is in order. This is all so formal. How about we have a few drinks at your place this weekend? I would invite you to mine, but to be quite honest I don't trust you enough yet."

Well, the man was certainly blunt.

"I don't know—"

"Your ex-boyfriend won't be there, will he? I trust you've taken care of that little problem."

I shook my head, caught in the crossfires of his threatening stare. That little problem would be in New York until Sunday, but Theo didn't need to know that. Let him assume that Jamie was gone for good. There was already a seed of an idea in my head about how Jamie and I could stay together without tripping Theo's wire. If he was staying in one of the Alcazar suites, maybe I could visit him on the sly at his place until this was all over. I wasn't sure if it would work.

"Jamie's gone," I said. "We can have drinks at my place."

"Great. How does eight o'clock Saturday night sound?"

"Sounds like a date."

And what the hell had I just said? Date? What if Theo took it to mean we were having a *date* date? I had no idea where his interests lay within the gender spectrum, but in his journal, Peter Santori had claimed that Theo tried to seduce him one night. He'd made it sound like a pity seduction, but I had my suspicions about that. I was pretty sure straight dudes who got a lot of action didn't typically offer to fuck their hard-up guy friends as a birthday present.

Theo actually smiled at me. "Then it's a date."

I made a quick escape so that I could worry without an audience.

When I cranked up my car and started to back out, I got a text message from Aaron. Or I assumed it was Aaron since it was a confirmation for a time slot at a nearby gun range. Was Aaron going to teach me how to shoot? The prospect excited me almost to the point of giddiness.

I headed back to my place to grab my gun, and I almost made it through the lobby without anyone accosting me. Unfortunately, Steve saw me and followed me all the way to the elevator.

"What's up with Jamie," he asked without prelude. "He's in an awful mood today, and I can't get him to talk to me."

"It's personal. You need to mind your own business on this. He'll talk when he's ready."

Steve's face fell. "I don't know what's up with you guys, but you need to get your shit together. You can fire me if you want, but I'm not going to keep my mouth shut. You're my friends, and my friends *are* my business."

He stalked back over to the front desk and glared sullenly at me as I got on the elevator. I wasn't going to fire him. It was an absurd thing for him to even suggest. But I did wish he'd stop trying to intrude. Things were complicated enough without him browbeating me about our love life.

Pushing those thoughts aside, I retrieved the duffel bag that contained my gun from the closet in my apartment and hurried back to my car. I had an appointment with destiny, and my destiny apparently included being a badass motherfucker with a gun.

AS EXPECTED, Aaron was waiting for me at the gun range, dressed in his new casual style that still caught me off guard. I was so used to seeing him with his hair buzzed and wearing a suit, and now he was just a regular guy with hair, a beard, and street clothes. And the weight loss was probably the biggest difference of all. I had to admit the look suited him. Aaron was a good-looking man.

"Kage," he greeted with a smile. He could be deceptively charming, but I knew that beneath the friendly veneer he was all business. "You ready to learn how to protect yourself?"

"Hell, yeah. If you'd told me a year ago I'd be learning to fire a gun, I would have called you a liar. The fact that I have a need to learn now is a little disturbing. Do you think I can get good enough to do any damage?"

"Nothing to it. You'll be a pro in no time."

I was pretty sure he was just trying to give me confidence, but I was excited to prove him right.

"Here's my gun," I said, showing him the 38 Special my uncle had left behind. It was a gorgeous gun, and it also had historical significance in my life. Call me a sap, but I liked the idea of using Santori's gun even if he and I hadn't seen eye-to-eye when he was alive. Like it or not, he was the only family I had.

"Actually, I brought you a present," he said, pulling a black gun out of his bag and holding it out to me. I turned it over in my hands, thinking that it wasn't nearly as attractive as the 38 Special. "It's a Gen 4 Glock 19. Same gun I carry, right down to the modifications."

"But I like my gun. It reminds me of old-world gangsters or something. This black one screams street thug."

"I know you like it, and it's fine to learn how to use it and enjoy it. It's a fantastic gun. But you're going to be at a disadvantage if you're talking about concealed carry and protecting yourself against people who are much better armed and better trained than you."

I frowned, unconvinced. I really wanted to use my gun.

"Let me put it this way," Aaron said. "Would you rather have six rounds or fifteen? And would you rather deal with single bullets or a clip."

"Okay, that's a good point." I returned the 38 Special to the duffel bag and got familiar with my new gun.

Aaron was a patient instructor. He started with proper handling and safety. Then we moved on to grip and squeezing the trigger. I'd never imagined there was a right and wrong way to pull a trigger. It was fascinating stuff. Eventually, he had me decked out in safety gear with my ears protected as I tried firing at the target. I have enough humility to admit I sucked at first. It wasn't as easy as it looked to fire a gun. There were so many things to consider: kickback, foot placement, aiming, squeezing, and working with the unique characteristics of my gun. By the end of our training, I was more than a little discouraged, but Aaron gave me a cool holster that fit inside the right front of my waistband and could be concealed easily beneath a shirt. That cheered me up a little, because damn. I had a holster in my pants.

Then I realized... Shit, I have a *gun* in my pants.

"Am I going to shoot my dick off?" I asked Aaron point-blank.

He chuckled. "No. The appendix carry may seem dangerous, but it's not any more dangerous than any other position. The trigger guard of your gun is protected at all times while in this holster. The only time you have to be careful is when you're unholstering and reholstering your gun. Practice it a lot with the gun unloaded, making sure that you keep your finger clear of the trigger guard until the gun is pointed downrange." He demonstrated. "When you're reholstering, be aware of bits of clothing, especially drawstrings, which could potentially breach the trigger guard. That's really it."

"Okay. Since you wear one of these, I'm not too worried. Now I just have to learn to shoot. After that sorry excuse for shooting I exhibited here today, I don't know if I'm even capable of learning."

"You'll get the hang of it," Aaron said. "There's a reason firing ranges exist. You have to practice to get good, and I expect you to be here at least a few times a week. My buddy Hank will take care of you."

He introduced me to Hank, who was a burly, bearded man in his forties, and Hank instructed me to ask for him any time I came to the range. He and Aaron exchanged a hyper-manly hug, and then Aaron took me to an empty snack room and got both of us a bottle of water. We sat at one of four tables and got down to business.

"What have you learned so far?" Aaron asked.

I laughed. "I've only seen Theo twice since you and I talked. Not much time to learn anything."

"Sometimes seemingly insignificant details can be important. You need to be paying attention to everything."

"Well, I do know he's got a hard-on for pain, and especially pain he's inflicted. The bastard got me to show him the bruises his goons left. He put his hands on me. Squeezed my bruises to make me flinch. He's kind of a sick bastard."

Aaron gave a quizzical look. "But isn't that the kind of thing you go for?"

"No, asshole, it's not. I like to beat people up in the Octagon, and I like to get rough in bed. What I saw in that man's eyes is something different altogether. I don't gloat over the damage I do to my opponents, and I certainly don't hurt people in bed just for the sheer torture of it. It's—" I wasn't sure how to explain my kink to Aaron, and it wasn't really his business anyway.

"It's what, Kage?"

I sighed. "It's more of a power thing for me, I guess."

"Do you think he's any different just because he enjoys a different kind of pain? I see a lot of parallels between the two of you. And let's not forget Santori. As I see it, the three of you are cut from the same cloth. I just hope you don't turn out like them."

Shame flooded my every cell. I felt like a pre-teen who'd been caught jerking off and was now forced to sit through his parents' lecture. Aaron seemed to think that my predilection for pain had the potential to make a monster of me. Could that be true? Was pain more than just a bedroom kink for me? Was I destined to end up like Santori and Theo Brown? The thought made me shiver. I didn't want to be like them. I hated them.

"Is that really how you see me? I asked, fearing the answer as much as needing it.

Aaron ran his fingertips distractedly through the condensation on his water bottle and shrugged. "I think you have a shot at being something better. A really good shot. I don't believe you're evil at heart, but then what man has ever been born evil? We all start out the same. It's up to each of us to decide what we will become in the end. But I didn't mean to get into a philosophical discussion with you about good and evil. My purpose in questioning you about Theo was to get you to explore what you know about him. That's an important skill when you're working undercover. I don't have time to train you properly in all of the nuances of the job, but I can give you some quick pointers that could mean the differences between success and failure."

"I'm down for learning anything you can teach. I don't mind telling you I'm scared shitless right now. I'm trying to be what you need me to be, but as you know, I'm just winging it. I don't know what the hell I'm doing. There were several times when I was talking to Theo that my nerves nearly got the best of me. I never know if I'm doing or saying the right thing, and I'm terrified that I'm going to make one wrong move and get myself killed." I paused and bit my lip. "He *would* kill me, wouldn't he? If he thought I was a real threat."

"I imagine so. That's why you have to pay attention. The fact that you and Theo have a similar fascination with power and pain should be an asset to you in figuring out how to deal with him. Like minds and all that. Does that make sense?"

"Now it does. I thought you were just giving me a lecture. Trying to make me feel like shit about my kinks."

He shook his head. "It's not my place to judge you, Kage. All I can do is make observations. What else have you learned?"

"Well, most importantly I've learned that he doesn't trust me. Or Jamie. I know you told me not to share any information concerning our arrangement with Jamie, and I fully intended to do as you asked. Now that's not so much an issue anymore since Theo told me I had to break up with Jamie or else."

"Really?" Aaron scrubbed his fingers through his beard. "Hmmm. I hadn't expected that. What beef does he have with Jamie other than the fact that your uncle didn't approve of him?"

"Your guess is as good as mine. He seemed very serious about it, though. Told me it was non-negotiable."

"Do you think Theo could be attracted to you?"

"No," I replied, my voice loud with vehemence. Then I put my disgust aside and considered it. "Well, I suppose he could be. I haven't gotten all the way through the journals, but at the beginning, Peter mentioned that Theo had offered to have sex with him on his birthday. I thought that was a little strange."

"You really need to finish those journals, Kage. I can't stress enough the importance of getting to know this man through your uncle's eyes."

"I want to read every word. I just haven't had the time with all this other shit going on. I was also trying to keep them a secret from Jamie. It seemed easier that way. If he'd known I was reading them, he would've had all kinds of questions, and I wasn't ready to deal with that."

"So he's gone now?"

"Not exactly. I told him we needed to take a break while I try to get in good with Theo. Again, let me reiterate that I did not, nor do I plan to, expose your agenda or involvement to him. Without that information, my excuse for working with Theo is thin at best, but I really had no other choice. I don't want to break Jamie's heart, and I don't want to put him at risk in any of this. I also don't want him to go and find someone else to fall in love with while we're working all of this shit out."

"It may be inevitable."

"Thanks a lot." I shot him a petulant glare that didn't seem to bother him in the least.

"You have to consider all possibilities realistically. In this line of work, there are sacrifices. It's nearly impossible to hang onto the people in your life no matter how much love you feel for them. Sometimes it's better for them to just set them free to have normal lives. It's selfish to keep them hanging indefinitely in the hopes that someday it will work out. This job takes a lot from us and gives back very little."

"Well, I'm not actually in this line of work, remember? This is your job, not mine."

He nodded. "You're right. But you're still involved, and nothing can be done about that. Your unfortunate parentage is to blame for that, but it doesn't change the facts. Do your best to help us out on this, and I'll do my best to see that you're safe and happy afterward. I just want you to realize there are things beyond my control, and Jamie is one of those things. You have to let him make his own choices. When the smoke clears, maybe he'll choose you and maybe he won't."

"Maybe you could keep an eye on him for me. Step in if he starts getting too close to someone or doing something I wouldn't like. That would give us some measure of control."

Aaron grinned and raised an eyebrow. "My God, you sound just like your uncle."

Jesus. He was right. I thought back over my words and was appalled that I had been the one to say them. I had just asked Aaron to spy on Jamie like he'd done for Santori, only this time it would be to keep Jamie tied to me instead of driving him away. In that moment, I sickened myself. For what I'd said, and the fact that even the shame of knowing all of that didn't make me want to do it any less. I didn't want to be like Santori, but dammit I still felt the urge to control Jamie by any means necessary. I hung my head and admitted to myself that I was fucked in the head, and that I was more of a bad guy than I'd thought.

"Hey, don't beat yourself up," Aaron said. "I know why you want to do it. Don't think I haven't been tempted in the past to use my resources to keep someone in line. But if you love him, I don't think it would be a good idea. You would just feel guilty and ashamed for doing it, and if he ever found out, he would resent you. Consider this: Santori thought he was doing the right thing for you by getting rid of Jamie. I'm sure there was a lot of selfishness mixed in there, too, but for the most part, I think he truly believed he was helping you. Now that you know that, do you forgive him?"

"No," I admitted. "I hated him for it. Still do."

"Exactly. And I don't think you should expect Jamie to be okay with you manipulating him, either. Even having someone tailed in the name of physical protection can be a slippery slope. Too easy to get turned around about what your true motives are. I can't tell you what to do, but my advice is to let him go in the hopes that you can be reunited someday when this dark cloud isn't hanging over your heads."

Damn. That's not what I wanted to hear. It made sense, but I still didn't want to hear it. What if Jamie got with someone else in the interim? I couldn't stand the thought of some other guy's hands all over him. Some other guy's dick inside him. Some other guy telling him he loved him, and worse, getting his love in return. It made me want to hurt somebody, and not in a good way.

CHAPTER NINE

KAGE

WHEN I GOT BACK HOME, Jamie was gone. I'd spent a lot of time at the gun range and talking to Aaron, and then I'd stopped by some random bar I'd never been to and had three or four beers. Probably enough to register a DUI, but I was beyond caring. I wanted some weed, but it was too close to my fight to risk it being in my system, so I opted for going home and loading up on painkillers.

Jamie had never responded to my text from the night before, but at least he had my number. Just in case he needed me. Was it wrong that I hoped he would need me? That he would get himself into some situation and force me to go back on my decision to cut him loose? Hell, I still hadn't decided for sure. The idea of giving him a suite in the Alcazar and visiting him in secret still held a lot of appeal, even though I knew it was risky.

Maybe his trip to New York would give him time to think everything through, and he would decide that making himself scarce while still waiting for me was something he wanted to do. It was going to be hell without him beside me in bed every night, but at least it was better than most of the alternatives. I thought about his job. The fact that he worked out of the Alcazar at the moment. Something would have to be done about that. I needed to get him another office, but I wasn't sure where he would be. Georgia? With Cameron?

I knew it was childish to keep hanging onto my jealousy of Cameron, but the images Santori had shown me of the two of them together were burned into my memory forever. It had hurt so much seeing them getting cozy. Cameron kissing him up against his car, then stripping Jamie's shirt off in the bedroom.

Ugh. God. Get out of my head. I scrubbed at my eyes as if that would do any good.

And what of Layla, the gorgeous but infuriating Mexi-bitch? Would Jamie want to get back with her if I wasn't around? If he decided that's what he wanted, it wouldn't be difficult to make it happen. Layla seemed to like Trey a lot, but he was no Jamie Atwood. She would be stupid to pass up the opportunity to get Jamie back, and I could see it in her eyes every time she looked at him that she knew it, too.

No, Jamie probably didn't need to go back there. I was trying to control the situation again, but fuck it. The compulsion was too strong to ignore. Maybe I could get him a place in Vegas. An apartment and an office, or an apartment *with* an office. He seemed to really enjoy getting out of the apartment to go to work, saying that it motivated him and made him feel legit, so it would definitely need to be both. Of course, I could always just give him money, which I planned to do anyway, but money wouldn't ensure that he stayed close by. He could take the money I gave him and do like I once suggested—buy a house on the golf course for him and Cameron. Jesus, that would burn me up inside.

By the time the three hydrocodone pills I'd taken started to kick in, I was nearly crazy with worry. My plans for Jamie had gotten increasingly nonsensical, and in the end I had circled back to keeping him with me and telling Theo to go fuck himself.

I don't know when I got up off of the sofa and moved to bed, but that's where I woke up the next morning with a killer case of cotton mouth and about two gallons of pee in my bladder. After I got myself presentable, I decided to go downstairs and be the boss for a change. I'd been MIA for days, and I needed to at least make an appearance and remind everyone who was in charge.

Steve was still upset with me. I could tell because his usual incessant banter was absent. He was distant and cool, and I wondered if he and Jamie had been talking. If he knew I'd tried to break up with him. I say tried because I had no idea if I'd succeeded or failed at it. He'd said we would talk when he got back, so I guess I'd find out then.

"How's Jamie?" I asked Steve finally. I leaned against the front desk and watched for signs of hostility in his expression, but he seemed resigned.

"Fine. He called me at noon and told me a little about what's going on. He'd already talked to some fighters and gotten some pictures. Seems like he's having a really good time."

I got the feeling the implication was that Jamie was having a good time despite me being an asshole.

"That's good," I said. "Did he send you any of the pictures?"

"Why don't you look on his blog if you want to know what he's up to? I check it every day. He incorporates a lot of humor into his articles, and it's really entertaining even if you're like me and know nothing about fighting."

Okay, that made me feel as bad as I'm sure Steve had intended. Why hadn't I been following Jamie's blog? I paid for it, but was that really enough? I should have been a more supportive partner. I'd just been so preoccupied with other shit I hadn't noticed I wasn't giving enough. On the other hand, Jamie had helped me every step of the way with the spa and with anything else he could.

"Have you finished choosing decorations for the spa?" I asked, trying to change the subject.

Steve sniffed. "Decorations? You make it sound like we're using Christmas lights and streamers."

"I didn't mean it that way, and you know it. Hell, I don't know design speak."

"If you want to see my plans, come take a look."

He led me over to the nearly-finished spa, which I'd already checked out when I first came down. All of the basic structural things were done. The sheetrock was up and painted. Flooring and wall tiles in pale shades of salmon, sand, and dusty blue had been installed, as had crystal chandeliers and high-end cabinetry. There was a good bit left to do, but it was actually beginning to look like a spa rather than a construction zone. It was breathtaking.

Steve brought out a thick scrapbook in which he had collected tons of samples. Paint chips, flooring, furniture... All manner of things that would eventually come together to create the finished look. He showed me everything from massage tables to sunken tubs. He'd even chosen a sound system so that soothing music could be piped in.

"Wow, you've really taken this seriously," I said, genuinely impressed. "It's going to be gorgeous. In fact, it already *is* gorgeous."

"And you thought I was going to make it look like what? A unicorn pooped glitter or something?"

"I think I told you I didn't want it to look like it was decorated by a unicorn with a Bedazzler, but please accept my apologies for ever doubting you. This looks absolutely amazing. I never would have thought to mix these colors. And the chandeliers are a nice touch. It's opulent but relaxing at the same time. Damn fine job." I patted him awkwardly on the back.

"You don't think I spent too much, do you?"

"To be honest, I barely glanced at the proposals before I signed them and sent them back. I wanted no expense spared for this thing, and despite the fact that I mentioned unicorns and Bedazzlers, I really trust you when it comes down to it. I just enjoy giving you a hard time."

"What is this, bonding time?" The angle of Steve's brow said he thought I was full of shit.

"No, it's Kage-being-grateful time. Now stop giving me grief."

"Fine. I'm glad you like the job I'm doing for you." Still so formal. He was really fucking pissed.

"You know, something occurred to me concerning you and this spa, and I wanted to get your opinion on it."

"Okay, shoot."

"How would you feel about getting away from that front desk and managing the spa instead?"

His eyes stretched to the size of softballs. "Don't tease me, Kage. Are you serious?" When I nodded, he said, "Hell yeah I'd like to manage it. Does that mean more money?"

"Of course. I haven't worked up the numbers yet, but you would be making significantly more money. It's time you got a raise and a promotion, and I can see how much you love working with the spa."

"But do you think I'm qualified? I mean I don't want to talk you out of it, but I've never done anything like this before."

"Had you ever done interior design before?"

"Well, no. Not for money. Just decorated a little for friends and family. But I watch design shows all the time, and I guess I just picked it up."

"Then you shouldn't have any problem learning the skills needed to run the place you decorated. We'll get you some classes. There must be some resources online to help you learn how to run a spa. Let me know what you find, and we'll get you trained up. This is something new to all of us, and there's going to be a learning curve. I know I could advertise for a manager with experience, but I'd rather give the job to you. Why don't you take a little time to think about it before you decide?"

"No," Steve blurted. "I don't need to think about it. I just need to get busy figuring out how to do it. Oh, my God, I swear you will not regret this."

I smiled and looked around the new spa again. "I know I won't. And I'm giving you a bonus for the design work you've already done. I'll go right now and make sure they get it into your next paycheck."

Steve touched a hand to his chest and blinked away tears of joy. "You might be a complete and total asshole right now because of the way you're treating Jamie, but I love you anyway." He threw his arms around me and tried to squeeze me to death.

I was suddenly all too aware of the gun—Gen 4 Glock 19, I reminded myself—concealed in the holster at my waist. What had Aaron called that position? Appendix carry. Hell, yeah, I was learning. I was also noticing how much more powerful I felt with a gun strapped to me.

Steve backed away from me and glanced at my waist. Right at my gun. I could see the suspicion written all over his face, but he didn't call me out on it. He just took a deep breath and changed the subject back to the one thing I didn't want to discuss.

"Now about Jamie. You need to set things right, Kage. I know you love him, and he's insane over you. Trying to get along with your uncle's business partner is one thing, but when you let it ruin the only real relationship you've ever had... Well, that's just tragic. I know how you feel about that boy. I can see it in your eyes every time you look at him. You were so different before you met him. I can't believe you'd let go of that happiness just to please someone else, let alone someone you just met."

I ran a hand through my hair and wished I could teleport out of there. "You don't understand the whole story, Steve, and I'm not at liberty to share it with you. Just know that I love Jamie more than my own life. I would die for him, okay? I would actually die for him, and that's all you need to know. Conversation over."

I left Steve with his mouth hanging open. Let him chew on that for a while. I was done wasting time trying to explain myself to people who couldn't possibly understand.

CHAPTER TEN

JAMIE

IT WAS hard to focus on work with Kage occupying my every waking thought. Damn him for ruining my excitement for the event. I moved through the hotel's crowded spaces like a zombie with a camera and hoped nobody would speak to me unless I chose to speak to them first. I wasn't in the mood for small talk. Just let me get enough content for next week's blog posts and get the hell out of there.

The worst part is that I had no idea where I'd go. If Kage and I were really going to split up, I needed to collect my things from the apartment, and then what? I really didn't want to go back to Georgia. That felt like a death sentence.

I managed to keep my mind clear enough to ask a few

questions at Friday night's press conference, which was held in the hotel, but I was more than relieved when it was over and I could head up to my room and breathe. I just wanted to lie down in my bed and worry. God, I was pathetic.

I shouldered my camera and pushed my way through the crowd that seemed to grab at me like human quicksand. I was getting claustrophobic.

When I finally reached the exit, Anthony Rodriguez stood in the doorway, blocking my passage out. I had seen him lurking around, talking to reporters and bloggers, doing early promo for the upcoming fight. Kage had declined to do any live promo this time around because of the responsibilities of his new business, but Anthony seemed more than willing to make the rounds. I had avoided getting anywhere near him so far, but now here he was. Forcing me to interact with him. The way his eyes met mine and held, I had no illusions that this was an accidental meeting.

His dark hair was slicked back, and his natural deep tan contrasted with the white dress shirt he wore open to the third button, revealing the beginnings of an impressive nest of black chest hair. His bio said he was born in Spain but raised in America, the only son of a successful businessman and a fashion model. I hadn't been able to resist the temptation to google photos of his parents, and my suspicion was confirmed. Both of his parents were out-of-this-world gorgeous. Anthony wore the same neat beard as his father, who had also passed along his six-foot-one stature and perfect body proportions to his only son, but the warm brown eyes, high cheekbones, and full lips had definitely come from his mother. In other words, Anthony Rodriguez was not at all hard to look at.

He was also Kage's upcoming opponent.

I took a deep breath and prepared for the worst, because as handsome as he was, the guy was intimidating as hell. His kicks were the stuff legends were made of, and he had knockout power with his fists and elbows. As if that weren't enough, the lethal striker was just as dangerous on the ground as he was on his feet. He was a good match-up for Kage— a scary one, really— because their skill sets were so similar. Fighters who were known for their superior striking rarely had high-level jiu-jitsu skills to match, so when two of these unusual athletes met in the Octagon, you could pretty much bet it was going to be a bloodbath. No doubt this would be the most challenging fight either Kage or Rodriguez had ever faced.

I was so damn wrung out, and I just wanted to get to my room without an altercation. There was a lot of testosterone flying around at these UFC events, and if any one of the fighters had reason to give me a hard time at this particular point in time, it was this one.

"Baby Kage," Anthony said under his breath as I approached, just loud enough for me to hear. The Spanish accent of his parents was barely detectable, but I had noticed it a few times in the way the occasional R rolled off of his tongue.

"Cute." I smirked at him, cursing the tell-tale irritation that I was certain showed on my face. "You can just call me Jamie."

He didn't move, even when I had to stop to keep from walking into him. I raised my gaze from his chest to his dark brown eyes that bored into mine as he leaned a hand casually on the door frame, making it clear that he wasn't quite ready to let me pass. "So you and the Machine are living together, huh? I saw it on Twitter."

"Fucking Twitter," I growled. "Nobody can have any privacy anymore."

Anthony surprised me by laughing. His eyes crinkled at the corners, and suddenly he didn't look so intimidating. "You're a celebrity now, kid. You signed on the dotted line. What did you expect?"

"You make it sound like I sold my soul to the devil or something."

"Didn't you?" At my awkward silence, he continued. "I know I did. This business is the devil."

I was thinking more along the lines of Kage being the devil in my case, but I didn't say so. Instead, I said, "It was nice chatting with you, but I really need to get to my room."

"Chatting with me?" Anthony didn't move, but his smile broadened. "But you didn't ask me any questions. Isn't that your job, to ask questions? You asked that human blanket Mark Felder a couple, and the girl fighters. I feel a little cheated. Do you not find me interesting enough for your blog?"

"Of course I find you interesting," I said. "I find all fighters interesting, but that doesn't mean I interview all of them. I've never interviewed Michael Kage, either." It still felt funny calling him that, but I had to be careful to maintain a professional distance when I was in this world.

"I noticed that," Anthony said. "But then you probably know everything there is to know about him. You don't know anything about me."

"I know that you're of Spanish descent and that you train at Ludwig's gym in south Florida. I know your record is 10-2, you're a decorated kickboxer, and you earned your jiu-jitsu blackbelt under the Gracies."

"Wrong. I recently left Ludwig's and moved to Vegas to train with the Alphas." He wagged his eyebrows. "That makes us neighbors."

"I'll make a note of that," I told him, tugging nervously at my camera strap where it dug into my shoulder.

"Hey, not to be rude, but you really don't seem like a real reporter. I feel like maybe there's a conflict of interest going on here. Like maybe you're favoring Kage over me. Is that what they taught you in your journalism classes, or do you even have a degree? Some people think you just got involved in reporting MMA news just to try to give your boyfriend a media advantage."

"Of course not," I said. "This is my job. I went to school for it, and I earned it. It has absolutely nothing to do with Kage."

Anthony shrugged. "Sure seems like it. You're not interested in interviewing the number two Welterweight contender? MMA Daily just asked me for a video interview, and I turned them down."

"Why did you do that? They're huge."

"They wanted an exclusive, and I thought it would be interesting to be interviewed by you. I couldn't do both."

I frowned. "So you chose me? Why? I'm nobody."

He grinned. "You're my opponent's boyfriend. I could really use some dramatic press, and that's pure drama right there. How much do you want to bet it goes viral? Think about what that would mean. I guarantee it would help you just as much as it would help me."

The guy had a point. Interviewing Kage's opponent before their fight would cause a lot of drama, and people loved drama. Social media would be ravenous for it.

Anthony must have seen the change on my face the moment I began to consider his proposition, because he gave me a smug wink. "Meet me in my room tomorrow?"

I sighed. "Sure, why not?"

He pulled his cell phone out of his pocket. "Give me your number, and I'll text you the room number and time." He tapped in the digits as I rattled them off, and then he slipped his phone back into his pocket and stepped aside to let me pass. "Thanks, Jamie. And don't worry. This is a brilliant idea."

I waved to him over my shoulder without looking back as I made my way to the elevators, wondering what kind of shit storm

Anthony and I were about to start. Regardless of whether or not our video went viral, Kage was certainly not going to be thrilled. But this was journalism, dammit, and I couldn't allow Kage to dictate my future. Especially one who was in the process of trying to break up with me. I was an adult now, and I had a career to build, and Kage might not be in the picture much longer.

IT WAS hard to drag myself out of bed the next morning. My mind had kept me up worrying all night just like I had known it would, and the last thing I remembered was crying into my pillow. I felt like I'd gotten no sleep at all. A quick glance in the bathroom mirror revealed a face I didn't want to claim, with pale skin, puffy eyes, and hideous dark circles. I took a long shower, and that helped some.

After my shower, I had a text message waiting. My heart jumped when I saw the notification because my first thought that maybe Kage had come to his senses and was texting to apologize and beg me back. Instead, it was Anthony Rodriguez. He wanted me to meet him in his room at noon for a room service lunch and interview.

Room service. My stomach growled.

I ordered breakfast of scrambled eggs, bacon, toast, and strong coffee with a shot of espresso. It tasted like nothing, but I forced myself to eat half of it. The coffee was the only thing I finished because I needed the caffeine kick in the ass to get me going.

At noon, Anthony Rodriguez opened his hotel door to me wearing nothing but a pair of jogging shorts and a smile. I tried to keep my eyes trained on his handsome face, but that dark expanse of exposed skin was like a magnet to my gaze. Shit. Couldn't he have put some damn clothes on?

It didn't help that his physique was similar to Kage's. Thick shoulders, rock hard pecs, and perfect abdominals that could have been chiseled from stone. I had to admit the guy was a work of art, but I did wish he'd throw a shirt over that body.

He invited me in, and I took a seat on the small sofa pushed against one wall. It wasn't a fancy room, not like the one I'd reserved on Kage's credit card, and it was small. Too small for his presence as he moved around the space to tidy up the clothes he'd discarded the night before.

"Sorry. I fell back to sleep after I texted you, and I haven't been up long. This place is a wreck."

"It's not that bad," I said. "Mine doesn't look any better."

He grinned sheepishly and ran a hand through his dark hair. "Yeah, but you didn't invite somebody to come into yours. I should have straightened this up before you got here. You don't think I'm unprofessional, do you?"

I laughed. "You're a fighter, not a housekeeper. Cleanliness is not a prerequisite for a UFC contract."

"True." He came to stand directly in front of me, and I had to look up to see his face. "Where do you want me?"

"Ummm..." I looked around the room. There was a bed, the sofa I was sitting on, and a tiny table and wood-framed chair in the corner. The chair looked more like a torture device than seating, and I didn't think I wanted Anthony sitting on the bed while we talked. That just left the sofa, which was really more like a love seat. "You can just sit with me. There's not much room, but I think we can manage."

He dropped down beside me with a smile, and it struck me that he had a really gorgeous smile. It was probably his best feature, and that was saying a lot considering all of the other things he had going for him: the muscles, the perfect bone structure, the exotic dark coloring, and the warm brown eyes. I tried to imagine him and Kage in the Octagon together and shivered. It would be MMA softcore porn.

"So are we on or off the record?" he asked. "Are you gonna be putting everything I say in your article, or can we just talk for a minute?"

Talk? Off the record? What did we have to talk about?

"I won't publish anything you don't want to share, if that's what you mean. This isn't a police interrogation. It's me trying to get news to MMA fans while helping you out, too. Like marketing for yourself. I'm not some hard-nosed reporter trying to dig up gossip on you."

He relaxed visibly and nodded. "Okay, I know you're the Machine's boyfriend, but I wanted to ask for some advice. Is that weird?"

"Depends on what kind of advice you want."

"Well, I've seen what you did for Kage. I read up on you and did a little digging on the internet. *And Twitter*." He nudged my arm playfully. "I know how you feel about Twitter."

I rolled my eyes and laughed. "Yeah, Twitter has caused me more problems than I care to think about." I thought of the night my Twitter exploration had led to Kage choking me out and then having a PTSD attack. But then I realized that if I hadn't been cruising Twitter that night, Kage might never have come to terms with what had happened to Evan, so maybe it hadn't been so bad after all.

"I like Twitter," Anthony said. "I can interact with fans, and I don't have to say a whole lot."

"So you're not a social butterfly, I take it?"

"No. I don't do well with that kind of thing. Talking to people like we're best friends or something. I'd just rather say my piece and get out of there."

"Do you get a lot of haters? I don't mean to imply that you're not popular, I'm just curious. I've had my share of haters, and they come out in droves to attack Kage."

Anthony shrugged. "I guess everybody has haters. They're everywhere. I don't let it get to me if some stranger doesn't like me. They don't know me."

"That's a healthy attitude to have."

"My mother is a model, and my father is a successful international businessman. I don't say that to brag. I just grew up with a little more attention on me, so I learned to ignore it at an early age."

"That's good that you don't let it get to you."

"What I wanted to talk you about is what you did for Kage. He was doing that underground fighting thing, but as far as the general public was concerned, he was nobody. Then he met you, and things changed for him. You were his publicist, right?"

I laughed. "We use that term loosely. I was a college student, and he brought me out to Vegas to be his intern. I'm afraid I didn't do a great job. I made him a website, which in retrospect was pretty crappy. But I took pictures of him and posted a little on social media. I honestly didn't know anything about social media then beyond cat memes and drunken bar selfies. I was so clueless."

"So he hired you because he wanted to sleep with you, huh?"

"What?" I couldn't hide my shock at his bold question.

"Sorry. I say what I'm thinking way too much. All I meant was that he hired you even though you had no experience, and then you two ended up together. I just connected the dots."

There wasn't much I could say to that, because Rodriguez had hit the nail on the head. But it made me uncomfortable, so I changed the subject.

"So what was it you wanted to ask me?"

"Well, I don't get a whole lot of media coverage. I told you I have a hard time interacting beyond an occasional tweet. I want to know what I could do to get what Kage has got. I know he doesn't do many interviews, and he's been pretty absent for the last few months, but people are still talking about him. His old pics still get tons of hits. He has more fans *and* more haters than I do."

"Well, for starters, I don't get why you gave up the opportunity for that exclusive interview with MMA Daily. They have a huge reach. That could have been a big break for you."

"Maybe. But I wanted to talk to you. I told you that."

"I'm not following your logic. Besides the sensationalism of being interviewed by Michael Kage's boyfriend, which may not even be relevant anymore, I don't see where I offer any advantage."

"May not even be relevant anymore?"

Oh my God, why had I said that? And of course, he picked right up on it. "I just mean you never know what the future holds. Hanging your hopes on that one small detail is a risk." There. Did that sound even remotely legit? I couldn't tell.

"So the blush has left the rose?"

"What is that supposed to mean?"

"It's something my mother likes to say. It means the new has worn off of your relationship and things aren't working out."

"Oh. Well, maybe. But we have no reason to talk about my personal life. I'm the interviewer, not the interviewee."

"I thought we were still off the record. Just two guys getting to know each other."

I shifted in my seat, suddenly very uncomfortable where the conversation was headed. "We'd better be off the record, because if you lured me to your room just to get something you can use against me for publicity, I'm going to be very pissed."

"That would be pretty shitty of me," he said, pulling his knee up onto the sofa and facing me head on.

"You haven't denied it, though."

He ran a hand absently down his ripped torso. It wasn't a

calculated move because he didn't even seem to notice he'd done it. I thought he probably did that a lot when he was deep in thought.

"You're way off base." His fingers lingered in the hair on his chest and scrubbed lightly as he stared at the ceiling, lost in thought. "What if I told you something personal about me? Would you chill the fuck out then?"

I gaped at him. "Do you ever censor what you say?"

"No. I told you I say what I'm thinking."

"Yeah, not the most endearing quality to have."

He shrugged. "It's who I am. I have a hard time putting up a front like everybody else. It takes too much effort, and I'm not good at it."

"So you're obnoxious because you're lazy?"

"Obnoxious?" He laughed, genuinely surprised by my assessment of him. "I don't think I'm obnoxious. Maybe you just don't feel comfortable with people who say what they mean."

Damn. He might have had a point. Was that really how I was?

"I'll bet you lie a hundred times a day." There was no accusation in his tone or his expression. "You sit behind your computer and type out what you think people want to hear, just like everybody else. I'm just saying I have a hard time doing that—trying to figure out who people want me to be."

I raised my eyebrows, surprised at how honest he was being with me. I really couldn't think of anything to say, so I just sat there staring at him.

"You didn't answer my question," he said. "If I tell you something personal about me will you calm down and quit thinking I'm some sort of gossip spy?"

I took a deep breath and let it out, feeling instantly more at ease. "Okay, fine. Tell me something."

"Sometimes I wear the same pair of socks two days in a row." At my unimpressed smirk, he added, "I'm also gay."

I blinked like a bewildered owl, because of all the things I could have imagined him confessing, being gay was not one of them.

"Did you ask me for this interview so that I could out you?"

He shrugged. "I don't know. Do you think you should?"

"Jesus, Anthony. It's your life. I can't make that decision for you."

"Well, I trust your opinion. You helped Kage, so help me."

"But you're his upcoming opponent."

"And you said you were professional, so that shouldn't matter."

Shit. He had me there.

"All right, tell me what your end goal is. What is it that Anthony Rodriguez wants?"

"Fame. Money. The truth is, my parents disowned me last year when they found out I'm gay. They were worried it might tarnish their reputations. I'm used to a certain lifestyle, and now I'm cut out. Fuck, I don't even know how I'm going to pay my rent next month. I need some big money fights. This one with Kage is pretty big, but even though he's ranked lower than me, he's the draw. I need some attention, and I need some fucking money."

"Okay. Well, that's certainly honest. We can work with that." Truthfully, I was getting excited thinking about making a difference in a fighter's life again. How awesome would it be to help skyrocket this guy's career and know that I was the one who did it? There was a sense of power attached to it that was almost irresistible to me. I remembered back to the feeling I got when I was posting pictures of Kage and helping to build a following for him. That rush I got every time I checked the stats and saw how popular he was getting.

"I'll make it worth your while," he said. "When I start making money again, I'll pay you to be my publicist like Kage did."

"No. Sorry, but I don't really want to be anyone's publicist. I'm just not qualified for the job. But maybe I could do a consultation or two with you. We could bounce ideas off of each other and see what sticks. I may not have the skills to be a publicist, but I do have a journalism degree and the knowledge I gained from working with Kage. I also pay attention to the business and do a lot of research for my blog, so yeah. I can probably help you out."

"That would be awesome. In the meantime, though, we need to figure out what to do on this interview. I was thinking I could talk about my fighting philosophy. Tell about my parents disowning me. I know they don't want me saying anything about them, but I figure it serves them right for turning their backs on me. It would be a good sob story, too. Don't people like sob stories?"

"For a guy who thinks it's too much energy to front, you sure do have a lot of ideas about manipulating your public image."

"Hey, I'm trying to learn. What ideas do you have for me? Maybe you could do some sexy pictures of me like you did Kage. It seemed to work for him."

"Well, I don't know—"

"I'm as sexy as him, right? I've got a hot body."

At the mention of his hot body, my gaze dropped to his abs, and again I found myself wishing he would put on some damn clothes. "Yes, you are very good-looking."

He laughed. "That's not exactly a ringing endorsement. Do you think I've got what it takes, or not? Be honest with me."

"Yes, okay? You're hot. Are you happy now?"

He did that maddening thing with his hand again, rubbing up and down his torso as he grinned triumphantly at me. "Thought so."

"You're also cocky. Probably to a fault."

He shrugged, unconcerned with that particular observation. When he'd said he didn't care what people thought about him, I had mistakenly thought he meant it like most everyone else did— the ones who *said* they didn't care but then set about trying to fix themselves to suit popular opinion. That didn't seem to be the case with Anthony.

He was also single-minded and bullish, constantly steering the conversation in the direction he wanted to take it. "So we can get some pics, right? For the interview?"

I held up my camera. "I didn't bring this thing for nothing, although I had imagined taking a very different kind of photo than what you're talking about. And I had imagined you wearing more clothing."

"Fighters are always shirtless in their pics. They wear their shorts and nothing else. I'm wearing shorts."

"I know, but—" I almost admitted that he seemed more naked than most in a pair of shorts, but that sounded all kinds of wrong. He had me off balance and had kept me that way since I walked through the door. Actually, since the night before when he'd first struck up a conversation.

I didn't have enough experience to deal with interviewing someone with such a strong personality. It was too hard to maintain my professional dignity when it seemed like I was constantly either defending myself or trying not to stare at his abs. I could refuse to continue the interview, but he did have a good point about the possibility of my blog post going viral. Who wouldn't be interested in Michael Kage's boyfriend interviewing his upcoming opponent? It would definitely get tongues wagging.

There was also the possibility that it would make Kage jealous, and I would have been lying if I'd said that didn't hold a lot of appeal for me. Kage didn't seem to have much interest in continuing our relationship. He had other things to worry about now, and I didn't want to play the part of the poor jilted lover. I needed to retain some of the power in our screwed up dynamic, and at the moment I couldn't think of a better way to do it than showing him that I was moving on and thriving. And spending time with hot guys.

So I interviewed Anthony Rodriguez. We worked up our angles for the story together. The title of the piece would be *Anthony Rodriguez: The Naked Truth*. It was fitting, considering his habit of saying whatever came to his mind—and the fact that we were going to feature some pretty racy pictures of him wearing very little.

We decided he would officially come out as gay in the interview. Once I'd gotten over my initial trepidation, I realized that any blogger with sense would have been salivating over the chance to get an exclusive on a fighter coming out as gay. It was big news, and I was going to be the one to break it. I tried to play it off to Anthony as no big deal, but inside I was doing a happy dance and fantasizing about all of the attention we were going to get when the story broke.

I wasn't sure what kind of effect his coming out would have on his career, but it hadn't seemed to hurt Kage much. There would always be haters, but overall the press had been positive. Even with Kage not being as much in the public eye since he took over the Alcazar, he was still big news online, and I had no doubt this fight would stir up interest for him again in a big way. Now I was working behind the scenes with Rodriguez to make sure he got his fair share of that attention.

I reasoned that skyrocketing the public interest for Rodriguez would also benefit Kage. Imagine all of the people dying to see a fight between two gorgeous, well-known fighters who had both come out as gay. I couldn't wait to see it all unfold.

In addition to Anthony's coming-out announcement, we decided to share the fact that he was born into a wealthy family and that his famous parents had now disowned him for being gay. He talked about his fighting style and his career path, his training, the physical challenges he had faced, and his past fights, but we both knew all of this was just window dressing for the real story.

We decided to keep everything under wraps until I figured out how and when to release the interview for maximum exposure and hype.

When we had finished working out the details of the written piece, we moved on to the photos. I set up my tripod and camera while Anthony dressed in workout clothes, hand wraps, and gloves. Then we proceeded to unveil him bit by bit in a photo story that would no doubt have its own Tumblr address within an hour of being published. By the last set of shots, Anthony had wet hair and was lounging on the bed in nothing but a white hotel towel.

"Turn over on your stomach," I said. "Let's get some more ass shots. People really seemed to go for the ones I took of Kage."

Anthony rolled over, pulling his towel off in the process, and ended up completely naked. He tossed the towel to the floor and looked up at me where I stood with my mouth hanging open.

"What?" he asked, and innocent little half smile tilting his full lips.

"You're naked."

"Yeah. Isn't the interview called *The* Naked *Truth?* We need to back that shit up with some honest-to-God nudity."

I opened my mouth to retort and ended up closing again. Dammit, the guy was right. Again. What good was a piece designed to get media attention if we didn't stick to the theme? It only made sense to have at least one nude. Otherwise the title was just clickbait.

"Okay, you're right. I love the idea. I'm just not used to photographing naked men, so I freaked out a little."

"I get it. It's not that easy taking my clothes off for you, either, but I figure we need to go big or go home."

I didn't believe for a minute that getting naked in front of me was any kind of hardship for him. He'd already shown me everything he had except his dick, and I suspected that before it was all over I'd be seeing that, too. And if his dick was anything like his ego, he was hung like a horse.

I had another moment of panic, because what the hell was I doing? I wasn't a porn photographer. I was an MMA blogger.

An MMA blogger who's taking naked photos of his boyfriend's opponent.

But then I thought of Kage breaking up with me, and that was all it took for me to embrace the stupidity. I settled in behind my camera and shot a series of photos that would undoubtedly end up in spank banks all over the world.

"Let's take a pic of us together." He rolled halfway onto his side, bending his knee so that it was the only thing protecting me from a gratuitous eyeful of dick. "That would be cool, right? The interviewer and the interviewee." He grinned.

I came out from behind my camera and glared at the smug fucker. How dare he suggest something like that? I wondered if what he was doing could be considered sexual harassment. It was certainly making me feel uncomfortable. "I'm not taking a picture with you naked and me fully clothed. That would be wildly inappropriate. Besides, it would end up on some fetish site somewhere."

He laughed. "I didn't mean like that. I meant with both of us decent. Keep it professional, Jamie. I'm not that easy." He winked.

Great. Now it seemed like *I* was harassing *him*.

"Sorry. I feel like an ass."

"Give me a minute to get dressed, and we'll get a *professional* picture of us." He pushed up easily off the bed, and...

Yep, there it was. The dick shot I knew was coming. I looked away and busied myself with checking my phone. Tons of social media notifications. Three texts from Steve. No texts from Kage. I sighed and slid my phone back into my pocket without reading any of it.

When Anthony was finally presentable in a T-shirt and shorts, I set up a shot of the two of us sitting on the sofa looking at each other with serious expressions, as if we were in the middle of the interview rather than tying up loose ends afterward. And in fact, this hadn't felt much like an interview at all. It had felt like plotting.

"You know, you should start doing video interviews," Anthony suggested.

"I would need a small crew for that. I plan to hire some people soon, but for now written interviews with photos is about all I can handle."

"Let me know when you do, and we'll get together again. Or hell, even before then. You have my number."

"I do." I waggled my cell phone at him.

"Oh, hey, that reminds me," he said, retrieving his phone from the bedside table. "You've got all kinds of pictures, but I have none. Let me get a selfie of us."

I hesitated, considering his request, but I couldn't think of any reason not to do it. "Sure. Come on." I patted the seat beside me, and he plopped down nearly on top of me. His hip was jammed against mine, and when he threw an arm around my shoulders, our entire sides were mashed together, and I was stuck in his armpit. I was grateful that at least he wasn't naked anymore.

"Smile," he said. We leaned our heads together in the requisite selfie pose, and he clicked the button. "Now stick your tongue out."

"What are we, in high school?"

He frowned into the camera. "Just do it."

"Fine." We both hung our tongues out, and he took the picture.

"Now show me that pretty smile."

"Pretty smile? Are you trying to take a picture or ask me to the prom?"

His eyebrows flew up. "You know, you're a terrible selfie partner. At least *pretend* you don't hate me."

"I don't hate you."

"Then smile."

After Anthony tortured me through another few selfies, I packed up and made my escape. Back in my room, I flung myself onto the bed and stared up at the ceiling. Now that I didn't have anything to occupy my mind, my thoughts went to Kage again. I wondered what he was doing. Was he working in the Alcazar? Training with Marco? Plotting bad guy stuff with Theo? Was he missing me at all?

I dreaded going home, but at the same time, it's all I wanted to do. Kage and I needed to work things out properly because this state of relationship limbo he had me floating in wasn't going to cut it. Either we were going to be together, or we weren't. I couldn't stand the thought of losing him, but the not knowing was even worse. It made me feel like a chump. Like he was just stringing me along. If we were committed to each other, then maybe I could give in and do what he wanted. We had been apart before. If he could promise me beyond a shadow of a doubt that we would be together when the two years were up and he could finally sell the properties he had inherited, then I could wait for him. I loved him that much. I could immerse myself in work and build my business up.

But going without sex for eighteen months or so would be a challenge for both of us. I was less worried about me than Kage. I knew I could last if I had him to look forward to at the end, but what about him? I liked to think that he was strong and that love would prevail, but what if he couldn't make it? And it wasn't just about sex. It was about love and connection. What if he fell for someone else? What if I waited all that time and then found out at the end that he wasn't mine anymore?

I sat up and growled into the silent hotel room. I had planned to attend the fight in the evening and then catch my flight out in the morning, but I couldn't wait that long. I was angry and frustrated, and all I wanted to do was find Kage and work things out. All that blustering I had done before I left meant nothing now. I made the decision to do whatever he wanted because he was mine, and I couldn't imagine a future with anyone else.

I called the airline and changed my flight to the earliest one I could get. I was going home.

CHAPTER ELEVEN

KAGE

IT WAS SATURDAY EVENING, and I was sweating bullets waiting for Theo to show up at my place. I'd given Steve instructions to have a temporary key card waiting for Theo that he could use on the elevator to unlock the penthouse floor. I'd spent the afternoon playing with my guns, standing in front of the mirror and practicing holstering and unholstering smoothly. Truth be told, I was also practicing my gun face, because I was just vain enough to want to look good while I was gunning somebody down.

When Theo arrived, I answered the door in a T-shirt and sweats, the holster and gun firmly secured beneath my waistband and hidden by my shirt. I said a silent prayer to no one in particular to please not make me have to use it. I wasn't even close to good enough yet.

When Theo looked at me, being strapped didn't make me feel powerful in the least. It made me feel vulnerable and exposed. What would he think if he discovered my little secret? I had already prepared the excuse that if I was going to be playing with the big boys, I needed to know how to use a gun. But the excuse wouldn't be of much use if he didn't give me a chance to explain.

"Michael," he said, drawing my name out like Santori always did. It made me wonder how much the two of them had talked about me in the past.

"Welcome to my castle," I said, realizing too late how cheesy that sounded. "Can I get you a drink? I didn't know what you like other than the Macallan, so I ordered a bunch of different stuff delivered. Beer, whiskey, wine... Hell, I don't even know what all is in there. I just told them to bring an assortment of their best stuff."

Theo brought his hands out from behind his back and showed me the bottle of Macallan. "I figured we'd have at least a glass of this to get things going."

"Good idea," I said. "Let me grab some glasses."

We sat on the sofa and shared our first drink, and the conversation was actually easy for a change. Theo could be downright charming and *normal* when he wanted to be. We discussed the hotels, a little politics, fighting, and our favorite restaurants. Regular stuff. I was so relieved. If I could get through this night with him thinking I was cool, maybe he would soon trust me with the secrets of his business. I wasn't naïve enough to think it would happen quickly, but maybe over the course of a couple of months. That wasn't too long. I could handle that.

After we drained our glasses of Macallan, we went into the kitchen and chose our next drinks. I wanted to try a little of everything we had, so I started at one end of the counter, planning to sample my way to the other end over the course of the evening. One small drink of each should have me feeling good, but not so drunk I couldn't function. The idea was to get Theo loose enough to open up more to me, and I couldn't expect him to get wasted while I watched. I had to lead by example and make a big show of having a good time.

About halfway down the countertop of alcohol, I realized that I may have been putting on too much a big show, because I really was having a good time. Theo was recounting a story about him and Peter getting drunk and peeing on a sidewalk when I noticed my head was spinning.

"They hauled us in for indecent exposure," he was saying. "Pete was mortified, but I thought it was fucking hilarious. I don't think he ever forgave me for that." He glanced at me, and the smile faded from his lips. "Kage, are you feeling okay?"

"The room is starting to go a little sideways. I think maybe I overdid it. I'm not used to drinking this much alcohol."

"Hey, don't flake out on me now. We haven't even gotten to the good part yet." He pulled a thin gold case from his pocket and grinned evilly at me. "You ever do cocaine?"

I swallowed, my mouth suddenly feeling very dry. "Tried it a couple of times. I can't do that, though. Gotta fight soon."

"You said it was a couple of months away. Coke only stays in your system for a few days. It'll be fine."

"Nah, man. Really, I can't do that. I—"

Dammit, I was supposed to be making Theo think I was cool. Would refusing to do coke with him ruin my chances of gaining his trust? Even as drunk as I was, I knew it was a really bad idea. But I had enjoyed the couple of small lines I'd had before, and if it wouldn't stay in my system longer than a few days, what was the harm in doing one line?

Theo pulled the coffee table closer to the sofa and set his little gold case on it. Then he opened a vial, dumped white powder onto the mirrored glass inside the case, and used a credit card to cut two lines, one long and thick, one thin and short. He scooted closer to me.

"What's your currency?" he asked, holding both hands out to me palm up. One held a rolled up hundred dollar bill, the other a small gold straw that matched the case.

I took the hundred.

"A cash man," he said. "Personally, I prefer gold." He made quick work of the larger of the two lines, zipping it into his nostril with practiced ease. "Your turn." He pushed the case in front of me and sniffed, rubbing his nose to clear the residue that lightly powdered the edge of his nostril.

Fuck it, I thought. I bent down and snorted the tiny line, relieved that Theo had the decency and the sense to at least go easy on me.

After that, everything was a blur of rushing and snorting. Time passed between the lines, but I didn't feel it. All I knew was that he kept pushing lines in front of me, and I kept snorting them up. After the first line, he hadn't even had to ask again. I got up and turned some music on, cranking the volume louder than I normally did. The music took on a life of its own, and I even did a little solo dancing, which I never would have done sober. Theo was a rapt audience.

Between everything was the intermittent volley of the coke tray. Slide and snort, slide and snort. It seemed like every time I turned around Theo was sliding it in front of me again, though in retrospect it couldn't have been nearly as many times as I'd thought.

Even though there were only two of us, it started to feel like a real party. At some point, Theo got a phone call. He stepped out of the room to take it while I wallowed on the sofa, lost to the music and the distinctive bitter taste of cocaine draining down the back of my throat.

I was barely aware of Theo returning to the room, all glittery-eyed and nervous from the coke. Had I missed him? It felt like I'd missed him.

He patted his pockets and pulled out his temporary key card. "I'll be right back. Don't you go anywhere."

I nodded, only vaguely curious about where he was going. When it seemed like he had been gone forever, I took over his job and slid the tray to myself. With trembling hands, I tried to cut a line in the powder Theo had left in the case, but all I ended up doing was fumbling the case onto the rug face down.

"Fuck!" I yelled, the word lost in the pounding music. I dropped to my knees and tried to do damage control, but the powder was clumped on the carpet. Thank goodness I could still see it. With no other option, I grabbed my hundred-dollar straw and snorted frantically at the scattered coke, feeling and tasting it as it filled my nostril.

I pulled myself back up onto the sofa and sank into the cushions. This was some good shit. I didn't ever want to stop. How had I not been doing this every fucking day?

My door swung open, and Theo was there again. I had no idea how long it had been. A minute? A year? It was all the same to me.

"I spilled it," I said, my voice extremely slow and slurred despite my racing mind. "I spilled it, but don't worry. I snorted it up. Snorted it up. Like a Hoover." I laughed.

"Did somebody say Hoover?" A tiny dark-haired twink pushed into the room from behind Theo. Another, slightly taller dark-haired twink was close on his heels, carrying what looked like a box under his arm. They looked almost like twins, with high cheekbones, perfect noses, and glossy pink lips.

"Get out of here with your cheap-ass Hoover," Twink #2 said. "Haven't you heard a Dyson never loses suction?"

"Hey, I didn't say it. He said it." Twink #1 gestured toward me.

"Michael..." Theo said, interrupting their animated exchange.

"Call me Kage."

"Okay, Kage." He smiled, and if he liked the idea, and pointed at the shorter of the two boys. "This is Noah." Then he gestured toward the taller one with a dramatic flourish of his hand, a grand presentation. "And this one is Felix."

The two boys waved at me. "Hiii," they said in unison. Noah smiled cordially, while Felix shot me a megawatt grin and eyed my body like a starving man at a buffet table.

God, were they even legal?

"Nice place," Noah said. "But it's too bright in here." He set about dimming lights without bothering to ask if I minded. I didn't. At the moment I didn't mind much of anything.

"Are these friends of yours?" I asked Theo, feeling a bit confused as to how they even ended up here.

"Very good friends. I think you'll like them." He came over to the sofa and grabbed the tray. After he added more coke and cut lines into it, he snorted one and offered the straw to Felix, who took him up on it without a second's hesitation. Noah was still busy messing with the lighting in the apartment, which was now almost completely dark. Suddenly a bright blue light started pulsing on and off, making everything look jerky and out of sync.

"What the hell," I said.

Felix pulled his head up from snorting his line and waved a hand dismissively. "He carries that strobe light everywhere he goes. It would be annoying if it weren't so cute." He made a kissy face at Noah, who flipped him the bird.

I thought nothing had ever looked as cool as Noah flipping his friend off in the strobing light. Everything had gone dreamlike and surreal, like a scene in an Andy Warhol movie, and I liked it. It occurred to me that I shouldn't have company here, and especially not a couple of twinks who were obviously looking to have a good time. But it was just so cool, and Theo was obviously enjoying himself. In my apartment. As if we were friends.

He held the straw out to Noah without a word. Noah made his way over to the sofa and took it, snorting a line loudly and rubbing his nose afterward. Now that they both had some coke in them, Felix and Noah started dancing in the middle of the floor, looking uber-cool and edgy in the strobing light. When their dance turned into a grope session, it took me a few minutes to realize what the hell I was watching, and I looked away in shame. Toward Theo.

He was watching me watch them, and it was a little disconcerting.

"What do you think?" he asked.

"About what?" I bounced my knee nervously, not wanting to acknowledge the truth of the situation.

Theo inclined his head toward my makeshift dance floor. "The boys. Felix and Noah. Which one do you like?"

I blinked. "They both seem nice."

"Nice, huh?" He chuckled and passed me the coke. "Noah is my particular favorite. He understands me."

I ignored his comment and snorted the baby line on the tray. That was really all I cared about.

Sometime later, we were all dancing. Well, Theo wasn't so much dancing as he was feeling Noah up, but Noah wasn't complaining. Felix came close and put a hand on my shoulder, shaking his head from side to side as he looked at the floor, lost in the music. Then he looked up at me and smiled, and I had a moment of clarity about what was going on here. Every move the boys made said they were down to fuck, especially now that the coke had kicked in. Shit. Was it time for another line yet?

Keeping a firm grip on my shoulder, Felix flattened his other hand against my chest and moved it slowly down my body, fingers trailing over my abs. Then he froze and swallowed before snatching my T-shirt up. "You're packing heat?" It sounded like a cheesy line from a cop show.

I grabbed his wrist and squeezed hard, forcing his hand up and away from my gun. My grip was strong, unforgiving, and the fearful look in his eyes quickly morphed into lust. The fact that he responded to being manhandled shouldn't have excited me, but it did. It lit a fire in my belly, because dammit that's how I was wired. I couldn't help it.

I let go and jerked my hand away, putting some distance between us as Aaron's words echoed in my mind. *Do you think he's any different just because he enjoys a different kind of pain? I see a lot of parallels between the two of you.*

"You're carrying?" Theo asked. "Aren't you just full of surprises."

"Yeah, I carry a gun. So what?" My voice slow and garbled, but there was an unhealthy dose of bravado in it even though I still couldn't shoot worth a damn.

"Put it away before you scare the boys." He didn't seem pissed. Only vaguely amused.

"But I like it," I slurred at half speed. "It won't go off. It's got this hard stuff to protect the trigger thingy. It's fine."

"I think it's hot." Felix smiled and moved closer, running his fingertips lightly over the holster through my pants. "Two guns for the price of one." His hand moved over my dick and traced the outline for about two seconds before I realized what was happening and grabbed his wrist again.

"Stop that," I growled. "I have a boyfriend."

Felix's eyes flitted to Theo in alarm.

"Ex-boyfriend," Theo said with a casual wave of his hand. "Who's up for another line?"

"Meeee," the boys chimed together, bouncing lightly on the balls of their feet. I thought they must have spent a *lot* of time together, because they even acted like twins.

I wanted to say no to another line. I wanted to tell them all to leave and let me go to bed and get my head straightened out. But instead, I sat down on the sofa and took the line Theo offered. How many times had I put that fucking hundred dollar bill to my nose? I had lost count. The lines Theo was cutting for me were tiny compared to his, but I wasn't used to doing any at all. I thought I should probably just decline the next one and send them home, but that was before the rush seized me again and I was lost.

Time passed, but I couldn't track it. Was it slow or lightning fast? Was any of this really happening?

There were snippets of sentences. Disjointed words like whispers in a dream. Noah's youthful lilt: *Glad you called us...been too long...* Theo's voice laced with misery and shame: *Sorry... happens sometimes with coke.* Slurping sounds and Noah's voice like a caress: *It's okay. Let me help.*

"Jesus, what happened to you?" Felix cried, startling me back from wherever I had been.

I glanced up out of my stupor to see him kneeling between my legs, looking flushed and pretty in the strobing blue light. My shirt was off, and Felix was staring in horror at my bruised flesh. I wasn't sure where my shirt had disappeared to, but even more alarming was the fact that my pants were shoved down around my ankles, and my dick was out.

What the fuck? Had I just been doing something? I had no clue, but I was half hard.

"Jamie." My voice came out slow and deep, not sounding at all like me. I looked frantically in Theo's direction. Noah was kneeling between his legs and swallowing his cock like a pro, but Theo's lust-hooded eyes were trained directly on me. He leaned his head against the back of the sofa, but he didn't take his eyes off of me.

"You look so much like Pete. I just can't get over it." He reached out to me, his fingertips grazing my bare shoulder. Then his arm dropped limply to the sofa as if all of the bones in it had suddenly disintegrated.

I swallowed, thinking maybe I was in the throes of a really bad dream. I only remembered Felix was there when he ran his warm hands up my thighs. I jerked at the touch and instinctively bent down to pull up my pants, appalled that I'd gotten myself into such a fix, but Felix distracted me by sliding the coke tray in front of me. There was one tiny line on it.

"That's the last of it," Theo said. "I saved it just for you."

Fuck. It was all gone? Without even bothering to pull my pants up first, I bent down and sucked it all up through my nose, making sure to get every grain. Then I leaned back on the sofa, cock out, and enjoyed the bitter taste of heaven seeping down the back of my throat.

And that is when Jamie came home.

CHAPTER TWELVE

JAMIE

WHEN I STEPPED off the elevator and onto the penthouse floor, I was assaulted by the sound of music blasting from our apartment. What the hell? Rolling my suitcase behind me, I approached with caution. It was late, and Kage rarely played his music that loud.

Was he having a party? The idea was unthinkable, and yet I had to admit there had been lots of unthinkable things happening lately. As I slid the key card into the slot, my skin prickled with apprehension. Images flashed through my mind, possibilities of what I might find in that apartment, yet none of them even came close to the horror show I found when I pushed open the door and stepped inside.

The apartment had been turned into a nightclub, with pulsing music and strobing lights, and it smelled like alcohol and sweat. When my eyes finally adjusted to the lights and I spotted Kage on the sofa, I think my heart actually stopped.

He was laid back on the cushions, eyes closed, with his pants down around his ankles. A young man—or a boy more like it—was kneeling between his legs with his hands resting on Kage's thighs. I dimly registered another couple on the sofa beside him. An older, long-haired man had a carbon copy of Kage's boy between his legs. The boy's head bobbed rhythmically to the music, while the man's face was turned toward Kage.

I wasn't able to observe unnoticed for more than a few seconds, because the light from the hallway spilling into the room brought everyone's attention straight to me. Well, everyone but Kage, who seemed to be completely oblivious to life going on around him.

The shock of what I was seeing held me frozen in place, my broken heart stuttering in my chest, and it took everything in my power to speak. "What the fuck is going on here?"

Kage turned his face toward the sound of my voice and looked sluggishly up at me with eyes that didn't seem able to focus properly. It took him a few seconds to narrow his gaze on me, and his words were like molasses as he said, "Jamie. You're home."

Something—the faraway look in his eyes or the lethargic sound of his voice—snapped me out of my shocked daze, and suddenly my feet were carrying me across the room toward him. As I went, I barked orders at the vagrants who were currently stinking up the place. "Anyone who doesn't live here needs to get the hell out. Now."

The two pretty twinks hopped up from the floor and started fumbling around, presumably trying to locate their personal effects. One of them ran to the wall and snatched the strobe light cord out of the outlet, plunging the room into near darkness. The only light came from the hallway, where I had left the door open, and the master bathroom, which cast a faint glow that was only visible if you looked directly at the bedroom door.

The long-haired older man, whom I assumed to be Theo Brown—because who else would it be?—got slowly to his feet. He towered over me, long and lean and intimidating. And it wasn't just his size that made me tremble. He had an aura about him that was unmistakably evil. Never in my life had I gotten such a strong negative vibe from a human being, and I had spent time with Peter Santori.

If Santori was the devil, then Theo was the devil's henchman, and that was infinitely more frightening. Because how fucking bad did you have to be to do the *devil's* dirty work?

"What did you give him?" I grated, pulling myself up straighter under Theo's contemptuous gaze. I sensed the dark-haired twinks lurking near the door, but they were of no consequence. Theo was the problem here, even if one of the boys had been about to take my man's cock in his mouth.

Or had he already? The thought sickened me.

"Why don't you ask him what he's taken? He's not a child."

I glanced at Kage, who was still embarrassingly uncovered and vulnerable to every eye in the room. "Compared to you he is a child," I sneered. "Especially in his current state." I bent to pull his pants up over his limp legs and work them under his ass, getting little help from him besides a twitch here and there. I sucked in a breath when I noticed the gun. Terror gripped me. Was there a chance it might go off and shoot me in the face, or maybe blow Kage's dick off? Mine shriveled just thinking about it, though it might serve the bastard right.

"He was having a perfectly good time before you got here," Theo said. "He said you were sort of provincial, and he wanted to blow off a little steam while you were out of town. Don't be too hard on him. He's a young, vibrant man, and he deserves to have a good time every now and then. You can't expect him to give up everything he loves just because he has a boyfriend."

My heart clenched. Had Kage really called me provincial? I knew he thought I was sheltered, but I had a hard time imagining he could be so condescending, whereas I had absolutely no problem believing Theo would make up such a thing. I went with my instinct, at least for the moment, and got a little feisty.

"Well, excuse my provincial ass for depriving the poor guy. I had no idea he had given up drug overdoses and date rape to be with me." I heard the twin twinks murmuring from the corner near the door, and I turned to face them, unsure of which was which. It didn't matter; they were interchangeable. "That's right, boys. Sucking someone's dick while they're passed out is rape, and last I checked that's a criminal offense."

One of them said, "We're just gonna head out, Theo."

"He wanted it," the other mumbled unconvincingly.

Theo waved a hand without even looking in their direction, and they took off down the hall. Thankfully, they left the door open. Otherwise I would have been plunged into darkness with Theo, and it wasn't as if Kage would be of any use in defending me. He couldn't even fend off a hundred-twenty-pound twink. Assuming he'd wanted to.

I had the sudden urge to grab the gun from Kage's holster and blow Theo away. With him out of the picture, things would be like they used to be. But I remembered everything Kage had told me about him. The fact that Theo intimidated him enough to break up with me on his order. I think at that moment, I wanted to kill Theo worse than I'd ever wanted to kill Santori—and that was something I had actually done.

Funny there was no guilt when I thought of it this time.

But what could I do? It wasn't like I knew how to use that gun, even if I could have managed to get it out of the holster. I'd probably have been dead before I'd even gotten my hand on it, like in those old gunslinger movies where some smug asshole gets blown away by the fastest gun in the west. And good luck luring Theo out onto the balcony and trying to throw him over like I'd done Santori. More likely, Theo would have locked the door after me and left me there to watch impotently through the glass while he debauched Kage in myriad twisted ways.

No, I had to tread carefully. Kage had said he needed to protect me from Theo, and I believed him. I had to swallow my ego and my instinct, which were both telling me to hurt Theo before he hurt us. I had to be smart. If I played my cards right, maybe I could get rid of him until Kage came to his senses.

"Look, Theo. We don't know each other, and I'm afraid things have gotten off to a rocky start between us. I just don't like coming in and seeing my man in this condition. Let's call it a night, and I'll get Kage cleaned up and tucked into bed." I looked at Kage's face again. He was pale and sweaty and completely out of it. I could tell he wasn't asleep, but he wasn't responding to anything that was going on, and that scared the shit out of me. "You don't think he needs to go to the hospital, do you?"

"No," Theo said. "And I doubt he'd want you to take him there. It would be all over the news tomorrow. Better to ride it out. He'll be fine when the cocaine is out of his system."

Cocaine. My heart jumped. "He's not used to cocaine. And he's been taking hydrocodone for days since the—" I was going to say mugging, but then I remembered it wasn't a mugging at all and that Theo had been the one behind it.

"The beating," Theo supplied, unrepentant and almost gloating. He stepped closer to Kage and bent to run a hand down his bruised side, glancing at me once with steely eyes as if daring me to stop him.

I didn't. I just stood there, feeling like the most impotent lowlife that had ever lived, and let the devil's henchman touch the man I loved. My stomach lurched, and the taste of bile burned a trail up my throat.

Thank goodness Theo wasn't in the mood to torture me long. He pulled his hand back and smiled coldly at me. "Healing nicely," he said. "And for what it's worth, I don't think he took any pain pills today. He was perfectly lucid when I offered him the coke, and he didn't mention it."

Perfectly lucid. I was *perfectly* sure Theo's comment had been a passive-aggressive dig at me, letting me know that Kage had done everything of his own free will. In fact, most everything he'd said to me so far seemed designed to push the illusion that Kage wanted me gone, and that it had nothing to do with Theo.

Fucking asshole.

Theo went into the kitchen and grabbed a bottle of liquor. "This one is mine," he said, waggling the bottle at me. "Tell Kage I'll be seeing him soon. Or don't. I'll be seeing him whether you pass along the message or not. Tootles."

I gaped at his back as he sauntered from the room. *Tootles?* What kind of self-respecting bad guy said tootles?

He pulled the door closed behind him as he left, knowing full well he'd be leaving me to stumble around in the dark. Why the hell didn't we have lamps on the end table like normal people? As I made my way to the nearest wall switch and flooded the room with light, I found myself wondering how much coke Theo had snorted. He wasn't exactly a spring chicken. Probably had a bad ticker. Maybe he'd have a heart attack on the way out and put us all out of our misery. Doubtful considering how in control he had seemed, but a man could dream.

"COME ON, Kage. Let's get you to the bedroom." I slid my arms around his muscled frame and tried to lever him off the couch. I got him about halfway up, but his limp weight was too much for me, and I lowered him back down with an irritated grunt. "Get your big ass moving. I can't carry you."

He opened his eyes and stared at me, his brows coming together in confusion. Then recognition seemed to dawn. "Jamie." He spasmed and went for the waistband of his pants, as if he was still living the moment where he got caught cheating on me.

"I've already pulled them up," I snarled. "Now get your butt up and move. We need to get you to the bed. Can you stand?"

"I think so." He sat up, suddenly looking much more lucid, and scooted to the edge of the sofa. "Where did everybody go?"

"Away, where they belong."

He made a move to pull himself to a standing position, but something on the floor caught his eye, and he bent to retrieve it. When he sat back up, he had a rolled bill stuck up his nostril, and he was sucking on it so hard it sounded like there was a tiny elephant loose in the room. Before I could react, he had pulled the bill away from his nose and inspected it for residue before shoving it back to his nose and unleashing the elephant again. It was pathetic, and it hurt my heart to see him like that.

I snatched the bill from him. "No more of that," I said. "You've had enough."

"But I think there was a little left on there," he said, his words unnaturally slow. "Wait, I spilled some on the carpet earlier. I don't think I got it all up." He dropped to his knees and started crawling around on the floor.

I shoved the rolled-up bill into my pocket and dragged him up just before he face-planted in the rug. "Kage, please. You're not in your right mind. Come get in bed, and I'll take care of you. Do you need to go to the bathroom?"

He scrunched his face in thought, and it was clear he wasn't going to be much help. I made the decision for him, walking him into the bathroom and holding him steady while he emptied his bladder. I avoided looking at his dick, because all that did was remind me of what I'd walked in on. At the time, I had just wanted those guys out of the apartment so I could deal with Kage, but now I was having retrospective fantasies of dragging the little twink up by his hair and slamming him face first into the coffee table. Or stomping his guts out like Theo's men had done to Kage.

Jesus, I'd had more violent thoughts in the last half hour than I'd ever had in my life, and they were still coming. It seemed the more I thought about it, the more pumped I got to do some damage. God, I should have beaten that kid's ass. And then Theo would have beaten my ass. And then probably shot me. Okay, so maybe I did the right thing.

When Kage was done, I maneuvered him into the bedroom and helped him onto the bed. He was already barefoot and shirtless, but he still had that damn gun on. It looked like it had to be uncomfortable, especially with him so bruised and sore, and I wondered if he'd been wearing it for protection. If so, I guess that went out the window when his pants hit the floor.

I fumbled around with the holster and managed to get it off of him without shooting anyone. Then I hid it in the back of the closet. When I returned, Kage was snoring loudly, as if his nasal passages had been roughed up with 40-grit sandpaper. But at least he was in bed.

When my body sank into the mattress, I groaned, realizing for the first time just how tense my muscles were. I tried to relax, twisting my neck from side to side and taking slow, even breaths. After a couple of minutes, I felt a little better. The snoring stopped, and his eyes flew open. After a minute of looking around the room, he closed them again.

"God, Kage. What were you thinking?" I said quietly, not

expecting an answer but needing to get the words out anyway. "I'm just so confused and scared right now. It's like I'm living in a nightmare and can't wake up."

I turned to face him and kept vigil all night. His eyes were usually closed, but he was in and out of sleep and moving constantly. Every now and then he'd start talking, but his words were so garbled up I couldn't understand what he was saying. At one point, he started coughing so violently, he doubled over in bed and curled into the fetal position while the coughs wracked his body. I wondered if he had swallowed wrong and choked on his saliva.

"Kage, are you okay?" No answer. "Kage, please tell me if you're okay. Do I need to call 911?" When he still didn't answer, went into a dead panic. I rubbed his back and kept talking to him, occasionally demanding that he answer me or at least give me a sign he was okay, but he seemed unable to respond at all even though his eyes were open.

For a solid minute he gasped and convulsed, sometimes coughing out so hard and so long I didn't know if he'd ever be able to breathe in again. Then he'd catch his breath, and my heart would start up again. Just when I was about to call 911, his hacking coughs slowed to the occasional quiet puff of air, and he settled back down. I rubbed his head lightly, not wanting to disturb him now that he was calm. When relief finally set in and I reached up to run a shaky hand over my face, I felt tears on my cheeks.

CHAPTER THIRTEEN

KAGE

THE LIGHT of midday assaulted me when I cracked open my eyes. The first thing I noticed was that it felt like I hadn't actually been sleeping. The next was that it was really hard to breathe. I snorted hard and swallowed down the thick, bitter sludge that had collected in the back of my throat.

I'd never felt so bad in all my life, and not just physically. I felt like I was smothering under a blanket of sadness, and I didn't have the energy to claw my way out.

There were images in my mind, as if I'd woken from the middle of a dream when the memory was still fresh and accessible. There were flashes of faces. Theo with his lion's mane of blond hair shot through with silver, looking at me like he thought I was someone else. Two boys, nearly identical in every way, with dark brown hair and pink pouty lips. And Jamie, fierce in anger, tormented with tears, and so damn beautiful it made my heart ache.

I remembered his hand against my back. His fingers running through my hair. His frantic shouts. *Kage, answer me! Are you okay?*

More memories threatened to break through the fog in my brain, but the thoughts were ugly, and I tried to push them away. To force them back into the haze where I couldn't see them anymore. To look at them would bring more shame, and I already felt enough of that.

God, I'd fucked up. Even without details, I knew that much, and the vague awareness was all I could face right now.

I turned my head and found Jamie's side of the bed empty. He'd probably left me. He should have left me.

I wanted to call out to him, but that would bring me closer to confirming that he was gone, so I kept my mouth shut and my body still. I didn't want to move again. Not ever. I wanted to lie unmoving in this spot until I died from shame and lack of water. A gun would be quicker, and lord knows I had enough of those now, but I didn't want to expend the energy to shoot myself. I wanted to die just like this. Still.

Already halfway there.

I closed my eyes and slipped back into blissful unawareness, and the next time I opened them it was nearly dark outside. Night was coming, and with it an unbearable ache in my soul. I didn't want to feel it, so I closed my eyes again.

I woke sometime later to the sound of the blender. Morning light streamed into the room, not yet bright enough to be obnoxious, but I blinked against it just the same. It seemed I was in the same position I'd been each time I woke. I hoped I hadn't moved. I needed to be still. To die this way.

"You're awake." Jamie's voice came from the doorway. Not exactly cheerful, but...kind. Like him.

My heart responded with a gentle throb, but my body remained still. I didn't look at him, and when he came closer to stand over me, I closed my eyes. Maybe if I couldn't see him, he wouldn't see me. I didn't want him to see the shameful wreck I had become.

He lowered himself onto the bed beside me. "I made you a shake. You haven't had anything to eat or drink for two days."

Two days? I'd thought it was one. Two days was better. Closer to death.

"Kage, you're dehydrated. Open your eyes and let me help you drink this. Or at least have some of this water." He squeezed a water bottle, and I winced at the annoying cracking sounds of plastic collapsing in his grip.

I didn't answer. I didn't move. I wanted him to go away and find someone more deserving of his love, because I was tainted now.

"If you don't open your eyes and drink some of this, I'm going to try to pour it down your throat. I hadn't planned on waterboarding you back into the land of the living, but I'm getting desperate here."

Part of me wanted to laugh, but that part was buried beneath the blanket of sadness.

Jamie sighed loudly. "I called a doctor, and he said it's normal for you to feel depressed after all of the cocaine you ingested. Especially since you mixed it with alcohol."

I didn't respond.

Jamie's voice got louder. "The doctor is on his way over here to see you."

My eyes flew open. "What?" God, was that even my voice? It sounded like I was gargling marbles. "I don't want a doctor here. Too risky."

"What do you think they're going to do, call the UFC and tell them you did coke?"

I ran a hand through my hair, shuddering at the film of oil and sweat that coated it. Then I groaned, belatedly realizing I had moved. And spoken. Now I would have to start all over again with the dying.

"Tell you what," Jamie said. "Sit up and drink some of this water and take a few swallows of the shake. Then I'll call the doctor and tell him not to come. But you need to hurry so I can catch him before he leaves."

I growled, but I sat up halfway in bed. Jamie set the drinks on the bedside table and propped some pillows behind my back. Then he handed me the water bottle.

The water was cold, but not so cold that it was a shock to my system. I appreciated that because it made it go down easier. After I took a few swallows, Jamie handed me the shake. It was too thick to be palatable, and it tasted different than it normally did since my taste buds were hibernating, but I took as many swallows as I could stand. Then I chased it with more water and handed both containers back to Jamie.

"We good now?" I asked.

"Yeah, we're good. Thank you."

"Just call that damn doctor."

He winced. "Actually, there's no doctor coming. I just said that to get you to drink."

"So you lied to me."

He shrugged. "I told you I was desperate. You can lie back down if you want, or if you'd rather get up, I can run a shower for you."

"I don't want a shower. I just want to sleep." *And to die.*

He raised a brow at me. "You may not want a shower, but you need one. I'm considering sleeping on the sofa tonight."

I growled and threw the covers back. "Fine. I'll get in the goddamn shower. But for the record, it's against my will."

"I'm fine with that," Jamie said, hurrying off to run the shower.

I hated him nursing me when I didn't deserve it. After the things I suspected I'd done—the things I couldn't quite remember and didn't want to remember—he should have been gone. Letting him do things for me made me an even shittier human being than I already was. But I got in the shower because he wanted me to, and because I didn't want him to have to sleep on the sofa.

When I got out of the shower and brushed my teeth, I actually felt a little better physically, though emotionally I was still all kinds of messed up. Jamie had changed the sheets in my absence, and he had fallen asleep on the fresh bedding. I wondered how much sleep he'd managed to get. I doubted it was much, because it seemed like every time I'd opened my eyes his side of the bed had been empty.

I pushed an errant lock of hair back from his forehead and replaced it with a soft kiss. Then I snuggled under the covers beside him and slept again.

THE NEXT TIME I WOKE, it was to the sensation of fingers ghosting over my skin. A gentle, tickling touch that started at my hip and traced down the side of my thigh and around to the front. The fingers swirled circles in the crisp hair at the front of my thigh, then followed an invisible trail around to the back of my thigh and up to my ass cheek, lingering there to grasp lightly at the swell of my cheek.

Jamie. I would know that touch anywhere. There was no

motivation behind it other than worshiping the thing that he loved, and no one had ever touched me that way but him.

I groaned, feeling a stirring between my legs as my dick responded to the gentle caress. "If I didn't know any better, I'd think you like me."

"Maybe a little," he said, his voice soft and vulnerable at my back. He trailed his fingers along the curve of my side until he hit a ticklish spot.

I jerked involuntarily and grunted. "Then again, you might be a really talented torture artist sent to discover all of my secrets."

"I don't know if anyone would be up to that task." He hit the ticklish spot again, on purpose, making me squirm. Then he dragged a fingertip tortuously down the crack of my ass until he was right...there. "But I'm willing to give it my best shot."

My dick was hard now, and getting harder with every passing second. He wiggled his finger into the warm space between my thighs and pressed up firmly against my flesh, sending a pulse of sensation up and into my body.

"That magic button," I groaned, my dick pulsing in anticipation.

"Mmm hmmm... Looks like it's working."

I made a move to turn toward him, but he pressed his body up against my back firmly enough to let me know he wanted me to stay just like I was. I glanced over my shoulder at him, and he smiled sweetly, so I settled back down to let him play.

He moved slightly away, and there was a vague shuffling behind me. Then something thick and wet pressing up between my cheeks. Jamie's dick, lubed up and hard as a rock. I shuddered and bent my knee to give him better access, and he pushed into me, sheathing his entire length in one firm stroke.

I hissed as the burn tore through me, the sudden stretch all but cleaving me in two, but my quiet conqueror gave no quarter as he claimed my ass. I surrendered, pressing back onto him even as I winced against the pain. Even with no words exchanged to spell it out, I think we both understood what this was. Jamie was taking back what I'd stolen from him—his power and his dignity. And I wanted him to take it. I owed him my surrender and so much more.

If it had been me in his position, I would have taken him with the force of an army, violently and without thought for his comfort. I would have battered his body and demanded his submission, forced every grunt and ripped out every moan until he was begging for mercy. And for forgiveness.

But Jamie wasn't me. He wasn't the cold creature I had been raised to be. He was kind, and he was loving, and he was innocent in a way I would never be. And in being so, he wielded a special kind of power over me. He held the ability to bring me to my knees the way no amount of violence ever could.

He conquered me with love.

"Put your hands over your head," he coaxed, pulling swiftly out of me as I reached up and grabbed onto the edge of the headboard. I sucked in a breath and then let it out as a deep groan as he wrapped his arm tightly around my waist and plunged back in. At this new angle, his dick glanced off my prostate and sent a wave of ecstasy through me.

"God, yeah, that's the spot." My fingers clenched until I was white-knuckling the headboard. "Don't stop, Jamie. Please don't stop."

He tightened his arm around my waist and cinched his body to mine, kissing my back over and over with soft lips that made my skin tingle everywhere they touched. He started moving steadily in and out of me in an unhurried rhythm, massaging my inner walls with the most delicious slow friction I'd ever felt. Now that he'd found my G-spot, he didn't let up on it, dragging the head of his cock over it until I was panting. The rhythm was excruciating, building the pleasure steadily until it seemed too much to endure. Marching me toward a climax that promised to be everything and more if only... I could... get there.

"Ahhh..." My balls tightened, and I started to crest, gritting my teeth against the overwhelming sensation. Jamie groaned and stopped his movements, then snatched out of me and started huffing breaths against my back so fast I thought he would hyperventilate.

"I'm close," he whispered, dropping more kisses onto my back. "Your ass gripping my cock feels so... fucking... right." He pressed the length of his body tightly against mine, the pounding of his heartbeat mingling with my own until the two were indistinguishable. "It's been a long time since I fucked you."

"Too long," I said, dropping my hands from the headboard and reaching back to rub his hip. I'd nearly rallied and caught my own breath by this time, and I was ready to feel him again. I rocked my ass back against him in a silent plea for him to finish what he'd started.

He didn't seem to be in any hurry as he rolled me over and pushed my legs apart. He looked down at me, eyes blazing with affection and lust, before pushing his cock back into me. I spread my legs even farther apart, giving him complete access to pound me into oblivion. But he didn't. Not yet. Instead, he hovered over me, a sad little smile curving his lips.

"I love you, Kage. You know that, right?" He started moving inside me, driving me wild with that same rhythmic friction, drawing out my pleasure like a rubber band stretched too tightly.

I bucked my hips up, begging for more, but he just kept up that maddening pace, grazing my prostate on nearly every inward plunge. Then he rested his weight on me and brought his soft lips to mine.

Our kiss was slow, just like the fucking. Tentative touches of lips, nudges with the tips of our tongues. Every now and then Jamie would dip his tongue deep into my mouth and plunder until I was breathless, and then he would pull back and continue with sanity-stealing gentle licks.

A few more minutes of relentless teasing, and I was mad with desire, writhing beneath him pleading for him to pound me hard. "Baby, please. I need to get off."

Jamie sat up and grinned. "Well, I'm not ready yet. And since I'm the one in charge, I guess you'll have to wait."

"You are definitely trying to torture me." I bit my lip, giving him a very deliberate fuck-me look, and wiggled my hips.

Jamie pounded a couple of hard thrusts into me, then stopped again, poking his bottom lip out in that beguiling pout that made me want to fuck his mouth raw. "Don't you think you deserve to be tortured?"

I swallowed, my throat constricted with a tangled mass of guilt and lust. "I do. And I'm ready and willing to take any torture you and that hot dick of yours feel inclined to dish out. But that doesn't mean I'm not going to beg for relief."

"Beg all you want," he said, leaning forward and latching onto my neck with his teeth.

I groaned as he clamped down hard on my throat and sucked, pounding stroke after stroke into my ass in time with his merciless sucking. When I cried out, he let go and moved his mouth down to my nipple, biting and sucking it just as hard as he had my throat. He was a man possessed, intent on devouring me piece by piece.

I let out an anguished cry that would have disturbed the neighbors if I'd had any. "Oh, God yeah. God... Jamie."

He moved to the other nipple and tortured it even more than the first until I had to grit my teeth against the cries. My dick was so hard I thought I would explode, especially when he leaned back

154

and drove up into my prostate enough times to make my toes curl and my balls ache.

"Fucking... *yeah!* Jesus." I reached down and stroked my cock when I realized that my orgasm was mounting no matter how much I wanted to hold off and please him. I needed to come, and I needed to do it now.

He pulled completely out of me and lowered his head to my cock, sucking the head into his mouth and working it hard while I stroked the shaft. God, it felt so good with both of us stimulating me.

"I'm about to come, Jamie. I can't—"

He pulled his mouth off of me and rammed back into me, grunting every time be bottomed out. I drew my legs up, stretching myself open for him and let out a broken cry as I shot my load, striping my bruised and sweaty chest with thick ropes of semen. *Finally.* Glorious relief washed over me, and I melted into the bed. I barely noticed through my fucked-out daze when Jamie ground to a stuttering halt and buried his dick deep inside me to unload.

Then he collapsed on top of me, our skin slicking together with sweat and semen. When had it gotten so hot in the room? With trembling hands, I coaxed his head up and his mouth onto mine for a sloppy kiss, our tongues tangling lazily.

I couldn't remember ever feeling this incredibly sated after sex, it wasn't just the orgasm-induced feeling that my muscles had turned to jelly. This was something deeper—the profound sense of peace that Jamie's forgiveness left in its wake. It was the closest thing to a religious experience I'd ever had. Mere hours before, I had been ready to die. But now... I couldn't imagine leaving a single minute on the table of life. Not if it was a minute I could have spent being loved like this.

I'd heard of unconditional love, but I'd always believed it was a fairy tale. The love of my mother was something I would never be privileged enough to feel, because whatever feelings she may or may not have had for me died before I was old enough to comprehend them. If my father was still alive, his love had not been strong enough for him to stick around in the face of tragedy. And my uncle's love? Well, as far as I was concerned, it had never existed. For whatever reason, his heart had been dead before I came along. I was certain the key to what had changed him was hidden in the bedside drawer—in the pages of his journals—but for now, I could only speculate and wish for what had never been.

But Jamie...

He had shown a level of compassion for me over the past days that bordered on insanity. If my fractured memories of the ill-fated party I'd hosted on Saturday night were anything close to the reality of what happened, he should have left me that night. Should have turned around in the doorway and never come back. But he didn't. He stuck around and nursed me through my debilitating hangover and the depression that accompanied it. If that wasn't unconditional love, then I couldn't imagine what was.

I didn't deserve love like that. I knew it all the way down to the darkest corners of my soul. And yet what happened next still knocked the wind out of me.

Jamie ran a lazy circle over my chest and sighed. "Are you good now?"

"Huh?" I asked, still dazed and running on about a quarter of my brain cells.

"You've been pretty wrecked since Saturday night. Are you feeling better?"

"Hell, yeah." I wrapped my arms around his trim body and squeezed, marveling for the millionth time at how perfectly we fit together.

"Thank God." He squirmed out of my grip and rolled to his side of the bed, then sat up on the edge and went completely still.

"You know, I was really worried about you. I thought you would never snap out of that funk you were in. When you didn't move or react for so long, all I could think of was that time you went catatonic, and Dr. Tanner had to shoot you full of drugs to try to bring you back. And then the hypnosis..." He shuddered. "That was so fucking awful."

"Good thing I had you there to take care of me." I stretched my arm out and ran my index finger down his spine, loving the little shiver my touch drew out of him.

"Yeah, it was," he said. "And this time... If I hadn't shown up, that crazy bastard Theo might have pumped enough drugs in you to put you in the hospital." He paused. "No, I'm sorry. He would have killed you, judging from the fact that he advised me not to take you to a hospital."

"I was okay," I said, more from embarrassment than anything else. I hated Jamie thinking I was weak.

Jamie choked out a laugh. "You were crawling around on the carpet trying to snort up spilled coke. You had your fucking pants around your ankles and some bubbleheaded twink on his knees—" The last word wavered and got hung in his throat. "You were not okay. You're *not* okay."

"I won't ever do that again," I said, a distinct note of pleading in my voice. I rolled onto my side and massaged one of the adorable dimples above his ass with my thumb, trying to reassure him with a touch. It was all I had to work with. "I swear, Jamie. I won't do any more drugs. I was just trying to get him to trust me."

"Yeah? And what's next on your list of trust exercises? Letting him fuck you? Because I assure you he would jump at the chance. The way he was looking at you gave me chills, Kage. And not in a normal way. I don't know how to describe it, but the name Hannibal Lecter comes to mind. Are you going to keep trying to get him to trust you until he invites to over for dinner?"

157

I shrugged, even though he couldn't see me with his back turned. "As long as he doesn't serve fava beans and Chianti I should be safe."

"That's not funny," he spat, standing up and whirling around to face me. "I can't believe you're making jokes."

I let out a nervous laugh. "You started it. Calm down."

"No, I will not calm down." But he did calm down. He took a few deep breaths, and when he spoke again, his voice was even. "The fact is you are putting yourself in danger by continuing to try to get in that monster's good graces, and I can't stand by and watch it happen."

I swallowed and stared blankly at him. "What are you saying?"

He paced to the door and back again, then crossed his arms over his chest. "I've made plans to stay with Steve for a while. He's got an extra bedroom, and he won't charge me rent until I get some more revenue coming in from the blog and my YouTube channel. But I'm going to need to borrow a little more money from you to get some video equipment. I'll eventually need an assistant, but I can start out small."

I continued to stare blankly, my mouth hanging ajar. I tried to say something logical, to present an argument that would allay his fears, but all that came out was, "Please don't go."

He glared at me. "A few days ago, you couldn't wait to get rid of me."

"I was trying to keep you out of all of this. To protect you."

"And suddenly I don't need protection any more?"

"No, you do, but—" I searched for words in my addled brain. Anything that would make a fucking lick of sense. "I don't know how I can do this without you. And you said you didn't want to go."

He dropped his head and stared at the floor as if he couldn't look at me when he said the next words. "I changed my mind. I can't walk in on another scene like the one I came home to Saturday night. I'm not strong enough to stand by and watch you kill yourself. If being partners with that monster is something you feel you have to do, and apparently it is, then go ahead and do it. But I'm not going to be around to see it."

"Please, Jamie. You can't just leave me like this. My plan was to try to see each other on the sly. I was even considering giving you a suite in the hotel and just keeping our relationship under the radar."

"Jesus, Kage." His lip quivered, eyes glistening with the sheen of tears. "Don't you think I'm worth more than that?"

God, I was losing my mind. Anger sizzled up from my gut until my limbs trembled with the need to lay waste to something. But the thing that needed wasting was the fucking situation, and that wasn't something physical I could beat into submission. If I could tell Jamie about my deal with Aaron, he would understand that I had no choice. The truth rose to my lips, but I couldn't let it out. Aaron had been very specific about keeping the mission from Jamie, and I couldn't ignore his implied threats. Even now he could be listening. Of all of the things that would put Jamie in danger, that one was the worst.

Jamie huffed and threw his hands up in exasperation. "Do you think I'm stupid, Kage? You're hiding something from me. I can see it written all over your face. Why won't you be honest with me? Ever since I moved in with you, we've steadily grown farther apart. You've driven a wedge between us, and I don't even know why. And do you know *why* I don't know why? Because you won't fucking tell me."

I looked down, unable to meet his gaze. "I can't." I didn't know what else to say. There was nothing else *to* say. Jamie was asking for the one thing I couldn't give him, and it was tearing me up to deny him, especially when the price was him walking away.

Jamie nodded. "Okay, Kage. You can't be honest with me? Fine. I get it. But I can't be in a relationship based on lies and half-truths."

"Please," I whispered. "Just give me a little more time. Move into one of the suites for now. We'll work it out."

"I'm sorry," he said, his voice choked with emotion. "I love you more than life itself, but what you're offering isn't acceptable to me. I just— I can't live like that."

"Well, can we at least make a pact to wait for each other? To not be with anyone else?"

Jamie laughed. "The pact you already broke? Yeah, that's really fair to me, isn't it?"

"I didn't mean to—"

"It doesn't matter. The choices you made put you in that position." He bit his lip and looked at the floor, watching his feet as they shifted with nervous energy. "If I thought—no, if I could believe—that was an isolated incident that would never be repeated again, I would forgive you in a heartbeat. Hell, I've already forgiven you for that. I know you wouldn't have cheated on me if you'd been in your right mind, just like I know you wouldn't have been rooting around in the carpet for drugs like some coked-out pig. But I can't trust that it or something similar won't happen in the future. Not when you insist on continuing to fuck around with this Theo piece of shit."

He went into the closet, dressed in clean clothes, and came out with his suitcases. Already packed. Apparently, he'd been busy while I was wallowing in bed like an ignorant asshole. Fuck.

"So this is it?" I asked, my voice wrecked and trembling.

Jamie nodded resolutely, but I could see that the resolution was forced. He was doing what he thought was right, but deep down it wasn't what he wanted.

"And you won't wait for me?"

His eyes darted away as if he was second-guessing himself, but they ended up right back on me. He was showing a level of strength I'd only seen glimpses of before, and it made my heart throb in my chest. How fucked up was it that him breaking up with me was making me respect him even more? At that moment, my desire for him was so strong it was like another being in the room with us.

"I love you, Kage. Today I love the person you are and have been since the day we met, and I hope you will remember that in the days to come. But who knows what twisted shell of a man you'll be when this is over? *If* it's ever over. I can't wait for someone I may not even recognize anymore. I'm sorry."

And with that, he wheeled his suitcases out of the room. I jumped up from the bed and hurried after him, naked and not giving a damn. I grabbed one of his suitcases and wheeled it to the door. "Give me a minute to get dressed, and I'll help you takes these down."

"Thanks, but I can handle it on my own." He opened the door, handed me his apartment key card, and kissed me on the cheek. "Watch yourself."

He was quoting the mystery note, and hearing those words come out of his mouth made me absolutely certain the note had been a friendly warning. Someone had believed I was headed for rough times, and unfortunately, they had been correct.

As I watched Jamie get on the elevator and descend out of my life, I resisted the urge to run after him. Because he was absolutely right. When I finally woke from the nightmare that was my life, would there be anything left of the man he had fallen in love with? Or would I, like my uncle, allow circumstances to shred my humanity until there was nothing left?

PART II

CHAPTER FOURTEEN

PETER

THE NIGHT of Gio's boxing party came too soon. I was living with him now, sleeping in his bed, and letting him fuck me night after night. He had claimed me body and soul, and I was terrified that everyone would be able to sense it. Already it was getting difficult to remember how we were before.

"You look nervous," Gio said, coming up behind me as I finger-combed my wet hair in front of the bathroom mirror.

I glanced at his reflection, my stomach flip-flopping at the sight of his muscles filling out the sleeves of his black Polo. He pressed his chest against my back and rested his hands on my shoulders, massaging as he bent to place a soft kiss on the side of my neck. My dick stirred at his proximity, clearly visible beneath the towel tucked around my waist.

"A little. I'm just—"

Gio's eyes grazed along my body, and his gaze got hung up on the bulge beneath the towel. His fingertips squeezed hard where they had been massaging, and I flinched.

"Sorry." His lips tipped into an apologetic smile, and he gentled his touch. "You were saying?"

"I'm just worried that people will be able to tell that we're... *you know*." I met his gaze in the mirror, brows knotting in a silent entreaty for him to *please* know what I was saying without me actually having to utter the word.

"Fucking." His voice was little more than a growl, and the grin that graced his handsome face as the word crossed his lips let me know that he got some perverse pleasure from making me squirm. His right hand slid from my shoulder and trailed down my back, fingers loosening the towel around my waist and dropping it to the floor. He gave my bare ass cheek a gentle squeeze and eyed my ever-increasing erection. "You and I are fucking, Peter. It's not easy to hide something like that, especially when I can't look at you without wanting to bend you over."

I shivered at his words, and at his warm breath against the shell of my ear. "You're not making me feel better about this. What if I forget, even for just a second? What if I say something incriminating?"

"What if you do?" He sucked my earlobe into his hot mouth.

"I don't know, Gio. What if—" Focusing on what I wanted to say was impossible with him molesting my ear. My world centered on the warm, wet pressure of his gentle sucking, and what little sense I'd had in my brain slid down into my cock.

Gio finally removed his mouth from my ear with an obscene slurp. "I can hardly bring myself to care."

He brought his left hand down to join the other in worshiping the curve of my ass, running his palms so lightly over my skin it tickled. When he dug his fingers into my hips and used his thumbs to spread my cheeks, I let out a broken whimper and pushed back on him, all reflex and instinct.

"Are you my little slut?" With the pressure of his palms, he spread me wide enough to set the nerve endings on fire and ghosted the pad of one thumb over my hole. "Hmmm? Tell me, Peter. Are you daddy's little slut?"

I groaned, unable to form words, and leaned against the front of the counter. My dick pressed against the drawer facing until it was almost painful, but I didn't lean back in search of relief. The pressure grounded me, and I needed grounding when he said those things that made me feel dirty and wrong and so fucking turned on that my dick throbbed.

"Climb up onto the counter." Gio wrapped his arms around me and hoisted me up, not waiting for me to do it myself. I had thought he meant for me to sit on the countertop, but instead, he positioned me on my hands and knees with barely enough room to keep from slipping off the surface. Tipped off my center of gravity, I tensed with the effort to hold my body upright.

"What are you going to do?" My voice wavered with a Molotov cocktail mixture of excitement and apprehension.

Instead of answering my question, he kissed a hot trail down over the swell of my ass and then followed the crease at the top of my thigh. He dragged his tongue over the sensitive flesh at the inside of my thigh, then nipped playfully with his teeth, sending little pinpricks of delicious pain shooting through me.

"Oh, God, Gio," I moaned shamelessly, losing my balance and careening forward. The side of my face smashed uncomfortably against the mirror, but in my ecstasy, I couldn't bring myself to give a shit.

"You like that?" He teased deeper along the crease of my thigh with languorous licks and kisses, and from the hint of a smile in his voice, he knew very well he was driving me mad.

"Yes," I said, trembling. "Yes. Yes." The word became a mantra as he buried his face between my thighs and dragged his tongue up from the base of my sac. My muscles seized up when I felt the wet tip of his tongue touch my hole, but when he started painting lazy circles around it, I nearly melted into a puddle on the counter.

Was this okay? It was nearly inconceivable to my inexperienced mind that Gio had his mouth *back there*. It was so unbelievably naughty and dirty and filthy and—

Oh, God! He touched the tip of his tongue to the very center of me... and pushed. I nearly flew up off the counter as his tongue invaded me, working the tight muscle loose and sending shocks of hot and cold pleasure racing up my nerve endings. It was so fucking intense. More intense than anything I'd ever felt in my life.

My balls drew up between my legs like a couple of shooter marbles, and I knew it wouldn't take long. Especially not with the way Gio was moaning as he lapped at my hole, as if he couldn't get enough. If the vulgar grunts and groans coming out of him were anything to go by, he was just as turned on as I was. The thought made me want to come.

He kissed my hole, suckling and nipping around the sensitive perimeter before pressing back in and making me gasp. Over and over he repeated the movements, establishing a hypnotic rhythm of suck and plunder until I was mindless and begging. My face was jammed so hard against the glass I was afraid something was going to break, and still, I just moaned out strings of nonsense. My harsh breaths sent streaks of fog across the mirror, pulsing like bars on a stereo equalizer.

Through my delirium, I was aware of Gio's fingertips tickling over the tightened skin of my sac, touching the base of my cock, and running up its length. It was too much sensation. Too much to handle at once. I pushed back on his tongue and let out an anguished cry as strands of thick, white semen pulsed out of me and onto the countertop.

Muscle control was a thing of the past, and if Gio hadn't been holding me steady, I could have crumpled. In all my years of working myself to climax, and even in the limited but overwhelming experiences I'd had with Gio, I had never felt anything so intense in my life.

With my breath still uneven and little post-orgasmic pulses of sensation still dancing through my limbs like twinkling stars, I allowed Gio to work me gently down to the floor. My face peeled away from the mirror, leaving a smudge from my cheek and a haze of fog that quickly dissipated. My knees ached from grinding into the countertop, and the joints had stiffened from being locked in such an awkward position. I straightened my limbs out slowly, like a newborn colt unfolding into the world, and tried to stand without falling over.

"How do you feel now?" Gio asked with a knowing grin. He wiped the back of his hand, and the obscene reminder of what he'd just done brought heat to my face. "Are you sufficiently relaxed, or do I need to take you into the bedroom and fuck you until you can't think at all?" He palmed the very obvious bulge in his pants and raised a brow.

"Gah," I said, my tongue as rubbery and useless as my limbs. "I already can't think, and my muscles are like jelly. Can I just go to sleep?"

"Not a chance. You're not getting out of watching boxing that easily." He looked at his gold Rolex and frowned. "We only have twenty minutes. Just enough time for you to dress and get situated in the great room before people start arriving. I'll go and make sure the caterer has everything ready."

"There's a caterer here?" I turned wide, horrified eyes toward the door. "I thought we were alone."

Gio shook his head and smirked. "He got here while you were in the shower. Been out there the whole time setting up. He should be finished by now, but I have to write him a check before he leaves."

"Was I..." I swallowed hard as heat crept up my throat. "Was I loud?"

Gio laughed. "Like porn with the volume cranked up."

"Oh, Jesus." I ran a hand through my disheveled hair and whisper-screamed, "How could you let me do that? Why didn't you tell me to shut the hell up?"

Gio ran a hand around the back of my neck and attempted to rub out the tension that had crept back into my muscles. Then he leaned in and captured my lips in a gentle kiss. "Don't worry. We're fine. I wasn't exactly using my library voice, either."

My mouth fell open as I studied Gio's relaxed expression. "How can you be so calm about everything? I don't get it. Do you *want* people to find out about us?"

"No." He looked perplexed for a split second, as if he, too, was confused by his own conflicting statements. Then his face relaxed again, and he smiled. "Sometimes, maybe. It's difficult hiding you away and pretending there's nothing between us. I'm so damn proud of you, Peter. I wish I could show you off."

I turned away and grabbed the towel I had been wearing. The evidence of my orgasm was splattered across the countertop like a Jackson Pollock painting, and I mopped up the X-rated artwork as I turned Gio's words over in my mind. His mixed signals had me reeling. "But... we *don't* want people to know, right?" I pressed.

Because I wanted to show him off, too. I wanted every person in the entire world to know that I was his.

"At this time, I think it's best if we keep the true nature of our relationship a secret. But we need to make the announcement tonight—subtly, of course—that you are living here now. If they found out on their own, it would seem like we have something to hide. And we don't. We have nothing to be ashamed of." He nodded resolutely as if trying to convince himself as well as me.

"Does anyone know about you?" I bit my lip and dropped the soiled towel into the wicker laundry basket before turning to face Gio. "That you like men?"

"No one suspects as far as I know. I—" He took a hesitant step toward me, uncertainty etched on his handsome features. "I used to be married, Peter." He scrubbed his fingertips through the meticulously-groomed stubble at his jaw, the sound too loud in heavy silence following his confession. He searched my eyes for a reaction. "Does that bother you?"

I shook my head, a jerky movement that was nothing more than a lie—because it did bother me. The thought of Gio with anyone else, man or woman, gnawed at my insides, and the more I thought about it the worse it got. Had he kissed her? Jesus, of course he had. He'd fucked her, too. My belly twisted in on itself and I had to resist the involuntary urge to clutch at it, to ease the incredible pain that had lodged itself there.

How many other people had he been with? How many people had he slid his dick into before me? How many people did I need to despise without even knowing their names?

I felt my eyes water. How pathetic.

I was nothing but a jealous, naive kid, and I'd been living in a fantasy world. The moment Gio had touched me, I'd slipped into sweet oblivion, my heart whispering to my brain that I was the only one. Now reality had come crashing down on me, and I didn't like it one little bit. I wanted the oblivion back—needed it—and yet I knew it would never again be mine.

Married. Jesus H. Christ.

Gio closed the short distance between us and folded me up in his arms even as I struggled ineffectually against him. I didn't fight hard, because I needed those arms around me more than anything. Even more than the oblivion. And I needed to hear his voice, soft and soothing as he spoke against my ear. "I'm sorry, baby. I didn't mean to hurt you. Dammit, I shouldn't have said anything. At the very least, I could have chosen a time when you weren't already anxious."

I slumped against his chest, dampening the fabric of his shirt with my ridiculous tears. "I'm glad you told me. Knowing doesn't feel good, but being lied to would be worse." My heart wasn't entirely convinced, but I pressed on anyway, trying to be strong. To be *mature.* "Did you love her?"

"I cared about her," he admitted. "In the beginning. But over time, things went sour. She knew I didn't love her the way she needed, and eventually she came to understand—" He took a deep breath and let it out slowly against my hair.

"Understand what?"

"I wanted children. A son to carry on my name. It's kind of strange to think about now, but I was raised to believe I was supposed to have that—the wife, the children, and the heir. But as time went by and Victoria failed to get pregnant... Well, there was no real interest there on my part beyond making babies, and she figured it out. How could she not? It was painfully obvious. After four years, the lack of chemistry between us and our inability to get pregnant weighed heavily on her. She started drinking, we started fighting, and then she cheated on me and fell in love with someone else. End of story."

"Did it hurt you that she cheated?" I kept asking questions I didn't want the answers to.

"In a way," he said. "But I had no right to be angry. I should have been relieved, but pride is a funny thing. I guess there's a certain power in being the one to say goodbye. We were both unhappy, and we both had lovers, but in the end she was the one who had the guts to end it."

Now my jealousy shifted from the wife to the lovers, and my entire body tensed. "Were your lovers men or women?"

Gio felt my reaction and chuckled softly. His lips touched my temple, and I could feel the smile on them. "Men."

"And did you love any of them?"

He hesitated. Shifted against me. "Only one."

Those two little words reverberated through me, forcing out a sound that was almost a sob.

He had loved before.

"I'm sorry, sweet pea. If I could change the past for you, I would. I'd make it so that you were the only person I had ever looked at."

"Really?" I burrowed into his chest, nudging for affection like a needy kitten.

"In a heartbeat." He kissed my hair. "Now get dressed before people start arriving. It wouldn't do for you to come strolling out of my bedroom in front of everyone."

Gio left the room, and I set about getting ready, moving through quicksand. The news I had learned in the past few minutes had wrecked me, watering down the memory of Gio's hot tongue against my ass until it seemed like something that happened a long time ago. Or not at all.

Married. Lovers. I wished I could erase his past like chalk on a board.

I pulled on the Polo and jeans Gio had chosen for me to wear. Our outfits nearly matched, but my shirt was hunter green instead of black, and my Calvin Klein jeans were tighter than his. When I'd modeled them for him at the mall, he'd glanced around to make sure there was no one around and then shoved me into the changing room, groping me relentlessly until the saleswoman returned. At her confused inquiry —*Are you in there, sir?*—Gio had slipped out of the dressing room and calmly explained that the jeans were so tight I was ashamed to step out.

"Oh, I can get you a larger pair," the woman had said.

"That won't be necessary," Gio told her. "He'll get used to it."

I had emerged from the dressing room red-faced and was unable to make eye contact with the woman the whole time she was ringing up our purchases. Now my face got hot again thinking about strutting around the great room in front of all of those men in such tight jeans. I was used to wearing loose skate shorts in my downtime and suits while I was working.

The doorbell rang as I was contemplating putting on a pair of comfortable shorts, and I rushed out of the room and flung myself onto one of the beanbag chairs I'd talked Gio into getting for the party. Then I realized I couldn't have looked any more like a kid if I'd had a juice box in my hand, and I switched to the sofa. Gio stood patiently by the door until I got into place, then he opened the apartment to the first of the guests.

CHAPTER FIFTEEN

PETER

Z WAS the first one in, striding confidently into the room in a bold red Hawaiian shirt and jeans. The black spikes in his hair were cemented into place, and a gold earring caught the light where it dangled from his left ear. He was striking in a disturbing way, with his pale skin, blue eyes, and sharp features that had undoubtedly been very handsome before partying had ravaged his body. Now he was painfully thin, as if he'd been living on a steady diet of hardcore drugs and not much else.

"Gio," he said in his laid-back drawl. "How's it hangin?"

I cringed. Gio wasn't the kind of man you talked to like that. He deserved reverence. Z's blatant show of disrespect made me want to punch him in the face. Why did Gio let him talk to him like that?

Z's eyes sparkled mischievously when he caught sight of me, and he winked. I thought of the day we met, when I was taking notes for Gio in the one business meeting I'd attended, and Z had asked to see my notebook. He had looked at my childish doodles and the lack of actual notes, but he hadn't given me away.

It confused me and made me wonder what his angle was, because Z didn't seem like the type not to have one.

Gio grasped him around the shoulders. "Good to see you, Z."

As if they didn't see each other all the time.

Frank, the big Italian, waddled in after Z and grasped Gio's hand with his sausage fingers. His chubby cheeks were flushed, his breathing labored as if he'd hustled up the stairs instead of taking the air-conditioned elevator. "Gonna be a good one tonight," he said.

Teddy, who was Frank's opposite in almost every way, waited politely until Frank was finished pawing Gio's hand. He wore what I assumed to be his usual attire—a faded button-up shirt and slacks. His thinning hair was slicked back with pomade in much the same way my father wore his, which gave it an unwashed rather than neat appearance. Somehow, though Frank's hair was slicked similarly, it looked shiny and clean in contrast. Like freshly Armor-Alled black vinyl.

"Hello, Gio," Teddy said with a habitual sniff, swiping at his thin nose with nervous fingers before reaching out to shake Gio's hand.

Gio clasped his hands behind his back in a blatant refusal to shake, and I remembered he had also refused to shake my father's hand. I couldn't blame him on either count. Teddy's hands had been all around his nose, and my father's fingernails were always filthy.

Gnawed and filthy and full of anger. Thank god those hands couldn't touch me in anger anymore.

At least not for now.

A bolt of panic coursed through me, because in my cloud of love and oblivion there was something else that hadn't occurred to me. What if Gio got tired of me? Would I have to go back to my father? I figured I probably had enough money saved up for about six months of living expenses, but then what? Would I still be able to work as Gio's assistant, or would he cut me loose? It was unlikely I'd be able to find another job that paid so well, even if I worked my ass off.

I glanced at Gio's face and found him staring back with a concerned expression, as if he had smelled my fear from all the way across the room. His supernatural ability to read my thoughts was both unsettling and comforting.

Z plopped down on the sofa, startling me out of my eye-lock with Gio. "I see you rated an invitation this time. How does it feel to be rubbing shoulders with the big dogs?" He bumped his bony shoulder against mine to illustrate the point, and I instinctively flinched away.

"Ummm... Good, I guess." It was a lame as hell answer, but I couldn't say what I *really* wanted to. That I'd rubbed more than shoulders with the alpha of this dog pack. And that less than an hour before, I'd been on my hands and knees with said alpha licking my ass until I came.

"Good, I guess." Z mimicked me in a childlike voice and burst into laughter that bordered on maniacal. He fidgeted, then looked around at the others in the room and lowered the volume of his voice as if he was sharing a juicy secret. "You're cute, you know that? Drawing pictures and shit while you're on the clock."

"I was just—" I froze, trying to come up with a plausible excuse. If I'd known he wasn't going to let the matter drop, I would have worked something up before I faced him again. But I'd underestimated his interest in the subject.

He clearly thought he had some dirt on me, and possibly on Gio, too. I couldn't be sure what he was insinuating with his comment, because he was so damn cryptic in everything he said. As if he thought he was the wiliest person in the room and couldn't deign to speak directly about anything. It was exhausting trying to decipher his riddles, and I wondered if it was even worth the bother.

"Hey, don't worry about it, kid." He ruffled my hair, laughing when I scowled and reached up to check the state of it. "Oh, I didn't mess anything up. You look fine." His eagle-eye gaze dropped down and back up as he scrutinized my outfit. "You and Gio are like the fucking Bobbsey Twins. He's been paying you good, huh?"

I nodded, caught in his baby blue high-beams. He was fishing for information. Dropping random comments and questions like bombs on Space Invaders until my head was spinning with the effort to dodge them. I slowed my breathing, calmed my heartbeat, and tried to focus on not giving anything away.

"I was lucky to get this job. I could have ended up flipping burgers for minimum wage. Instead, I'm working for a great boss who isn't afraid to pay me what I'm worth."

I thought it sounded mature. Savvy. But if the raise of Z's eyebrow was any indication, he wasn't buying it.

"And what's the going rate these days for kids who draw little pictures instead of taking notes like they're supposed to? Did Gio see that notebook of yours after the meeting? Did you show him all the hard work you were doing?"

I huffed. "For your information, Gio told me I could ease into the notes thing. It was something new he'd added to my job description, and I didn't have much experience at it. He said it was kind of like a dry run to see what it was like, so I doubt he would be mad."

There. A fine explanation considering I had come up with it on the spot.

Z grinned, but he didn't look amused in the least. "I don't know how I feel about some kid who doesn't know what the fuck he's doing listening to me talk about my business. Like I can't quite figure out what Gio was thinking bringing you in on us like that. I thought assistants were supposed to keep up with his appointments and pick up the dry cleaning. Keep the house clean and shit."

"That would be a maid," I said, meeting his intense gaze with one of my own.

"Excuuse me," he drawled. "I stand corrected. You're not a maid. But we both know you're not a note-taker, either. What exactly is it that you do around here?"

I opened my mouth, prepared to recite the short list of things I had done for Gio at one time but didn't really do anymore. Why did he make me so nervous? Why was he giving me the third degree?

"Get over here, Z," Gio called from across the room. "Stop giving Peter a hard time. I don't want to have to hire a new assistant because you ran this one off."

Z sucked his teeth and pushed up to standing, rudely using my knee as leverage. "Later, alligator." He strutted across the room and joined Gio and the others, talking too loudly as if he thought he was the life of the party.

"You're fucking crazy," Z yelled in response to something Gio said. "There's no way this thing is gonna go past round three. Tyson's gonna knock him out in seconds."

Gio scoffed. "I still think it's gonna go past round three."

"What makes you think that?"

"Because I bet that it would, and I rarely lose. I stand to gain a lot of money, not to mention the chance to say *I told you so*. It's gonna be a sweet payday."

Z laughed. "Yeah, for you and a lot of people. I just don't know how you think Bruno has a chance in hell of dodging that fist for three whole rounds. You know if Tyson lands it, it's lights out."

"Bye-bye, Bruno," Frank chimed in gleefully.

"We'll see," Gio said. "But I've always been unnaturally lucky. Admit it, Z."

Z smiled. "Yeah. It's annoying as fuck."

They went back and forth about it for a while. I, of course, had no opinion on the fight. I knew who Mike Tyson was, because... well, I had a pulse and a TV. But I still had no interest in the fight itself or in hearing other people talk about it.

When the doorbell rang and Gio swung the door open to reveal my best friend standing on the other side, I perked up. *Finally*, something to do besides listening to boxing talk and getting harassed by Z.

Theo stepped inside at Gio's urging, and his eyes immediately sought me out, like a geek scanning for his prom date across a crowded dance floor. All that was missing was the corsage.

"So glad you were able to make it," Gio told him. "Peter is over there on the sofa. Bored to tears by now, I'm sure."

"Thank you, sir. Thank you for having me." He all but bowed.

Wow. Formal Theo. This was something new.

His entire face lit up when he saw me, and he hustled over to the sofa, grinning like mad. "Dude, this place is ridiculous." He slid in beside me, eyes bugging. "You're so fucking lucky, man."

I smiled, trying not to let his gushing go to my head. "Yeah, I guess. It's a lot nicer than my dad's place, that's for sure."

"So you were serious about staying here?" he asked. "You're like a live-in assistant now?"

"Yep. Twenty-four-seven." My pride conveniently ignored the fact that the live-in assistant thing was nothing but a smokescreen.

"What a hardship." Theo watched the men, who were standing in a loose circle and talking. His eyes seemed to zero in on Gio, cataloging every detail of the man now that he could observe him from a distance. "What's he like, your boss? Now that he's got you on the clock day and night, I'll bet he runs you ragged with all his rockstar demands. Do you have to pick out all the green M&M's for him? Does he send you out for cigs at two in the morning? Or pickles and ice cream?"

I gave him my *what-the-fuck* face. And then, to be thorough, I said it, too. "What the fuck, Theo? He doesn't smoke, and he's not a pregnant woman. He's a businessman, and he's not hard to work for at all. No midnight runs, no green M&M's, and definitely for God's sake no pickles and ice cream. It's basically the same as before, but I don't have to get up early to come to work. I just wake up, roll out of bed, and get dressed." Then I couldn't help adding, "In designer suits."

Theo shook his head. "You're turning into one of those posh types, aren't you? Before you know it, you'll be sitting around in a smoking jacket and eating bonbons on the clock."

I wanted to argue, but Theo was dangerously close to right. From the outside looking in, I looked suspiciously like a high-dollar prostitute. Gio didn't treat me like one, and I didn't feel like one, but the circumstantial evidence was piling up to the point that I was pretty sure a jury would convict.

"So have you talked to Mr. Rivera about hiring me?" he asked.

"Oh." I froze, realizing I had forgotten my promise. "I haven't gotten around to it yet. I figured I ought to wait until I was more... you know, settled in my own job."

"Looks to me like you're pretty settled," he pointed out. I couldn't argue.

"I'll ask him soon. Probably tomorrow."

"Thanks, man. I sure could use a job." He smiled and rubbed his stomach. "I could use some food, too. I saw you had some snacks laid out on the table over there. Are those for us?"

"Yeah, we got a caterer." I stood and motioned for Theo to follow me to the kitchen. The island and breakfast table were covered in finger foods, but that was only the beginning. The table in the formal dining room beyond held heavier dishes like enchiladas, fried chicken, and a couple of mystery casseroles. My heart melted when I saw a pan of chili cheese dogs stuck right in the middle of everything.

For me.

Theo grabbed a plate and loaded it down with two chicken legs, three enchiladas, and a chili dog. I got two chili dogs and added a handful of potato chips when we passed by the breakfast table on our way back to the great room. Then I doubled back and pulled a couple of beers out of the fridge, holding them between the fingers of one hand while balancing my plate precariously in the other. Just as we approached the living area, Theo slammed on brakes in front of me.

"What the hell, Theo?" I took a step back, cringing when I noticed a little beer had sloshed out onto the floor.

"Somebody took our seats," he said, gesturing toward the sofa where Teddy and Z had made themselves comfortable. They were watching the enormous big screen TV, which was normally hidden behind the doors of a wall-sized shelving unit.

Gio was chatting with two guys I'd never seen before—a smallish black man of about thirty, and an older man with pale, weathered skin and a wave of wispy white hair swept back from his forehead. Carlos hung back near the door, nursing a beer. The driver looked out of place, especially because I was used to seeing him dressed for work in a suit instead of a t-shirt and jeans. He smiled when he saw me, and I waved awkwardly with the beers I was holding.

"We have bean bags," I told Theo.

He shook his head. "I ain't sitting on no beanbag while I try to eat, boy. Let's go to your room. Some privacy would be nice, anyway. I'm feeling weird with all these old dudes."

"Shhh..." I hissed. "That's rude. Besides, Gio is *not* old." I hoped my comment didn't sound like I wanted to take Theo's head off, even though I did.

Theo raised an eyebrow at me. "Dude might look like a movie star, but he's still old. He must be in his late thirties."

"Thirty-seven isn't old," I muttered under my breath, wondering if Theo would catch on if I protested too much. "I'll check back with you when you're in your thirties and see how old you think it is then."

"Whatever," Theo said with the infuriating apathy of an eighteen-year-old who thought he was immortal and did not have a thirty-seven-year-old boyfriend. "Where's your room? I'm tired of standing here holding this plate."

I hesitated, because it suddenly occurred to me that I didn't have my own room, and taking him to Gio's room was not an option.

"Dude," Theo pleaded.

Resigning myself to what was happening, I sighed and spun around, skirting the kitchen and heading down the hallway that ran along the back wall of windows. We passed the darkened office, and I heard Theo laugh quietly behind me.

"It's dark back here," he said. "Kinda spooky."

"Can you open this?" I asked, indicating the closed door of the guest room. "And get the light, too. My hands are full."

Theo reached around me with his free hand and opened the door to the bedroom that should have been mine but wasn't. Then he followed me into the room, which was pitch black except for the glow from the city outside. He slid his hand along the wall for a few tense seconds before growling, "Dude, where's the damn light switch?"

"Just feel around for it," I said irritably. The truth was I had no more idea where the light switch was than he did. I'd only wandered into the room a couple of times, and always during the day. I assumed it was in the usual spot inside the door on the right side, but I couldn't chance a wrong guess.

It took Theo another few seconds to find the switch, and just when I had started thinking maybe there wasn't one at all, light flooded the room.

"Well, this is fancy," Theo said, his eyes appraising the heavy wood furnishings: a four-poster bed, mirrored dresser, armoire, and bedside table. Two gold wingback chairs sat near the window, a small reading table situated between them. The decor was as gorgeous as everything else in the apartment, but it was too pristine. A place where life never happened. "Hey, you even made your bed for a change," Theo said with a laugh.

I shrugged, already feeling like coming here was a really bad idea. "Gio has a maid come in a few times a week to tidy up."

"You've got a maid?" Theo gaped. "Couple months ago you were sleeping on a futon. Now look at you."

I shuddered at the thought of the rock-hard futon. Sleeping in Gio's bed was like floating in a silk cocoon, and I made a promise to myself that no matter what happened I would never go back to the uncomfortable slab in my dad's apartment. Even an army cot in the middle of a crack house was preferable.

"That futon sucked," I said, understating the obvious as I lowered myself onto the bed and settled my plate of chili dogs onto my lap. Then I offered Theo the spot nearest the headboard so he could set his plate on the bedside table.

"You got a TV in here?" he asked around a mouthful of chicken.

I took a swig of my beer and full-on panicked. *Did* I have a TV in here? The armoire at the foot of the bed was the most likely place to find one, but I was afraid to check it in front of Theo and find it empty. "Ummm... let's not watch TV," I said. "I haven't talked to you in a while, and I've missed you. What have you been up to?"

"Same old same-old," he said with a shrug. "Hanging out down at the pool hall. It's not the same without you, man. Your boss needs to ease up and give you a little time off so we can kick it. You must at least have weekends off or something."

"I want to hang with you some, but—"

"But you're too good for the pool hall now," Theo filled in.

"No, I'm not," I said, appalled at the suggestion.

What he said was sort of true, but it wasn't that simple. The way he'd said it made me sound like a stuck-up asshole. I didn't think I was *better* than him or anyone else who chose to spend their time shooting the shit down at the pool hall, but now I'd had a taste of something better—life with Gio.

The pool hall had been an escape from the dirty little apartment. From the depression of poverty. From the fists and the belt. Now that I felt secure and fulfilled and oh-my-god happy, I didn't need the distractions that had helped me navigate the dark waters of my teenage years. And now that I had made it out, I had no desire to dip even a single toe into the murky bog that was my old life.

"Yeah," Theo drawled, his smile hesitant and almost shy. "You're definitely too good for all of that now. It's cool, though. I don't blame you. If I had a sweet setup like this, I wouldn't want to go sit in a smoke-filled dungeon with a bunch of losers, either."

I laughed. "You know, you're a lot of the reason that dungeon is smoke-filled."

He rolled his eyes and finished off his first chicken leg.

We ate in silence for a few minutes, neither of us quite knowing what to say. Life as we'd known it had morphed into something neither one of us quite recognized, and even with our knees touching on the bed, there was a distance already growing between us. Would this be the last time he and I would be together? Would we run into each other years down the road, virtual strangers with only a few vague memories of what we'd once been to each other?

Guilt rather than sadness clawed at my insides. Theo had been my lifeline over the past four years, and without him I would surely have drowned in a sea of loneliness and depression. But now that I was safe on shore, I was prepared to cut him loose and watch him drift away. I realized this with stunning clarity, with the same certainty that I would need another breath after this one was done, and yet I had no intention of trying to change it.

As I sat nibbling idly at my food and contemplating the depth of my own shittiness, Theo suddenly shoved his plate onto the bedside table and jumped up off the bed. Without a word, he stalked purposefully over to the closet and flung open the door to reveal... nothing. Inside was darkness and space. The scent of wood and paint and carpet. Of disuse.

Holy fuck. He'd figured it out.

"What the hell do you think you're doing?" I raged, vaguely panicked to hear notes of my father's voice in my own. "Get out of there, you nosy bastard."

But my anger wasn't directed at Theo. I was mad at myself. Why had I thought it was a good idea to bring him into this room? It was no more than a cardboard movie set. A shallow illusion that only barely masked the truth.

Theo turned back toward me, wearing an expression I'd never seen on him before. Judgment.

"I knew it," he said. "I fucking knew it." His tone wasn't triumphant, as in *aha! I knew it*, but disappointed, as in *I didn't want to believe it, but deep down I knew it.*

I stared down at my plate, feeling stripped bare and suddenly all too aware of what I had been doing. Of how this must look. And like Adam and Eve in the Garden of Eden, after they'd eaten of the fruit and discovered their nakedness, I was ashamed. But a fig leaf wasn't going to fix my problem.

Theo sat back down on the bed, gingerly this time as if something might break, and twisted his hands into his lap. "What are you doing, Pete? I—" His voice was so quiet. "I thought you had a job. I was so proud for you. I thought you were his *assistant.*"

"I am," I squeaked. "I mean, I *was*. I never lied to you, Theo. You have to believe me. It just... became something more."

"Something more," Theo repeated. "Like what exactly?"

"It's—" I closed my eyes, wondering if speaking it aloud would unravel it all. Make it nothing, and silly, and so utterly ridiculous as to be laughable. Because who was I to lay claim to a man like Giorgio Rivera?

Theo knew me better than anyone. He knew where I'd come from and how pathetic I was. If I spoke the word that was on my tongue, he would laugh at me, and then I would know how foolish I'd been to ever believe in...

"Love," I whispered.

Theo chewed on the word for a while. Then he turned more fully toward me and stared at the side of my face. "Is he at least paying you well? You're not giving it away for free, I hope. A man like that can afford whatever he wants, and you shouldn't let him take advantage of you because you're desperate to get away from your dad."

Theo couldn't have struck me harder with a two-by-four than with the harsh words he'd chosen, because he'd indirectly called me a whore, an idiot, a victim, *and* unworthy of Gio's love. There may have even been a few more insults hidden in there, but I was too devastated to ferret them out just now.

Could I protest, or would taking up for myself just be proving his point that I was naive? And what if he was right?

He put a hand on my shoulder and squeezed. "We'll figure this out together."

"Figure what out?" Gio asked from the doorway, relaxed and upbeat as if he'd just come to see about me and probably try to talk me into coming to watch the main event. But when I looked up at him and he caught a glimpse my face, his own expression turned frighteningly cold. He clicked the door closed, locked it, and pinned Theo in his ice-blue glare. "What on earth have you done to him?"

Theo stuttered, producing only sounds of confusion.

Gio sat down beside me, depressing the mattress with the familiar weight of his body, and wrapped a strong arm around my shoulders. "Are you okay? What's going on here? Talk to me."

"He found out," I said, followed by an embarrassing whimper. "I shouldn't have brought him back here. It was too obvious that no one sleeps in this room, and he figured it out. I'm sorry, Gio."

He tightened his grip on my shoulders and pressed his forehead to my temple. "It doesn't matter. He's your friend, right? Friends don't sell each other out." He lifted his head to look at Theo. "Isn't that right? Friends don't hurt each other." His tone communicated an unmistakable warning.

Theo swallowed audibly before nodding.

"He was only trying to protect me," I said, coming to his rescue even though he may not have deserved it.

"I was." Theo pulled himself up straighter and surprised me

by what he said next—with how fearless he was. "I'm not really digging the whole power dynamic here, Mr. Rivera. You know Pete doesn't have a lot of experience. It would be easy for you to take advantage of the situation."

Instead of getting defensive or angry, Gio nodded. "Your concerns have been noted, but I have a few of my own. The stricken look on Peter's face when I came into the room is something I don't ever want to see again as long as I live. I've worked very hard to make sure he feels safe, and tonight you've made him doubt his security with me. Do it again, and there will be hell to pay. Do I make myself clear?"

I shuddered. When Gio spoke to me, he was always so kind, his words soothing. But the fine-edged razor tone he used on other people—the one that said he was not pleased—chilled me to my soul. How could *that* Gio and *my* Gio exist together in the same body?

"Yes, sir," Theo said. "I didn't mean to cause trouble. It just seemed odd, that's all."

"I love him." Gio stroked my hair and pulled me against his chest. "He's mine, and I'm going to take care of him. Whether you or anyone else find that odd is of no importance to me."

It felt a little strange being talked about and deliberated over like I was an object, but at the same time, it gave me a sense of security and heart-swelling pleasure. Gio had come for me, and he'd done what I needed. He'd taken the confusion and the guilt and the question of whether what we were doing was right or wrong completely out of my hands. It didn't matter if I was sinful or stupid or naive as hell. Gio was more than capable of making decisions for both of us, and I was relieved to let him.

"Look, I'm gonna go," Theo said. His shoulders were slumped, face tight. He ran a hand through his blond hair and stared at the closed door, as if he found it difficult to look at us. I supposed it was a little weird seeing me all curled up against Gio's chest when he'd never seen me so much as touch another person.

"No need to rush off," Gio said. "I didn't mean to make you feel uncomfortable. I'm just protective of Peter, and if I think someone is confusing or hurting him, I'm going to react."

Theo finally looked our way. "Same here. But the truth is, I really don't belong here with all these people. Pete is my only friend here, and he's with you, so I feel kinda like a third wheel. I'd just be more comfortable down at the pool hall. Pete and I can hang out another day. Right, Pete?"

I nodded. "Yeah, for sure." The truth was, I wanted him to go. I wasn't mad or anything, but it did feel a little weird with him being here after everything that had happened. After all that was said. "I'll give you a call sometime, okay?"

Theo headed for the door but turned back to us before he walked out. "Don't forget to ask about that thing," he said to me.

That took me off guard. Even after everything he'd learned, he still wanted a job with Gio. "Sure. I'll definitely do that."

Theo made his uncomfortable escape, and Gio pulled away from me and tipped my chin up, forcing me to look at him. "What thing?" I should have known he wouldn't let that slip under his radar. I wasn't really ready to ask, but it seemed I had little choice now without making things even more awkward.

"Theo wanted to know if you have any place in the business for him. He really needs a good job, and I told him you might consider it."

Theo's brow crashed down in confusion. "Do you want me to hire him, or are you just being polite?"

I thought about it. After sticking by me over the years, he deserved some payback. It would also keep him close without me having to go hang out at the pool hall again. I was pretty sure Gio wouldn't go for that, anyway.

"I want you to give him a job. He's my only friend, and I don't want to lose him. He's dependable, and he's taken care of me over the years when my father—" I couldn't finish my sentence, but I was pretty sure Gio knew where I was going with it.

He nodded. "I suppose I could give him a trial run. I'm not sure what he would be qualified for, so I'll need to talk to him at length. He may just end up doing odd jobs for me."

"Like me?"

"Most definitely not like you." Gio ruffled my hair. "Give him a call tomorrow and have him come by. I'm not sure if it will work out, but I can't seem to deny you anything, Peter. If this is really what you want, I'll do it."

CHAPTER SIXTEEN

PETER

FOUR MONTHS into their working relationship, and my lover and my best friend were thick as thieves. Theo came over nearly every day and hung out with us when he and Gio weren't out working. I had only a vague impression of what the two of them did when they were gone. Meeting with people, conducting business transactions of some sort... I was a hundred percent sure that what they did wasn't legal. I'd already known from my limited dealings with Gio's business associates—Z, Teddy, and Frank—that this business I'd landed smack dab in the middle of was not the type of thing you'd admit to in Sunday school.

Not to mention Gio often carried a gun, and I hadn't patted

Theo down, but I was pretty sure he had taken to carrying one, too.

For my part, I kept my mouth shut. I got the distinct impression that Gio wanted to keep me separate from his professional life, though I wasn't sure if it was because he was ashamed or because he didn't think I could handle it. I doubted it was shame because Gio wasn't the type to make apologies for his choices, so that only left the other. I didn't mind. He knew me better than I knew myself, and if he thought I needed to know something, he would tell me.

At one point in the beginning of our relationship, I'd thought he was going to bring me into the fold. Having me come in and take notes on a business meeting between him, Z, Teddy, and Frank had seemed like a first step, but I quickly realized it had been nothing more than an icebreaker for the other guys' benefits. A way of saying, *This is my new assistant, and I trust him.*

Theo actually shared more with me than Gio did, but only on the rare occasions when we were alone. Like the day Gio left us watching TV and went downstairs to discuss something with Z.

"Where did you and Gio go last night?" I asked when *Saved by the Bell* broke for commercial. "I was already in bed when he got home."

Theo shrugged, not meeting my gaze. "Sometimes we gotta work late. It's not like this is a nine-to-five type of job."

I laughed. "That wasn't vague at all."

Theo picked at a thread that had come loose at the seam of his dress slacks. "Gio has already read me the riot act on telling you shit. He doesn't like for you to know details about what we do."

"Does he not trust me?"

"It's not that, and you know it. He just—" Theo wiggled nervously in his seat. "He treats you like a little prince, you know? Like you're too good to be tarnished by the bullshit we get up to.

He would beat my fucking ass if I went running my mouth to you, and I don't know why you want to know, anyway." He made a sweeping gesture with his hand, indicating the apartment. "If I could have all this without having to do anything but be the boyfriend, I'd be sucking Gio's dick night and day."

I frowned and punched Theo hard in the shoulder. "Dude, get your mind off my man's dick."

Theo scoffed. "I don't *wanna* suck it. I'm just saying you've definitely got the sweet setup here. You should chill out and enjoy what you've got."

"A few months ago, you were practically accusing me of being a whore."

Theo grinned. "Well, you are, kinda. But you're a fucking well-paid whore. I say enjoy it while it lasts."

"While it lasts?" The statement actually made my heart rate speed up, and not in a good way.

"Yeah, while it lasts. Nothing is forever, Pete." He picked at the thread on his slacks again. "I mean, you and me...we're forever. But all this other shit could go poof at any second."

That hurt. It also underscored the difference between how I felt about Theo and how he felt about me. In my mind, Gio and I were the forever, and Theo could go poof at any second. Of course, I didn't tell him that. He obviously valued me as a friend above all else, and it was flattering, but it also made me beholden in a way. To spare his feelings, I allowed him to have his little fantasy, but I did set him straight on one point.

"Gio and I are forever, too. I'll never love anyone like I love him."

Theo's expression soured. "He's too old for you. He's gonna die one day, and then where will you be?"

My heart flopped sickeningly in my chest. "Don't be morbid. He's not that much older."

"The fuck he isn't," Theo grated. "I mean don't get me wrong, Gio is a badass and a half. I've never met anyone so intimidating in my life, and I've met some thugs in my day. This cat is on a whole other level. But he's gonna break your heart, Pete. That's a fact."

I narrowed my eyes at him. "How is he gonna break my heart? Do you know something I don't?"

A humorless laugh burst out of Theo. "Jesus Christ, kid. I spend all day at the man's beck and call, while you get to cuddle and fuck and make goo-goo eyes at each other over candlelit dinners. You get Saint Gio; I get Gio *"Iceman"* Rivera. So, yeah. I know a fucking lot you don't know."

I gulped. "Iceman?"

"Yeah, that's what I call him. Like on the movie *Top Gun*. He hates it."

"Why do you call him that?"

"Because the man never smiles, and he's cool as a cucumber no matter what happens. I don't know what it would take to shake him, and to be honest, I don't ever want to find out."

I felt the need to defend Gio's honor, especially while he wasn't around to do it himself. He wasn't the cold-hearted bastard that Theo was making him out to be. He was kind and compassionate, and deeper than anyone I had ever met. His soul may have been hidden well beneath the surface of his skin, but to me, it was fathomless and contained all the wonders of the world.

"He smiles," I said in a pitiful attempt to redeem his image.

"Yeah, when he's with you. That's all you know, though. You don't see him in his element, when he's fucking around with all these shady cats he does business with. And when—"

Whatever Theo was going to say was lost to the sound of the door opening and Gio's smooth, deep voice. "Peter, get ready. I'm taking you out."

Theo and I both stared up at him with huge, guilty eyes, and of course he didn't miss it. He never missed anything.

"I get the feeling someone has been running his mouth." His eyes were trained directly on Theo.

"No, sir," Theo lied. "Pete was just trying to convince me that you were sweet, so I had to set him straight."

"Sweet," Gio snorted. "I don't know about all that, but you shouldn't be trying to destroy his illusions. If he likes to think of me as sweet, what's the harm in that?" As if to illustrate, he leaned down and kissed me, bypassing chaste and going straight to raunchy. He slanted his mouth over mine and forced his tongue between my lips. My arms went around his neck, and I pulled him closer, deepening the contact and chasing that drugging effect his kisses always had on me.

Theo cleared his throat. "You guys are embarrassing."

Gio pulled away from me and glared. "Why don't you leave, then? Peter has to get dressed, anyway. They have a dress code at Luigi's, and it doesn't include shorts and bare feet."

I flew up off the sofa like I suddenly had wings. "Luigi's? Can I get the goat cheese ravioli and a double order of calamari?" I had come a long way from chili dogs since I'd met Gio.

"Of course, sweet pea. You know you can order anything you want."

I danced off to the bedroom, but not before I caught Theo's exaggerated eye roll. "You treat him like a child."

"Well, he didn't have much of a childhood, did he? If I want to indulge him, that's my business. Your business is doing what I tell you to do, and right now I'm telling you to leave."

"Fine," Theo huffed.

I closed the bedroom door, muffling their exchange, but I did hear the distinct thud of the front door closing. Then Gio came into the bedroom and sat down on the bed. He leaned back onto the pillow and stretched his legs out, crossing his feet at the ankles. He had toed his dress shoes off at the door, but he still wore his black socks, and he alternately curled and stretched his toes within them as he watched me retrieve a suit out of the closet and drape it over one of several chairs in the room. The heat in his eyes as he tracked my movements made it almost impossible to concentrate on what I was doing, and I realized belatedly that I'd forgotten to grab my shoes.

When I went back into the closet and bent to get my favorite pair of wingtips, I caught sight of the large black box I had shoved into the corner days before. I'd been waiting for the right time to give it to Gio, and our first night out in what seemed like ages was perfect.

I pulled the box out of its hiding place and brought it out, my belly doing somersaults as I worried that he wouldn't like the gift.

"What's that?" he asked.

"Ummm... I got you a present."

His eyes widened. "A present for *me?*" He seemed genuinely taken aback that I would buy him a gift, and I supposed I couldn't blame him since he was always the one doting on me.

"Yes, I—" Doubt flooded me, and with every instinct telling me to *Abort! Abort!* I turned back toward the closet. "Ummm... Never mind. You probably won't like it. It was a dumb idea."

"Peter." Gio's stern voice had the instant effect of halting me in mid-step. "Bring me my gift. You can't take it back now."

I sighed, shoulders sagging, and approached him with the box tucked under my arm. He reached out to take it from me and had to pry it from my death grip.

He untied the gold ribbon that encircled the box and removed the lid, and my heart nearly stopped as he unfolded the gold tissue paper and stared down into the box. He didn't speak for a moment, and all I could think was what a stupid thing I had done. The gift was absurd and so out of character for Gio. What had I been thinking?

He looked up at me, his expression unreadable, before reaching in carefully and bringing out the black hat I had bought him.

"I noticed your dad was wearing a hat in the pictures you showed me of your family," I said, rushing to explain my logic, which now seemed faulty. Gio had never worn a hat, so why did I think he would want to wear one now? When he'd shown me the photos of his family, I'd gotten the impression that he revered his father and was shaken by his passing several years before, but that didn't mean he wanted to emulate the man's style.

Gio turned the fedora in his hands, inspecting the fine craftsmanship. The black fur felt, the wide brim, the black band that encircled it. He was quiet for a long time, leaving me to form my own dire conclusions. Did he hate it? Did he think I was an idiot for buying it? The waiting for a reaction was excruciating.

When he finally spoke, his words were strained with emotion. "This is the most thoughtful gift I've ever received, Peter. I don't know what to say except thank you, from the bottom of my heart."

I shuffled closer. "So does that mean you like it?"

He dragged his gaze away from the hat in his hands to stare up at me, his eyes glistening with unshed tears. "I love it. How did you—"

"I got your tailor to order it for me. I didn't know what kind of hat it was, and I didn't want to take the pictures out of the apartment, so I had Bill come over while you were gone. He special ordered it from Christys' in London."

Gio set the box aside on the bed and went into the bathroom. I watched from afar as he fitted the hat on his head and inspected his reflection in the mirror, angling the hat this way and that until he got it like he wanted it. Then a smile crept onto his face. "I look like my father," he said, his voice so quiet I barely made out the words.

"You do," I agreed. "I could tell you loved him very much, and I wanted to get you something that would remind you of him."

He left the bathroom and strode toward me, the small smile he'd aimed at the mirror reaching full power just as he got to me. "It does, and I love you for it." He took me into his arms and squeezed me to his chest until I thought I would break.

"You do so much for me, and I wanted to give you something in return to show you how much I appreciate everything." I blushed against his chest. "Plus, I just love you so much."

He pushed me away until he could fit his mouth over mine in a heartfelt kiss.

"So what do you think?" he asked, finally breaking the kiss and stepping back. He grabbed onto the top of the hat and struck a rakish pose, raising one eyebrow and giving what could only be described as a smoldering look. It made my knees weak.

"I think you look like a Hollywood movie gangster."

He raised his eyebrow even higher. "But not a real gangster?"

"Well, I don't know if real gangsters are as good-looking as you."

"Hmmm..." He moved closer, shrugging smoothly out of his suit jacket and letting it slide down his arms. His gun was strapped to his side in a tan leather shoulder holster, and I was glad he'd chosen that one. It was sexier than the one he wore inside his waistband. "How about now, sweet pea? Do I look like a real gangster now?"

I was shocked because he normally tried to downplay any sort of references to crime or to what he did for a living, but on this particular night, he seemed to be using it to turn me on.

It was working.

"Yes," I said. "Very real. You look hot. And... scary."

He reached out and snatched me up against him. "Scary, huh? Why is that? Are you afraid of what I might do to you?"

I gulped and nodded slowly, looking up at him with wide eyes. In that hat, and with the gun strapped over his white dress shirt, he looked like a different person—one who might not treat me with the same gentle care that *my* Gio did. His fingertips dug into my forearm as he pulled it to his lips and pressed a soft kiss to the sensitive underside of my wrist.

An involuntary sigh escaped my parted lips, and his eyes widened, the black of his pupils reducing the ice blue around them to a thin ring of color. With his free hand, he reached around and grabbed onto a handful of ass and hoisted me one-armed up his body. I wrapped my legs around his waist, heart beating frantically. I could feel the insistent press of his cock through his pants, nudging at the tender space just behind my balls.

He looked up at me, and I brought my mouth down on his, tentatively at first. But he mastered me even from his lower vantage point, sucking my lips into his mouth like they were his to devour. And they were. Everything I had was his to take, and the way he handled me said he was well aware of that fact. He used his grip on my ass to work me incrementally up and down, stroking his cock with my body until I thought I would die with the need to have that steely length inside me.

"Do you want to know what it feels like to be fucked by a gangster? To be owned by someone dangerous?"

"Yes," I whispered. "God...yes. Please."

He walked me over to the bed and dropped me so roughly onto the mattress my teeth clacked together. My head fell back, and I stared up at him, my limbs going all soft and useless with the tingling rush of need coursing through me.

"Take your clothes off," he ordered. "Show daddy what's mine."

My stomach flipped, and I nearly moaned out my pleasure at his words. Coaxing my body into action, I shucked my t-shirt first, followed by my shorts and underwear.

He picked up the discarded red Calvins from the bedspread and pressed them to his face, breathing in before tossing them onto the floor. "I love your scent," he growled. "It drives me mad."

I blushed as I lay naked and exposed to him. No answering words would come. I was mute with anticipation.

Gio was intimidating like this, fully dressed in his gangster wear, gun strapped to his side, and eyes full of nothing but me and the desire to have me. It occurred to me that I was completely at his mercy in every way. He wasn't just spouting sexy words when he said I belonged to him. I was his, body and soul. Bought and paid for with money and with love.

He removed the hat from his head, kissed it, and set it on the bed. Then he unbuckled his shoulder holster and discarded it onto the bed beside the hat. I got the distinct impression he was leaving the articles in plain sight to remind me that even when he was naked and fucking me, he was still a gangster. But the illusion wasn't really an illusion at all, no matter how many jokes we made about Hollywood gangsters. Whether we acknowledged it aloud or not, Gio was the real deal, and that fact alone was enough to make my dick stiffen.

He stood above me, raven-haired and crystal-eyed, with merciless determination to have me etched on his perfect features. He was a picture of dark perfection. The spread of meticulously groomed stubble at his jaw, the tawny skin of his throat, the masculine jut of his Adam's apple, the dusting of black hair on long, tanned fingers as they deftly worked the buttons of his dress shirt free.

I was so lost. From the moment my father had dragged me into this apartment, I'd never stood a chance. Gio had wanted me, and he'd taken me. Now I was his, and he was mine to worship for all of eternity. I doubted even death could diminish the consuming need to belong to him, and the obsession that laid waste to everything that had once existed on the periphery of *him*.

He was my everything, and without him, I would cease to be.

As if he could sense the depth of my thoughts, Gio chuckled, naked now even though I hadn't noticed him removing his pants. "Where did you go, sweet pea? Your eyes are a million miles away."

"I was just thinking about how much I love you. About how I would die if you ever left me." I was being more honest than usual, laying it all on the line because I had nothing to lose but him.

His expression hardened, brow creasing. "Why would you ever think such a thing? I'm not going anywhere. You're my baby."

"Theo said you would break my heart. He said he sees a side of you that I don't."

"What?" he asked incredulously.

"It's true," I pressed on, letting the doubts run free now that the door had been cracked open. "I don't know what you do when you're not with me. You keep me locked away here, and you come and go as you please. You have an entire life that doesn't include me. For all I know, you're out fucking other guys. You could have an entire stable of lovers, and I would never even have a clue. Hell, you could have a dozen apartments, with a poor clueless boy like me in each one just waiting like a desperate little puppy for his master to come home and pet him."

Oh, God. What was I saying? Were these really the thoughts that were in my mind?

Apparently so, because here they were spilling out all over Gio like some vile sludge of jealousy.

Gio literally growled, his expression murderous. "Theo needs to keep his fucking mouth shut before he finds himself in the unemployment line."

"Don't fire him because of me," I cried in alarm. "He didn't say all that stuff about other guys. All he said was that you would break my heart and that I didn't know the side of you that he sees. He just thought he was being realistic."

"Realistic." He huffed. "The reality is that Theo only sees what I want him to see. He *works* for me, Peter. He's nothing to me but a tool to use, but you... You're everything to me."

He climbed onto the bed between my legs, spreading my thighs wide and pushing them up toward my chest. He'd gotten the tube of lubrication while I'd been dazed and thoughtful, and now he slathered it onto my hole without preamble, pushing it into me with sure fingers.

I clenched around the sudden intrusion, stinging from the stretch but aching for more.

"Do you feel my love?" he asked. "Do you believe what I tell you is real? That I will love and care for you as long as there is breath in my body?"

I nodded, tears stinging my eyes. Because even though I could be temporarily swayed by paranoia, my heart knew the truth. I felt guilty for even voicing the doubts that Theo had tried to put in my head. He just didn't understand—couldn't possibly understand—because he had never felt anything like what Gio and I had. As unworldly and egocentric as I was, I could almost believe that *no one* had.

"I'm sorry," I said, consumed by shame. "I never should have listened to Theo. Never should have doubted you."

"Shhh..." Gio bent over me and ran a hand through my hair. "There's no need to apologize. You haven't done anything wrong."

"But I have." I turned my face away from him, the tears coursing freely now. "You give me everything in the world, Gio.

You've never once said a harsh word to me, you've gone out of your way to make sure I know I'm wanted and loved, and this is how I repay you? With doubt and accusations of cheating on me?" I squeezed my eyes shut and sobbed. "I don't deserve you."

Gio rolled off of me and sat down on the edge of the bed, running a hand through his dark hair. "Where is this coming from? One minute we're playing *Peter Gets Fucked by a Gangster*, and the next you're crying and saying you don't deserve me."

I recognized his attempt at humor to lighten the mood, but it didn't work. I felt miserable. I was also horny as hell, but miserable just the same. I didn't know how to make things right—how to get rid of the guilt that was choking me. I knew guilt. It had been my near-constant companion for as long as I could remember, and in my experience, there was only one way to eradicate it.

My father's words echoed in my mind. *An eye for an eye, and a tooth for a tooth.* Yet another snippet of a Bible verse, lopped out of the whole and perverted to suit his needs. But it rang true for me because it's how I was raised.

I hated myself for being that way. For needing something I shouldn't need. Just another cause for guilt.

"What can I do to prove it to you?" Gio asked at last. "What do you need that I haven't been giving you?"

I couldn't possibly answer that question. Not with words. Instead, I crawled off of the bed and bent over the side of it, presenting my bare ass like I had done countless times in the past. Only this time there was no fear. No anger. No desperation coiled in the pit of my belly.

I rested my cheek on the bed, face turned toward Gio, and held his gaze. I was making an offering. A way to even the score and set things right again.

I saw the moment realization hit him. His face went dark and stormy, eyebrows crashing down and mouth flattening into a grim line. He glanced down at my ass, then back up to my eyes, and shook his head. "You can't ask me to do that, Peter. I would give you anything you asked for, but the thought of hurting you makes me sick to my stomach."

At that point, all of my reasoning was out the window, and I wasn't even sure why I was pushing. It was sick, wasn't it? But I was single-minded with the unholy need, and now that it had been unleashed, and there was no calling it back.

"It won't hurt if you do it," I argued. But when there was no change on his face to indicate I was swaying him, I decided to play dirty. I bit my lip and wiggled my ass. "Come on, daddy. I've been a really bad boy."

"Oh, God." Gio closed his eyes and sucked a noisy breath in through his nose before letting it out through his mouth. "What if you hate me for it?" he asked, his voice a quiet plea.

"I could never hate you. I just need you to punish the bad thoughts out of my head, Gio. If I'm wrong, then *make* me believe."

And with that statement, I'd finally hit on the heart of my need. It wasn't only about punishment; it was also about proof. If my doubts were unfounded, then I ought to feel shame, and I deserved to be punished. But Gio wasn't the type of man who would punish me if I was right. If I was wrong, he would beat my ass if that's what it took to prove himself to me. And if he refused... Well, then I would know.

Gio glanced at my ass, then back at my face, and I could see his resolve cracking. Even more telling was the fact that his dick was still hard.

Emboldened by that little triumph, I pushed my ass back and begged. "Please, daddy. Show me how wrong I am."

Gio sprang up from the bed, apparently sensing what was at stake in our little game. All apprehension faded from his expression, and he was *my* Gio again. Self-assured and determined to set me straight.

He flattened himself over my back and ground his erection against the crack of my ass as he growled against my ear. "If I hurt you, you tell me to stop, goddammit. Do you understand?"

I nodded, swallowing a lump of fear and anticipation.

He pushed up off of me and rubbed his palm over one ass cheek. A gentle warning. I tensed and held my breath, waiting.

The first blow was tentative as if he was testing his strength.

"Mmm...harder," I breathed, pushing back for more.

He rubbed the other cheek before slapping it with more force than he had the first.

I gasped. "Yeah. More."

He switched to the other cheek, first rubbing then slapping, putting more of his body into it this time. The sting was divine, and I grunted in response.

The next blow was hard, as was the one that followed. I felt the shock reverberate through my balls and through my dick, and I scrubbed my straining erection along the bedspread for friction. A couple more hard strikes and I was moaning like an animal in heat.

Gio rubbed his palm over the tender flesh, reawakening the sting, and then he pushed his cock along the channel of my ass. "Is that good, baby?"

I nodded with a helpless squeak.

And then he struck me again, four blows in quick succession. And as I writhed in sweet agony on the bed, he flattened his body over mine and said through clenched teeth, "Don't you ever fucking doubt my devotion again. Is that understood?"

"Yes," I said.

He pushed roughly against me, the head of his cock nudging my hole. "Yes, *what*?"

"Y—yes, daddy," I stammered, mindless and aching.

"That's right," he said, pushing up off of me once more and raining down a series of hard blows that sent me into a frenzy. I was mewling now, and my dick was weeping, soaking the covers beneath in precum.

And then Gio spread my aching cheeks and slammed his cock into my already-lubed ass with such force I cried out. "Oh, God yes, Gio. Oh... fuck."

I had never been so turned on in my life. A shudder rippled through my body as he pulled almost completely out of me and pushed back in, balls slapping against mine and sending a jolt of pure pleasure into my groin.

Gio pulled out again and ran his palm over my abused flesh. "Your ass is on fire, baby." He slapped it again before slamming his dick back into me.

"Ohhh..." I moaned, my voice guttering into a lower register as the pain sharp pain radiated outward and dissipated into a rhythmic throbbing.

"What have you done to me?" Gio panted. "I never wanted to hurt you, but seeing you this way... so needy and... God, I'm so hard, baby. So close. I need to fill you up."

He dropped over me one last time, bracing with his forearms on either side of me, and I knew this was it. His sweat slicked my back, the scrub of his dampened chest hair yet one more facet of the delicious torture of my senses. Every nerve ending in my being was awake now, and Gio was master of them all.

His dick pulsed hard within the channel of my ass, a signal of his impending release, and then he was clinging to me. Lips pressed against the back of my head, shouting a string of barely coherent things. Dirty things. Loving things. And he unloaded all of his passion inside of me in wave after hot wave.

I writhed beneath him, pressed into the bed with by the weight of him, as every bit of tangled up lust and pain and humiliation spilled out of my untouched dick and onto the covers. My ass spasmed and quaked around him, muscles intent on wringing out every last drop.

And then we were still, both panting heavily into the silent room.

After a time, when his dick had softened and left me bereft, Gio rolled off of me and onto his side. He carded his fingers through my damp hair and sighed. Then his hand dropped to my sore ass, palm skating gently over the flesh.

I winced, and Gio's hand stilled.

"I don't want to be a monster," he said, voice broken.

I thought of my father. Of the cruelty in his eyes and the unbearable crack of his belt against my ass. Of the hateful words and twisted aberrations of Bible verses that spewed from his liquor-scented lips. Was he a monster? I thought perhaps he was, but he never would have imagined himself one. He was also nothing like Gio, who even after all of the kindness he had bestowed upon me, and even knowing I wanted his discipline, still questioned himself.

"What makes a man a monster?" I asked, staring into his haunted eyes.

He rolled onto his back and lay in silence for long moments, his chest rising and falling steadily as he thought. Just when I suspected he would never answer my question, he turned back onto his side and found my gaze again.

"I believe a man becomes a monster when he loses the ability to feel compassion for others. When he ceases to feel the pain of those he hurts, he's no better than an animal. Compassion is the thing that separates monsters from men. And you, sweet pea, are my compassion." He dropped a kiss onto my hair and sighed. "You are my love."

CHAPTER SEVENTEEN

PETER

I HADN'T MEANT to fall asleep. I'd planned on watching TV and maybe writing a little bit in my journal. I needed something to occupy my mind while Gio was gone on a rare overnight business trip. I wasn't used to being alone, and the apartment felt cavernous with just little old me in it.

It was disconcerting to realize just how dependent I had become on Gio's presence. When I lived with my father, I'd relished every moment I had to myself and had rejoiced every time I came home to an empty apartment. When he was gone overnight, I'd entertained dark fantasies of what may have kept him away and secretly hoped he would never return.

It was different with Gio. I wanted him with me every second of every day, so when he told me he'd be gone overnight, I was filled with dread. As soon as the door had closed behind him, I'd clicked on the TV and sat down on the sofa, staring blindly at the screen. Then I'd stretched out with a pillow beneath my head, feet propped up on the back cushions, and stared at the ceiling, willing the minutes to fly by.

Apparently, I had passed out within minutes because when a knock at the door startled me awake, I checked my watch. Less than a half hour since Gio had gone.

The knock scared me because I couldn't figure out who would be visiting while Gio wasn't home. Theo never visited when I was alone, and I suspected it was to avoid incurring Gio's wrath. My man was nothing if not territorial where I was concerned, and Theo had a knack for getting his hackles up. And besides, Theo was going with him out of town. That made me really jealous, but I had been the one begging Gio to hire him, so I had no right to complain.

Whoever was on the other side of the door knocked again, louder this time. I swung my legs down from the back of the couch and sat up, staring nervously at the door.

"Hey kid, I know you're in there." It was Z's voice, and that was even worse than not knowing who was out there. "Gio sent me to tell you something. Open up. It's important."

Suddenly worried about Gio's safety, I hurried to unlock the door, but what I discovered on the other side was instant validation that Z had just been lying to get me to let my guard down. My father stood beside him, dressed in his usual plaid blazer, buttoned up.

Somehow he looked even shabbier than I had remembered. Maybe the time away from him had given me a new perspective, or maybe he was taking even worse care of himself since I had left home. Whatever the reason, the old man looked like shit.

Before I could gather the words to turn them away, Z pushed the door open and sauntered into the room, my father close on his heels.

"I—I don't think you guys should be here right now. Gio isn't here, and I don't think he would like me having company." In fact, I *knew* he wouldn't like it, so why was I being delicate?

"Company?" my dad asked incredulously. "Is that what I am now? Last I checked, I was your goddamn father."

Z dropped down onto the sofa and turned to watch the drama unfold, one arm stretched along the back of the cushions.

"You guys need to leave and come back when Gio is here. He's not going to be happy about this."

"I don't give a damn," my dad yelled. "I have a right to visit my own damn son. This is ridiculous. When are you coming home? It's been months."

I toed the floor, wondering what I could say to get them to leave. "I live here now. Didn't Gio tell you I was staying with him?"

"Doesn't matter what he told me. He's not the boss of you. I am."

I backed up a couple of steps, putting distance between myself and the man who had bullied and tormented me for years. Even now, I could feel the sting of his belt across my ass.

"Why are you here?" Stupid question. I knew very well why he was here.

"I'm here to take you home. Now get your suitcases packed and let's go."

Instinctively, I looked to Z for backup, as if he hadn't been the one to bring my father here in the first place. The asshole just sat quietly on the sofa with that maddening grin still in place. At the moment I wasn't sure who I hated worse, him or my dad. But I was sure of one thing. I needed to get both of them out of the apartment before things escalated.

With no one to back me up, I pulled myself up straighter and gave my dad what I hoped was a look of fierce determination. "I'm not going anywhere with you. This is my home, and you need to leave now."

He scoffed. "This isn't your home. It belongs to your boss, and you're just a charity case to him. I know what you told him to make him feel sorry for you. Spreading lies about me."

"I haven't lied about anything," I said, cursing the nerves that always reared up inside me when I talked back to my father.

"He came to my fucking house the other day and threatened me, you little shit. All because of the lies you told him. But charity only goes so far. One of these days, he'll get bored of being your knight in shining armor, and then you'll be out on your ass. What will you do then? You think I'm gonna help you after you disobeyed me?"

"I don't need your help. I don't need you for anything." God, it felt good saying those words to him and knowing for the first time in my life that they were true. Even if Gio kicked me out tomorrow, going back home was not an option. Even the word *home* didn't fit anymore. The crappy little apartment was now just a place I used to live, and this man was just someone who used to make my life a living hell.

He growled, fingers twitching at his sides. If we had been alone, he would have been unbuckling his belt already.

"You need to come back home where you belong before I lose my patience. You get what I'm saying? Write Mr. Rivera a note and tell him you realized you wanted to go home. Tell him you made up all that stuff about me... *abusing* you." He grimaced in disgust, as if he truly believed it was all a lie. I wondered if he was that delusional, or if he was just putting on a show because we had an audience.

"Better listen to your father," Z said. The bored look on his face said he didn't have any real concern for my father or for our relationship. I doubted Z had ever been truly concerned about anything but himself.

I dug my toes into the rug I had gotten accustomed to feeling beneath my feet. *My* rug. *My* home. "I said I'm not going anywhere. Now get out."

The old man lunged at me and wrapped his fingers tightly around my upper arm, squeezing so hard I knew there would be bruises there. If I had seen it coming, I might have been able to get out of the way. But I had gotten too comfortable, too used to having Gio standing between me and the world. I'd forgotten what it felt like to have to be wary all the time, and it had made me lax.

"Heyyy," Z said from the sofa, his drawl lazy and unaffected. "Enough of that, Jack. Gio is already gonna be pissed off that I let you come in here. You said your piece, and the boy said his. Now it's time to go."

My dad jerked his head in Z's direction, clearly shocked at the lack of support. "But—"

Z cut him off by grabbing his upper arm, in much the same way my dad had just grabbed mine, and ushering him out the door. I took a moment to be almost impressed. Z may have been a world-class asshole, but he sure knew how to put my father in his place.

After he slammed the door shut behind him and turned back to me, I sank down onto the couch, relieved. That is until I realized I was now alone in the apartment with Z, who was nearly as unwelcome as my father.

"You're not going to go with him?" I asked hesitantly.

Z shrugged. "Why would I? It ain't like he and I are drinking buddies. I just told him I'd let him come up here and ask you nicely to come home. He did, you said fuck no, end of story. Right?"

I nodded, wondering if maybe Z was a little cooler than I gave him credit for. He could have let my dad come up without supervision, which would have been a nightmare. Somebody might have ended up hurt or dead. But he had supervised the entire exchange and then made my dad leave when he started to get unhinged. I figured I should at least offer the guy something to drink to show my gratitude.

"Would you like some lemonade?" I asked.

Z took his spot on the sofa again, pulling a knee up onto the seat and turning halfway around to smile up at me over the back of the sofa. "You got anything harder?"

He pulled a small cylinder from his pocket and unscrewed the cap. The top had a tiny long-handled spoon attached to it, the bowl filled with white powder. He snorted the powder up his nostril, stuck the spoon back into the cylinder to refill it, and snorted again. Three times he did this while I watched in disbelief.

I had seen cocaine a time or two before, but never in my living room. It freaked me out, but then what did I expect? Gio might not have done drugs himself, but I knew his business was connected to drugs in some way.

Ignoring my horrified stare, Z said, "I'll take beer, wine, bourbon... Something with some fucking alcohol in it."

He refilled the spoon and held it out to me, but I refused with a fierce shake of my head. He shrugged and snorted it himself before screwing the cap back onto the cylinder and sliding it back into his pocket.

"Thought you were gonna get me a drink," he said.

My brain rebooted. "Ummm...I think we have some beer."

"*We,*" Z repeated quietly. As I walked to the kitchen, he called out, "Hey, dude, I like your outfit."

I looked down and realized I was actually wearing very little. Lately, my lounging clothes consisted of tight t-shirts and loose jogging shorts that showed my ass if I bent over.

Gio liked me that way, and I was more than willing to please. I loved the way his eyes lit up when I pranced around in front of him in skimpy clothes, so I did it as often as possible.

My current outfit was a tight black Misfits T-shirt that cut off just above my belly button, and a pair of black shorts with hot pink piping. And no shoes, of course. I never wore shoes in the apartment.

"Thanks," I said self-consciously.

He was still turned around in his seat. Now he had his chin resting on the cushion and his arm draped casually over the back of the sofa. He watched me with a level of concentration I found unsettling, especially when I returned to the living room and handed his beer over the back of the sofa.

He wrapped his thin fingers slowly around the bottle, brushing mine as we made the exchange. Then, without missing a beat, he slid his free hand all the way up my shorts and palmed my ass.

Time seemed to stand still as he stared up at me with hooded eyes, his bottom lip caught between his teeth and his hand lightly gripping my ass cheek.

Finally, I found my bearings and staggered back and out of his reach. "You should go now. I—I'm tired, and I need to go to bed."

I felt like an idiot making excuses, but something about Z had always given me the creeps, and at that moment my creep-o-meter was registering off the charts. I was afraid to be blunt with him because he was unpredictable.

He had touched my ass. He wanted me. And I was alone with him.

"Hey, don't run me off before I've finished my beer." He turned the bottle up and took a swallow.

"And then you'll go?" I prayed he didn't hear the desperate ring of fear in my voice.

"Jesus, just relax and come sit down. I ain't gonna bite you."

"Relax?" I asked stupidly.

In a surreal turn of events, he started singing Frankie Goes to Hollywood and drumming along with his fingers on the back of the sofa. *"Relax, don't do it. When you want to go to it. Relax, don't do it. When you want to come."*

I ignored the impromptu concert as if it hadn't happened. "Uhhh... You can finish your beer, but I need to go change. I wasn't expecting company, so I'm just wearing my lounging clothes."

I started walking toward the bedroom to change, but about halfway there it occurred to me that Z knew which bedroom belonged to Gio. Everyone did. I couldn't go in there for clothes, and I had none in the guest room.

Fuck.

I swung back around and laughed nervously. "Never mind. I think I forgot to do laundry."

With little else to do short of trying to physically remove Z, I sat down and counted the seconds. I'd never been so uncomfortable in all my life.

Z didn't stop looking at me like I was his next meal. "So this is the kind of thing you lounge around in every day? Damn. Gio's dick must *stay* hard." He blatantly adjusted his own dick in his jeans.

I stared down at my lap, afraid of what else he might do if I kept looking at him. I wanted to play dumb and tell him I didn't know what he meant, but that would keep the conversation going, and I just wanted him to *leave.*

For God's sake, why did I have to be wearing such short shorts? They rode up my legs almost to my crotch, exposing way too much thigh. I pulled at the hems of both legs, trying to work them down, and slouched my posture in a vain effort to minimize the strip of bare abs visible beneath my cut-off shirt.

"Heyyy. Kid." Z slid closer. "If it makes you that uncomfortable, go change your clothes. You can go in Gio's room to get 'em. I already know you guys are fucking."

My head came up at that. How did he know? Had Gio told him or was he just hazarding a guess? There was no doubt in his darkening eyes—just a disturbing mix of amusement, lust, and some unnamable something that made my skin crawl.

"I'll change," I said quietly. At least it would give me a reprieve from Z's intense scrutiny. Plus, more clothing meant more work for his roaming eyes as he mentally undressed me. A three-piece suit and overcoat ought to do the trick.

I skittered off into the room like a frightened rodent, locking the door behind me. My eyes darted frantically around as I tried to work out a plan for getting Z out of the apartment. Maybe if I stayed put for a while, he'd get bored and leave. But I knew that was unlikely.

The balcony was always an option. Too bad I couldn't scale the outside wall like Spiderman.

Then I spotted the phone on the bedside table, realizing my brain must have shorted out in Z's presence, because duh... I could call Gio's pager. Surely he wasn't too far away yet. He'd said he had to go by the bank and then to pick Theo up.

I grabbed the handset and punched in his pager number. A tone sounded, and I keyed in our home number followed by the pound sign. There. Done. Now all I had to do was wait for the callback.

Z knocked on the bedroom door, and I nearly jumped out of my skin.

"What are you doing in there?" he asked.

"Uhhh... nothing. I'm just tired. I think I'm gonna take a nap.

Go ahead and finish your beer before you leave, though. I don't mind."

The doorknob jiggled. "Don't be like that, kid. I was just messing with you. Open up."

"Z, I'm really tired. Nothing personal."

He laughed, and I thought I saw the knob twist just a little bit. "Nothing personal? Is that your way of saying I'm not good enough for you? Cause you sure don't have any problem giving it up to Gio."

He wasn't making any sense. Why was he even trying to mess with me if he knew I was with Gio? Didn't he know that was the quickest way to get fired? Or at least I *guessed* Gio would fire him for hitting on me. Maybe not.

Suddenly the lock clicked, and the door swung open. Z stood smiling in the doorway, an evil smile twisting his lips.

I gasped. "How did you—"

He held up a small pouch and slid a thin metal object into it. "Boy Scouts always come prepared."

"I don't even want to know why you carry a lock picking kit around in your pocket." I gulped around a knot of fear. "But you need to leave. I'm serious. Gio will be back any minute, and he's not going to like you being here. He'll kick your ass when he finds you in his room."

"Wrong," he sang. "You don't think I know Gio's out of town?"

Z took a step toward me, and I lunged for the phone. All I could think to do was page Gio again, but there was no dial tone. The phone was silent.

Had I been transported into a horror movie? Maybe I was dreaming.

God, please tell me I'm dreaming.

"I took the phone off the hook in the living room," Z said. "I don't like to get interrupted when I'm trying to hang out."

I was pretty sure in this case *hang out* was a euphemism for *fuck*.

He pulled his cocaine dispenser out of his pocket and snorted a few more tiny spoonfuls. "Sure you don't want some of this? You need to chill."

"Why are you doing this?" I asked. "You don't even like me."

"I like you," he said, shoving the cocaine back into his pocket. "I definitely like that ass. Why don't you let me get up in there?"

"Shut up. You're freaking me out."

He took another step toward me and laughed when I flinched. "What's the matter? Why you wanna act like a little virgin?"

"I'm with Gio," I yelled. "I'm not cheating on him."

Z scoffed. "That man is twice your age, kitten. A few years down the road he won't even be able to get it up. And besides, what makes you think he's not cheating on you? I guarantee you he is. Our boss is not known for his *monogamous inclinations*." He laughed, celebrating his own wit.

It made me want to puke. But it also made me really fucking angry, and that was a good thing. The anger started to eclipse the fear.

"Z, I'm not kidding. Get the hell out of my house. I'm not interested in *hanging out* with you."

"No need to get all crazy," he said. "I'm just trying to get to know you better. Shit. Gio left you here all alone, so what's wrong with having a little fun? I know you have to get lonely."

He was steadily moving toward me as he talked. Slowly, as if he didn't want to spook me.

I stood taller, hoping I didn't look intimidated. "I love Gio. I don't need anyone else."

Z laughed. "I hate to break it to you, but he doesn't love you. I know it feels that way right now, but you'll find out in a year or so when he trades you in on a new model. That's what he does. Believe me, I know."

Was that sadness in his eyes? Was it possible that Z was one of the men Gio had been with before me? I had to know.

"Were you and Gio... together?"

Z smirked, stepping closer. "What do you think, Einstein?"

"I—I don't know."

"Of course he wouldn't tell you. He wants you to think you're the only one. Wants you to feel special."

I gulped, doubt tightening my throat to the point of pain. "How long ago were you together?"

A rueful grin twisted Z's gaunt face. "It's been a while. Guess I got too old for him." He looked me over in disgust. "Apparently he likes 'em young."

Oh, my God. Could that be true? Was it possible that Gio would cast me aside when I got too old to keep his interest anymore? Z wasn't even that old. He was still in his twenties.

My stomach twisted, and I wanted to hurl. Z was almost on me now, just a couple of steps away, and I didn't like the way he was looking at me. The expression of interest he'd worn earlier had changed into something much darker.

Resentment? Anger? *Hatred?*

He dropped his voice and spoke to me softly now. "Come on. I won't hurt you. It'll be fun."

"Gio—"

"Forget Gio. This will be our little secret."

He closed the short distance between us, and my survival instincts kicked in. What had started as an attempt at seduction had turned into something else. Something that frightened me.

I shoved him, and he stumbled back several steps.

He came back at me, his face contorted with rage, and I landed a solid punch on his cheekbone. Pain shot through my hand, but I wasn't about to show it.

Z righted himself quickly, and before I could even pull back for another punch, he backhanded me hard across the face. The skinny fucker was stronger than he looked. The blow knocked me off balance, and I fell onto the bed.

I shook my head, feeling a little bit dizzy, and scrambled back to my feet. But as I moved toward him again, he pulled a switchblade knife from his back pocket and ejected the blade.

I froze.

Z grinned wickedly, his hand twitching. "Boy Scout. Remember?"

I was pretty sure Boy Scouts didn't carry switchblades, but I wasn't going to argue the point.

"No need for all that," I said quietly. "Please put the knife away and let's discuss this calmly. I won't fight you."

I had been in a few scraps in my life, and my dad had beaten me plenty, but I'd never had a knife pulled on me before. It was a hell of a lot scarier than it looked in the movies.

"Lay down!" Z yelled. "And get those fucking shorts off. I'm done playing around with you."

Oh, God. This was really happening.

I did as he ordered, feeling the burn of bile in the back of my throat as I slid my shorts down my legs and laid back on the bed. A trembling started deep in my body and made its way to the surface, and with it came the ache of humiliation.

I felt so fucking weak. He was going to take what was Gio's, and I was going to have to let him.

Z undid his jeans and slid them to his knees, along with his boxers. His erection stood straight out from his body, hard and imposing and even more of a weapon than the knife he was using to subdue me. Because the knife was a threat; his dick was a promise he intended to keep.

He transferred the knife to his left hand and started to stroke himself with his right. "You got anything to slick this thing up with?"

I pointed wordlessly to the nightstand, and he reached into the drawer. I saw an opportunity to grab the knife and went for it.

My back was barely off the bed before Z was on top of me with the knife pressed against my throat. "Try that again, and you won't live to take another breath."

I nodded, my eyes wide and fearful.

He stood back up and slicked himself. Then he stared at my soft dick in a way that made my skin crawl.

"What's the matter? This body doesn't turn you on?" He lifted his shirt to reveal a wasted chest and belly, his ribs pushing painfully through the skin. "Don't look at me like that, you fucking prick. With that fucking disgust on your face. I used to be pretty like you."

I opened my mouth to deny that I'd been looking at him in any particular way, but he jabbed the knife at me.

"Shut your mouth, you nasty little whore. Get those legs spread."

I whimpered and did as he asked, resting the soles of my feet on the bed. He hooked his arms around my legs and pulled me to the edge of the bed, accidentally scratching my thigh with the tip of the knife and drawing a thin line of blood.

"Oops," he said. "Better be still. I'd hate to nick an artery." He studied my face, and his tongue along his lips. "Maybe I should accidentally cut up that pretty face of yours. Think Gio would still want you then? I'm betting he'd throw you away just like he did me."

I was trembling so hard it was like I had fever chills. Z stood over me, with that evil grin and the knife in his hand, and bents his knees to push inside me. I squeezed my eyes shut, a low moan coming out of me that sounded like an injured animal.

But then I heard Gio's steady voice. "I see you've discovered my plaything."

Z tensed, and my eyes flew open. Gio stood in the doorway, calm and collected as if it was just any other day. As if I wasn't lying on the bed with a man about to rape me at knifepoint.

"Gio," Z gasped. "I just—"

"Thought you could cut me out of the fun," Gio supplied for him. He stepped toward us, mild annoyance registering on his handsome features.

I was confused. Shouldn't he be alarmed? Shouldn't he be rushing to rescue me? To wrestle the knife from Z, or pull out his gun and tell him to step away?

If this had been a movie, he would have been drawing his gun and shouting, *Step away from the boy before I blow your fucking head off.* Not stripping his shirt off and looking at Z with an expression of... Tenderness? Desire?

I watched in horror, unable to speak or beg for help.

Gio came close, gripping his balled-up shirt in his left hand as he stroked Z's face with the right. "Why didn't you tell me you wanted him? You wouldn't have needed that." He jerked his head toward the knife, now held loosely in Z's grip. "Peter will do whatever I tell him to."

Gio leaned in and kissed Z gently on the corner of his mouth while running his free hand down his arm. A visible shudder rippled through Z's body, and his eyes fluttered closed as he relished the tender kiss.

"Gio." His voice was soft. Needy. "I wanted—"

"I know," Gio said quietly. "You missed me. And I've been spending time with someone else."

Z nodded, all of the earlier anger and bravado having drained out of him.

Gio unbuckled his belt, and my brain screamed, *Oh God, oh God, what the fuck is happening?*

Z was pliant as Gio gripped his hips and turned him back to face me, once again positioning him between my legs. I glanced down and saw that Z was just as hard, his dick glistening with lubrication. My consciousness nearly wavered.

Gio was going to let him fuck me? I didn't want it. I didn't want anyone inside me but Gio. Not ever. Tears slid from the outside corners of my eyes, and I didn't bother to wipe them away.

Gio pushed against his ass from behind, and Z groaned. Gio's right hand slid around and caressed up Z's T-shirt. Over to his shoulder. Down his arm. Toward the knife.

"Let's get rid of this thing," he said. "Someone might accidentally get cut."

Z's lips were slack as he nodded and gave up the knife, but he turned and watched as Gio deposited it on the nightstand. Satisfied, he turned back to me, looking just as bewildered as I felt.

Then suddenly he spun around and threw his arms around Gio's neck. Gio squeezed his frail frame tightly against him, and his eyes met mine over Z's shoulder. His eyes were haunted.

In that moment, Gio's words came back to me—*Only one.* The two words that had broken my heart.

Z was the one. The only other man Gio had loved.

I wanted to die as I watched them embrace, their hands wandering over each other. Z's long fingers trembling as they combed through Gio's hair. Gio's strong arms encircling Z's narrow back while he still clutched his shirt in one hand. The affection coursing between them was palpable in the room.

"I love you so much," Z whimpered, going limp and shaky in Gio's arms.

"I know you do," Gio whispered. "I love you, too."

I just lay there, naked and still, as a piece of me withered and died.

Z sniffed back tears. "Can we be together again?"

"We can all be together." He turned Z back around to face me, and I saw the gleam of tears in both their eyes.

"Forever?" Z asked, his voice breathy and full of childlike innocence.

"Yes, baby. Forever." Gio pulled Z's head back against his shoulder, kissed his cheek tenderly, then drew the knife across his throat.

CHAPTER EIGHTEEN

PETER

I WATCHED in horror as a spurt of red hit my belly before Gio could get his wadded up shirt to Z's throat to staunch the blood. My brain scrambled in search of any scrap of logic to explain the gruesome scene playing out in front of me.

Z's eyes stretched wide for a few seconds before his gaze grew distant and unfocused. The shirt Gio held clamped to his throat soaked through, and a wash of red started to pour down his T-shirt.

Gio, his face contorted into a mask of sheer agony until he was nearly unrecognizable as the man I knew. A low moan came out of him as he stumbled backward, Z's shoes trailing limply along the carpet as he dragged him into the bathroom. Still emitting that tortured moan, Gio lowered the man he had once loved gently into the garden tub.

I got up on shaky legs and staggered to the bathroom, moving on instinct rather than any conscious decision to do so. What I saw in the bathroom would forever be burned into my memory.

Z jerked violently in the tub, convulsing a few times in quick succession as if his failing body was trying to reboot. Then he gurgled a thick stream of dark blood out through his mouth and nose before going completely still. His eyes were fixed on some distant point, unseeing as he gave up his last, liquid breath.

Gio dropped to his knees and started to rock, keening like a frightened animal as he ran trembling fingers through the disheveled spikes of Z's hair. Tears coursed freely down his cheeks.

I couldn't do anything but stare, questioning reality and my own sanity. Gio's cries were driving me mad, echoing in my head until I finally covered my ears with my hands and squeezed my eyes shut against the horrific scene. My body started to quake from shock. I knew it, and yet I couldn't do anything to stop it.

I was cold. Like death. Like Z. So cold.

I was dimly aware of a hand resting on my shoulder, and I turned my head slowly to see who it was, half fearing a ghost. But it was only Theo. I hadn't even known he was there.

He pulled me away from the bathroom and guided me to the bed. Helped me to sit. Wrapped his arms around me.

I collapsed onto his shoulder and finally started crying. I could feel my tears soaking his shirt, but I couldn't bring myself to care. I went limp against him and shuddered as sobs wracked me. I could still hear Gio in the bathroom, his wails fading to whimpers, and I cried for him. It was the most heartbreaking sound I'd ever heard. I wanted to go to him, but Theo held me in place. He was the only sane one here.

He ran rough hands up and down my naked back, soothing me.

Eventually, I heard Gio shuffling in the bathroom, and I chanced a peek through watery eyes. He was scrubbing his hands where the blood that soaked through the shirt had gotten on him. There was surprisingly little blood anywhere but on Z, and I marveled at Gio's foresight with hanging onto his shirt.

The thought brought a realization that nearly took my breath away. Gio was already planning to kill Z the moment he entered the room and found us there. He had known even as he held him. Kissed him. Told him he loved him.

Gio staggered out of the bathroom, shirtless, his belt still hanging loosely where he had unbuckled it.

"Fuck," he cried, crashing drunkenly against the door frame as he entered the room. Then he took a deep breath, wiped the tears from his eyes with one hand, and looked at us. I thought I saw a flash of anger as he took in the sight of my naked body pressed against Theo's.

The last man who had touched my naked body was lying dead in the tub. Theo must have had that same thought, because he let go of me.

Gio held a wet washcloth in his hand. He sat down on the bed and pushed me down onto my back, inspecting me for something. Damage? Blood?

When he saw the small red smear across my belly, he worked it away quickly with the warm, soapy cloth.

"Is that all?" he asked? "You didn't get any more on you, did you?"

I shook my head. "I don't think so."

"What happened here?" He touched the fine scratch on my thigh that had already congealed and was on its way to healing.

"He accidentally scratched me with the knife."

"That's it? Just scratched you?"

"Yes, Gio. I'm fine. It was just a scratch and a little bit of blood."

"But the blood didn't get on your scratch?"

"No, Gio."

He carried the washcloth to the bathroom and dropped it into the trash, casting a troubled look at the body in the tub as he came back into the room. Then he let out a pent-up breath and laid down beside me.

Theo was still sitting there, looking toward the bathroom. Normally it would have been weird lying naked in front of him, and even clinging to him naked, but in the aftermath of a near-rape and brutal murder, it felt strangely okay.

I didn't even have the urge to cover myself. Perhaps it was because I was already so emotionally naked, and clothing couldn't hide that.

"You need to get everything cleaned up," Gio said.

Theo started and looked back at him. "Yes, sir."

"There are gloves in the kitchen under the sink. Be careful where you get that blood. He had AIDS."

Theo and I both stared at him in shock. "How do you know?" I asked.

"Because I was paying for his treatment." Gio waved a hand. "It's fine. Just don't get it in any open wounds or your eyes."

"Nah, I know how it works," Theo said. "I'm not scared. I was just thinking about what he was about to do before we got here. With Peter."

Gio nodded stiffly. "Just get him taken care of. And treat him with respect. No matter what he was about to do, he was someone I cared about. He deserves a proper burial."

"Where are we taking him?" Theo asked.

"The desert. We need a large moving box and a truck. And some plastic we can seal up."

"I'm on it, boss." Theo got up and left the room, presumably to go and find the items.

I had to wonder at how well Theo was handling everything. He had just been tasked with preparing and transporting a body to the desert to dispose of it, and he was taking it in stride.

Had he done things like this before? Had Gio killed before?

I didn't want to think about those things. I'd had enough trauma for one day, and I just wanted to curl up against Gio and sleep. And hopefully not dream. But there were some questions I needed answers to first, about what had happened with Z.

After Theo had thoughtfully pulled the bathroom door closed and left the apartment, I turned to Gio, who still had that haunted look in his eyes. I was sure there was a similar look in my own eyes.

"He was trying to give it to me, wasn't he?" I asked quietly.

Gio nodded. "He was."

"And he's the one you were talking about. You loved him."

"I did," he admitted. "I just didn't love him enough. It's why he was so angry at you. He knew how I felt about you, and he obviously couldn't handle it."

"What happened? How did he get sick?" I swallowed back the urge to ask Gio if maybe he was sick, too. If tonight had proved nothing else, it was that Gio hadn't been lying when he said he'd do anything to keep me safe.

"He and I were together years ago. We met at a nightclub after I got divorced, and we hit it off. He was very different then— always a bundle of energy. Such a goof, so wild and free. He was a freak for Elton John." Gio chuckled, and a lone tear slipped out of his eye.

"Sounds like he was a lot of fun," I said, feeling the inadequacy of my words.

"He made me feel alive. I cared about him very much, but over the course of our relationship, he changed. Got involved in drugs. Not selling them, but actually taking them. He was doing all sorts of things. Coke, crack, crank… heroin." He took a deep breath and let it out. "I got him into rehab, and he was able to kick the heavy stuff, but he was never quite the same."

"And you two weren't together anymore?"

"No. We had stopped seeing each other months before he went to rehab, but he came to my place one night, and he was in really bad shape. I had to do something."

"And you didn't want him back after he got clean?"

"I was already past all of that. Seeing other people. Like I said, I didn't love him enough." A flash of regret crossed his face. "I never loved him like I love you. Like I would move heaven and earth to keep you by my side. I gave up on him."

I ran a hand down his bare chest. "That's not your fault. You can't make yourself love someone more."

He chuckled lightly through his pain and pulled my hand to his mouth, pressing a gentle kiss to my fingers. "I know that. And Z was fine with it. He had moved on as well. But he came looking for a job one day, and I put him to work. He's been with me ever since, but only in a professional capacity. I mean, we were still friends, but there was never any spark. Never any thought of getting back together."

"At least not on your part."

He shook his head as if to clear some doubt that had only recently made its way into his mind. "He was fine. He never came onto me or anything, so it never crossed my mind that he still thought of me that way. But then he got sick. We're pretty sure he got it from sharing needles. I felt so fucking awful for him."

"So you paid for his treatment. That was really generous of you."

"It was the least I could do. The guy had pretty much been handed a death sentence, and there was no way he could afford it on his own. He didn't have any health insurance, so I offered to pay."

We lay there in silence for a moment as I worked to process everything. My brain was overloaded to the point of exhaustion.

"I had noticed a change in him lately," Gio said. "Not just in his appearance, but in the way he was acting. He got pneumonia last year, and it was really bad. He stayed in the hospital for a while, and ever since then he's been on a downhill slide, I think."

"He'd gotten really thin," I said. "I had noticed it, but I just assumed he was doing a lot of drugs."

"He was," Gio said. "I could tell he'd started back up. I pulled him aside a few times, but he just told me to mind my own business. When I think back, it seems like he started doing the drugs again around the time you came into my life."

"Oh, God," I groaned. "Did I cause all of this?"

"No, baby. Shhh..." He turned to face me and stroked my hair. "It's not your fault that he was sick and fucked up on drugs. It's not your fault that I fell in love with you. And it's not your fault that a desperate, depressed man decided to attack you."

At his last words, the memory of the fear I had felt when I was at Z's mercy came rushing back, and I started to shake. Gio pulled me sharply into his arms and crushed me against his chest. It was such an odd thing to notice, but the familiar tickle of his chest hair filled me with warmth and that sense of security I'd only ever felt with Gio.

"I'm sorry that happened, baby. So sorry that happened to you. I should have read the signs. I knew he was feeling jealous and getting a little unstable, but I never imagined it would come to this."

"He scared me," I whimpered against his chest. "I thought he was going to take what I never wanted to give to anyone but you. I thought he might even kill me. But now that I know the truth, I can't even imagine what he must have been going through. He knew that he was dying, and he had to watch the man he loved falling for someone else." I shuddered.

The sickening jumble of fear, disgust, and unease I'd felt for my would-be rapist had transformed into something else. Compassion. I ached inside for the once-vibrant man who had met such a tragic end, and even after what he had tried to do to me, I couldn't find it in my heart to hate him.

Gio ran a hand down my back and rested a hand on my ass. Not in a sexual way, but a gentle, possessive touch. As if he cherished the body I had so freely offered up to him, and which he now owned.

"I couldn't let him hurt you," he said. "And God forgive me, but I didn't want to watch him waste away to nothing but a shell of the man he once was." He sobbed against my cheek, a mournful sound that carried with it all the pain in the world. "I loved him."

I ran a hand down the back of his head and melted against his body. "Then I loved him, too."

THAT NIGHT we carried Z's body out into the desert, the three of us traveling in silence. Gio dug a deep hole, laboring far into the night. He only let Theo help when he got too exhausted to go on, but he wouldn't let me do anything.

"This is my burden," he said. "My work to do and my weight to carry."

Gio pulled the plastic back to reveal Z's body and removed his gold earring. He handed it to me for safekeeping, and I held it like a precious relic as I watched them lower his frail body into the ground and cover him with dirt.

Gio stood several yards away for a long time, broken and sweaty, staring off into the gloom. His anguish was palpable, his shoulders slumped with the weight of his guilt.

I grabbed the handful of emergency candles I'd found in Gio's kitchen cabinet and stabbed them into the dirt around the grave site. Theo lit them all with his cigarette lighter, then fired up a cigarette and puffed a plume of smoke into the dim gray glow of pre-dawn.

As Gio wandered back to us, I retrieved the boom box from the truck, and we all sat in a cluster at the side of the unmarked pauper's grave that would cradle Z for the rest of eternity. The silence was deafening as I pressed play on the cassette deck.

The haunting melody of Elton John's *Goodbye Yellow Brick Road* floated across the desert, and we cried until the sun started to break over the horizon.

PART III

CHAPTER NINETEEN

KAGE

THE JOURNAL ENTRY chronicling the death and burial of Z nearly brought me to my knees. I couldn't imagine the sorrow and guilt those three men had felt after the horror that unfolded that night.

My uncle had been attacked and nearly raped. Gio had killed a man in cold blood—a man he'd once loved and still felt responsible for. The emotions coursing through me were staggering, as if I had experienced that loss myself.

How did you move past something like that? I doubted anyone could come through such a tragedy unscathed. I imagined the guilt they must have all carried with them as they moved on with life and left Z behind, and felt the ghost of a hole in my own heart.

I flipped to the back of the journal and out pulled three photos that had yellowed and faded with age. I stared for a long time, shocked to finally be able to put faces to the names I had read about.

The first photo was of three men. My uncle at the age of eighteen, smiling brightly and looking so similar to me it took my breath away. Gio posed beside him in the fedora Peter had given him, looking gorgeous and intimidating with his dark hair and piercing blue eyes. A hint of a smile graced his full lips as he held Peter close, tucked in under his arm like the precious possession he was. Theo stood aloof on the other side of Peter, his flowing mane of hair looking the same as it did today.

It was strange to see my uncle and Theo so fresh-faced and unlined, especially after all I knew they had been through. I wondered if the photo had been taken before or after Z's death.

The second photo was of Peter and Gio in their bedroom, hugging and smiling sweetly at the camera. They looked so damn happy and in love. I wondered if Theo had been on the other side of the camera taking the picture.

The third photo was an even older one that featured a younger Gio and a black-haired man whom I assumed could only be Z. It appeared to have been taken in a nightclub. A crowd of blurry-faced people partied behind them as they posed for the picture, both grinning broadly as if they didn't have a care in the world.

Tears fell from my eyes, and I moved the photos quickly out of the way before the teardrops could land on them. It was unsettling how much I had come to feel for the people in these photos. I'd never actually met two of them, and the other two were people I despised. And yet I felt a part of them now.

I thought of Z, alone in the middle of the desert somewhere, and the tears fell harder. Jesus, what was wrong with me? How could their story affect me so deeply?

I flipped back to the photo of Gio, Peter, and Theo, brushing my finger lightly over Gio's face. Something about the man as described through my uncle's eyes had me mesmerized. I wondered if he was still around. I wondered if I could meet him.

My finger caressed over his hat—the one Peter had given him as a gift—and the gold chain that now encircled my own throat. Was it strange that I loved the feeling of having a piece of Gio so close to me?

God, I was getting weird. Fixated on the past and its distorted version of these four men.

And then I had a thought—a memory, really—and I rushed to my uncle's abandoned apartment and slipped inside.

The place was so quiet and still, it reminded me of a tomb. I suppose it was, in a way. It was a tomb for the memories of past lives, and of the joy and loss that had been experienced within its pristine walls. I thought of Gio and Peter and Theo and Z moving through the space, all vibrant and alive, and it made me so very sad.

I had come to the apartment for a reason, though. There was something in the bedroom I remembered noticing on the few times I'd been in there. I'd always thought of Santori's apartment, and especially his bedroom, as feeling like a museum or a shrine. Until now I hadn't known exactly why, but now I understood. It's because it *was* a shrine. A memorial to the life he and Gio had shared here.

I turned on the lights, feeling like it was a little sacrilegious to do so, and crept into the bedroom. I turned the light on there, too, and noticed that the furniture was much the same as it had been in the photo tucked away in the journal. It was hard to imagine that my uncle had been such a sentimental bastard, but I was standing right smack dab in the middle of undeniable proof that he was.

I moved hesitantly toward the master bathroom and looked

inside. My heart lurched when I caught sight of the garden tub where Z's body had lain as he drew his last breath, blood spurting from the gash in his throat. I imagined Gio crumpled to his knees on the floor beside him, running his fingers through his dark hair as he died, and my heart hurt almost as if I'd been there myself.

A chill washed over me, and I spun around, suddenly terrified that someone or something was behind me. I was overcome by the irrational fear that I would find Z's ghost standing there with his throat slit and his eyes full of pain. But I was alone in the room.

As I tried to calm my racing heart, my gaze snagged on the very thing I'd been looking for: Gio's hat. I'd never paid it much attention before, but now I realized it had always been there. As if it was just waiting patiently for Gio to come home and put it on his head. I didn't want to think of how Santori had ended up with it, and the serpentine chain I now wore.

No, I wouldn't think of that. The possibilities disturbed me far too much.

I crossed the room and picked up the hat in slightly trembling fingers. A thin layer of dust had settled on the fur felt surface, and I tapped the hat against my arm, watching the dust swirl in the dim light of the room. Then I placed it on my head.

I now wore his hat and his chain, and I touched a hand to the holster at my waist. The one that held his 38 Special. When I went out, I always carried the gun Aaron had given me, but when I was home, I wanted Gio's gun at my hip.

I was overcome by the strangest sensation of channeling Gio. Of becoming more like him the closer I got to his things. It was a delicious feeling, as if I was rebelling against the universe and doing something that was never supposed to be done. I couldn't explain any of it—the reason I felt this way, the reason I wanted his things. But the feelings were there and just as strong as any I had ever felt.

I wasn't going to fight it.

I left the apartment with the hat on my head, and when I was back at my place, I stood in front of the mirror and admired myself.

Gangster Gio.

Gangster Kage.

I shook my head and laughed at myself, but it didn't stop me from wanting this.

I imagined myself working alongside Theo, dressed like Gio Rivera as I spied for the government in an effort to take Theo and all of his associates down. The thought sent a thrill through me. Because as much as I'd felt drawn in by Peter and Gio and Z, I'd somehow never gotten that feeling about Theo.

It was puzzling, really. Maybe it was because I knew him in the present, and because I hated him.

He was the reason Jamie was gone, and I was left to face all of this alone.

I thought of Gio and Peter, and how Gio had said he didn't want to be a monster. How he'd confessed that Peter was the only thing keeping him from becoming one.

Compassion and love.

It had been a revelation, because that is how I'd felt about Jamie from the beginning. He'd always been the one thing that kept me grounded and made me want to be a better person.

God, I couldn't lose him.

Even with all of the espionage and danger, Jamie was still my biggest concern. My only concern, really. Without him, it would all be for nothing. Didn't he understand that everything I did was for him? To keep him safe? To earn the happily ever after we deserved together? It was so frustrating to have to watch him drift away from me, all the while knowing that he was the only reason I was doing any of this. That the things I was doing to keep him safe and by my side were the very things that were pushing him away.

I studied my reflection in the mirror—my modern-day rendition of Gio Rivera—and grinned, looking evil and so unlike myself. An image flashed behind my eyes of Gio slitting the throat of the man he had once loved. He'd done what he had to do to keep Peter safe, even though it broke his own heart to do it.

Jamie's face swam in my vision, looking up at me with wide brown eyes that held all of the innocence and beauty the world had to offer. Suddenly the confusion and fear I'd felt over the past months were gone, and I knew with surprising clarity what I had to do.

Jamie was my compassion.

My love.

My reason for existing.

I had to keep him safe and ensure that we had the chance to love each other for the rest of our lives.

I slipped my 38 Special from the holster and aimed it at the mirror, imagining my enemies lined up in front of me just waiting to take a bullet in the name of love. Like Gio, I didn't want to be a monster. But by God, I would become the worst monster the world had ever seen if that's what it took to get my Jamie back.

To be continued...

SANTORI RELOADED
Book 3 of
The Santori Trilogy

Coming soon

Books available at all major retailers
& MarisBlack.com

ALSO BY MARIS BLACK

Standalone Novels

Owning Corey

Soul Storm

SSU Boys Series

Pinned (SSU Boys #1)

Smitten (SSU Boys #2)

Undeclared (SSU Boys #3)

Initiation (SSU Boys Short)

Kage Trilogy

Kage

Kage Unleashed

Kage Unmasked

Santori Trilogy

Santori

Santori Reborn

Find my newsletter, other buy links, & extra content:

marisblack.com

ABOUT THE AUTHOR

My name is Maris Black (sort of), and I'm a Southern Girl through and through. I was born and raised in Georgia, but these days I call Nashville, TN home.

In college, I majored in English and discovered the joys of creative writing and literary interpretation. After honing my skills discovering hidden meanings authors probably never intended, I collected my near-worthlessEnglish degree and got a job at a newspaper making minimum wage. But I soon had to admit that small town reporting was not going to pay the bills, so I went back to school and joined the medical field. Logical progression, right? But no matter what Idid, my school notebooks and journals would not stop filling up with fiction. I was constantly plotting, constantly jotting prose, constantly casting the people I met as characters in the secret novels in my head.

Yep. I can blame my creative mother for that one!

When I finally started writing fiction for a living, I surprised myself with my choice of genre. I'd always known I wanted to write romance, but the first story that popped out was about a couple of guys finding love during a threesome with a woman. Then I wrote about more guys, and more guys, and more guys. I was never a reader of gay fiction, and I'd never planned to write it. The only excuse I have for myself is:*Hey, it's just what comes out!*

I adore the M/M genre, though, with all my heart.It feels sort of like coming home.I can't quite explain it. I've always had openly gay and bisexual friends and relatives, the rights and acceptance of whom are very important to me, so it feels great to celebrate that. But there's also something so pure and honest about the love between two men that appeals to me on a romantic level and inspires me to write.

Thank you, men. :)

Sign up for new release notifications at MarisBlack.com

Connect with Me:
marisblack.com
maris@marisblack.com

28061947R00146

Made in the USA
Middletown, DE
19 December 2018